I make no claim to tra... are
believed to be within t... ...ims of fair use.

Foreword by Lord Invid, edited by the Author

Mr. Ziblis asked me to write a foreword for this book, and, well? Here it is. I, like the creator of this world am a product of having grown up in the 70s and 80s. Those days were ones of great changes in this world. The Berlin Wall fell. Michael Jackson rose. Our parents were the hippies and vietnam vets of the world, and in the case of Victor's parents, disco lovers. As George Carlin said, the hippies went from cocaine to Rogaine, and we were the generation they spawned.

Victor and I grew up in places where the parents weren't hippies who turned to angry selfish Baby Boomers. Our parents were working class, they knew we were going to have to work hard just to get by. We lived by some different rules than what you see today.

The rules were simple: Know who to fear and who to respect; treat accordingly. Know that if you failed to do this, you could get hurt... or you could bring shame to your family who would then hurt you for it. If you were anyone, or from anyone; everyone knew who you were. You knew who everyone else was, and if someone was new it never took them long to get shit sorted out.

People cared about what you could do, and knew very well what you couldn't do. You figured out who it was you needed to know in order to get things done, and you learned (usually the painful way) who to just stay away from. Doing all this earned you a place in your neighborhood, for better or for worse.

One thing most kids like us didn't have was money, if you wanted money you had to earn it. So we, the children of Generation X, found ways to get money. If your family had money it could be as simple as doing chores or getting an allowance, but for most of us it just wasn't. We learned to scavenge cash deposit bottles, copper wire, dropped packs of smokes or whatever other things could be found for free and turned into cash. Others learned the art of the hustle, tricking others and working cons to get what they wanted.

Back in those transitional days only an idiot would try to steal something, because we weren't as secretive with what we had. Everything was known by everyone else and ownership was enforced by the community. If you brought something from somewhere else into your neighborhood? Everyone would know you left your circle to get it, and it was most likely hot. Sooner or later someone would come looking for it.

Despite being more open and trusting, people were also more territorial. We couldn't leave our neighborhoods because that was forbidden and honestly it was downright scary to do so. If you were out of your area, news of you going where you didn't belong (or coming back from there) would spread fast, and there would generally be hell to pay for it. Why? Because the odds said that you were up to no good out there.

It was also understood that once you stepped out of your neighborhood you were no longer under the protection of your community. I haven't yet read this book; when I see my writing here it will be attached to a book that is as new to me as it is to you, but it is from all of this I know I will enjoy it. This sense of community cause and effect carried over to the first book, and I enjoyed reading about those familiar ways. I loved that about Nick and Jessica's world, and I want to see more. I also don't speak or write "by the rules", so his style attracted me instantly.

Another thing about Victor, myself, and every one of us Gen X folks is that we speak Media as our first language. Our generation is the one of Saturday morning and after school cartoons. We know what Energon is, who was Destro and we knew to NEVER cross the streams. Important safety tip. We know what not to feed after midnight, and where no one can hear you scream. We know who created the Protoculture Matrix, what is at Boulder Hill, can name the fortress under which Man sleeps; the list goes on and on. For many of us? With but a quarter and a responsive joystick we could become gods.

Catchphrases and POP culture are our calling cards, even the poorest of us were united with the rich kids in these regards. The gap between financial classes was all but irrelevant to us. Nick Sakamoto speaks this same language, so enjoy the codes and callbacks to what could be 25 minutes into the future.

"Mereow roow merow meroo mew merorerro" - Bonecrusher the Kitty. (Translated) "I was only gone for three days and she sent a dog boy after me!"

Lord Invid

Faye Bosch pulled the rope about her frayed and ratty trench coat tighter. She had gotten it wet earlier entirely by accident and now that wetness had frozen. The rope being pure nylon did not help this situation; it just kept slipping. Though she had several layers on, the coat was an integral part of holding it all together. Sometimes during the fall or early spring she had to balance carefully. Too much and she would sweat fast and wear out her clothing, too little and BAM! You wake up teeth chattering and having nowhere to get inside from the cold, save for maybe a Dunkin' Donuts, if the clerk doesn't just throw you out instantly. But December in Chicago? The only fight worth worrying about was staying warm at all.

Having guarded against the worst of the cold, Faye looked around the street that could be seen from the alley she had her squat hidden in. Thanks to last night's overly generous trick, food wasn't an issue; in fact she could probably spare enough to get a warm-ish room at the Rosebrier Inn for a week. Faye didn't wish to do so until the cold was simply too dangerous to sleep outside. It marvelled her how plain out... odd people tended to be. If she were a well-heeled elven corp sort, she sure wouldn't pay good money to have a dwarf woman who hadn't showered in several weeks. The situation made her feel... icky. It wasn't the fact that she had rented her body out to survive that really got to her... it was the fact that she just couldn't figure the guy's reasons. He didn't even want SEX, he just wanted her to serve him food.

Her neck itched, and she reached up to scratch it. Her fingertip found something hard, and by reflex she grabbed whatever it was and pulled it into her field of vision. Of all things, it looked like a porcupine's quill. Like the ones she saw on TV when she was a kid… sorta hollow and thinnish. She didn't think porcupines had weird… pulsating… sacs on the other end? So interested in this was she, that it took her a moment to realize that her body wasn't… really responding correctly. She slumped to the ground face first. She tried to get up, and found that she could only move her arms to put her palms flat on the ground with monumental effort. She willed her arms to push her up, but they did not obey. A moment later, they slackened.

She could feel her legs being grabbed by the ankles, and she was turned using her face as a swivel so that her legs were now pointing deeper into the alley. Faye found she could still close her eyes and did so a few times, before even blinking became difficult. She allowed the lids to just lay slack, half open. Whatever was happening to her right now would probably wear off after her unseen captor did… whatever he wanted to her. And if she died this night? So be it. She was ready. The world was a pretty shitty place to be Faye Bosch in anyway.

The unseen attacker began to drag her away… not bothering to shield her face from the concrete. She could not move at all, could not even actually close her eyes anymore, all she could do was helplessly look at the alley wall, moving in jerks and stutters as she was dragged along. One of her ankles was let go, only to be taken hold of by another hand. She was now being dragged further down the alley at a decent clip. This was more painful than she had thought it might be, and her captors were picking up the pace as she was being taken… who knows where? The cold concrete started grinding the flesh of her cheek away, Faye began to fear that, as the old cliches would say… there might actually be fates worse than death.

Chapter One:
- "Proper Crimbo (Single Version)", Leigh Francis

Jessica Dombrowski looked up at the mirror and checked her lipstick. It felt odd to be wearing lipstick at all, much less BLACK lipstick, but here she was doing exactly that. Her nails matched... as much as they could considering her line of work and habit of chewing said polish off. She had to admit... it really did go well against her pale flesh considering her black hair did the same up top. The door to her right opened, letting the chill of winter into the warm vehicle. A man's hand came into view; with skin a few shades more tan than her own. As she took that hand, Jessica marvelled briefly at how soft and smooth the skin was, given the general rough and tumble nature of the man who used these hands. Jessica looked up into the eye of the man she loved.

Nikolaos Sakamoto. They had met less than three months ago, but she felt so secure with him it may as well have been three decades. Had they had a rough beginning? Oh, absolutely. When they met they were both broken, desperately sleazy people with little concern as to whether they would live to see the next day. Really he was just supposed to be a one night stand, perhaps even her very last, but things just didn't turn out that way. From their very first night together Jessica had come to know the man he wished to be, the man that he really WAS when you got past all of the masks he wore. Masks so subtle at times he did not even know he wore them himself.

Was their love flowing along an ideal path? Also absolutely not. Supernatural forces had actually pushed them together for mostly selfish reasons, and when Jessica found out about those manipulations, that had almost been the end of their tale together. In the end, Jessica realized that Nick was right; it did not matter how they got their love, it only mattered that they HAD that love. The path had been rocky from then on; they had even had angry arguments over the stupidest things and on two occasions Jessica had been ready to punch him out. Doctor Thorne had taught her an important skill though... to take a walk around the block, take some deep breaths, then come back to talk things over rationally. Of course, Jessica was also struggling with esteem issues. Though she logically KNEW that these nothing arguments were just her way of trying to convince herself she actually held power in this relationship, she had been unable to prevent the anger from rising up. But still, she was secure in this love.

Nick tended to be a man who could whip from boredom to child-like joy at a moment's notice, and she also knew he was capable of incredible brutality. Where Jessica met everything in life with flaming passion, Nick was patient with her in a fashion entirely unlike almost all other things in his life. It was true that they were both volatile, damaged people with little holding them on the good side of a shooting spree except their shared desire to try to protect others. Jessica was his exception. This is not to say he was devoid of passion involving her, in fact quite the opposite was true. When she needed it most, he was able to reach into some unseen reservoir of peace and tranquility. He would plant himself like a mighty oak, implacable against the wild storm that was Jessica Dombrowski. He was, in that way, the most reliable thing in her life. He was able to tell when it was time to stop fighting against her, to either let her leave and rage, or just hold her until her fears quieted down. A horrible paradox, it was how secure she felt with this very pretty man that brought those fears and angers out in the open. How was that for seriously fucked up? The one person she felt safest with got the very worst of Jessica unfiltered, but he also got the very best from her.

Looking him over, she felt her mouth open lightly. Every once in awhile Jessica caught sight of him just right, like now with a thick snowflake resting on his eyelash and the moonlight making his skin seem to glow a bit. Like every other time, she was struck again by just how… pretty he was. He was like something out of an Asian fairy tale, both animal and human at the same time. A beauty so ethereal that while Nick clearly was ON this Earth, Jessica felt he could not be OF this earth. The scars here and there did nothing to detract from this, even the terrible ones he usually kept covered with his eye patch.

Nick helped her out of the car and slammed the door shut after locking it. He turned eagerly, "C'mon, Jess! Brian says they have their Christmas decorations out, and I wanna go see!"
"Oh my God," Jessica said, touching the bridge of her nose, "Remind me why I willingly have sex with you again?"
"Because I have a working TurboGrafx-CD and every US release for it?" Nick asked, in a helpful tone of voice.

"So help me," Jessica said as she rolled her eyes, "If you weren't so damn pretty I'd drive you out to the woods and leave you there."

"I'm telling the ASPCA on you!" Nick countered.

Jessica threw her arms around his neck and went up on the balls of her feet to give him a kiss, "You're so pretty."

Nick grinned lopsidedly at her, "So you keep saying. C'mon, Jess, let's get going. Brian's already inside!"

"I don't get you, Nick, "Jessica said, "You haven't seen this guy in 4 years, and your idea of a good reunion spot is Wal-Mart?"

Nick broke from the embrace and took her hand.

"Honestly, Jess, you just don't get me."

"I just SAID that, you goof!"

Nick's lopsided grin lowered in intensity a bit, but did not leave. It was December, the most wonderful time of the year! This was the time of year when even most of the worst assholes would at the very least buck up and PRETEND to give a shit about their fellow man. Truth be told, Nick carried a little bit of Christmas around with him always. Jessica noticed that a few days before Thanksgiving, when she spotted him trying to decide between a red tie clip with a green tie, or a green tie clip with a red tie. Jessica pressed him, and found out that no matter what, he always wore some small portion of red and green.

It was also true that he listened to Christmas music every Sunday while making breakfast… it was a tradition he began after his first date with Akiko. Even as he held the hand of his new lover, he found himself reminiscing about when he first met his wife.

Nick had stayed the night; and what happened during the night was nobody's business, but Akiko's father had walked into the kitchen while Nick was making coffee during the morning after. Desperately seeking some way to redirect the old man's ire, the still-teenaged Nick turned on the record player in the room. Mr. Saotome had imported the 1977 "Snoopy's Christmas" album by the Peppermint Kandy Kids, and by happenstance that was on the player. Nick found himself almost immediately captivated by the jovial notes that began the story. When the actors began speaking, Nick had no idea what they were saying. The happiness and goofy quality of the dialogue transcended language, and Nick found he wanted to know what they were saying. On that day started not only Nick's English lessons, but also his love of all things Christmas. Through the years that came, that continued. He would make a special breakfast on Sunday morning, and play that music through the preparation and eating of said food, and he only missed one day of this tradition: the day after Akiko died. Even through the dark times that followed, he kept the tradition on; though it no longer made his heart leap.

Until he met Jessica, that is. She hit his life hard and got right past his walls, smashed her way into his heart, and had since then been busy webbing over all the weak parts in his heart. Christmas music made his heart leap again, cartoons were fun and innocent again. And the sex? Sex was no longer just an escape from the drudgery of life, a desperate reach for some joy. When Nick had finally decided to start dating again, he was never really that much into it. Though he was not on the level that Jessica had been... it was true he cared very little the identity of the women he was sleeping with. He was just going through the motions anyway, save for time spent in bed with them. That brought him to life again, even if for only a very short time. That was why he could not hold her past ways against Jessica; he was the same. She was just better at cutting through the bullshit and getting down to business.

Sex had been good, but now it was... amazing. He'd like to say the sex with Jessica was always stellar, but honestly they were still getting used to each other in bed. Even at it's worst, though, it felt... right. Nick found a line from Scrubs summed things up best: everything he does is more fun if Jessica is doing it with him.

Nick shook himself out of his reverie. Jessica had led him into Wal-Mart and was talking, "-you even listening to me?"
Nick leaned into Jessica, "Sorry, was just thinking about how much I love you, how much you just set my loins aflame," he leaned in and inhaled her scent, and started licking her along her jawline.
Jessica closed her eyes, enjoying the moment before she spoke, "I said, is THAT the guy you're looking for?"

Nick looked where Jessica was pointing. It was! There he was, Brian Braddock. His best friend. Nick had known this man for well onto twenty years now, since they first bumped into each other in England, Nick seeking out more of the men who took his family from him, and Brian seeking only to find out who the beautiful Japanese girl with Nick was. Brian was a man who was in the 22nd

SAS, and had been transferred over to Interpol to deal with international crime… such as the syndicate Nick was hitting over and over until they would leave him alone. When that was done, his sister-in-law Noriko had fallen for Brian, and their lives became intermingled since. Whenever Brian could get away on vacation in the US, or reasonably enlist Nick's services as a Private Investigator, they got together again and again. As time passed, they became closer and closer, forming a bond that went beyond mere friendship. They had only been able to exchange emails, chat online, or play MMOs together for the last five years as Brian had been too busy to get away.

Brian was not a hard man to spot… he was the only African-descended human male in this part of town who was clearly at the beck and call of his tiny wife. Their eyes locked from across the front end of the Wal-Mart, Brian was down by pets… and thus was clearly sneaking early glances at the Christmas decorations; and Nick was way over by the far entrance. On a whim, he set up his media player to belt out the theme song from "Chariots of Fire", and they began to run at each other.

Sort of.

Brian and Nick clearly had the same thing in mind, because they were engaging in a slow motion run, making overblown movie expressions at each other while the music swelled. Nick reached his hand out towards his best friend and spoke like a man slowed down on film, "Brrrriiiiiiiiaaaaaaaaan!" Brian, in response, reached out, still in slow motion as he passed the eye drops, and tore the package open, handing it back at normal speed to his wife. He proceeded to dump massive amounts of the drops into his eyes, making it look very much like he was weeping with joy... Brian raised his arms and shook his head, and called back, "Niiiiiiiiiiccccckkk I looooooooovvvveee yyyooooooou!"

Jessica walked ahead of Nick, reaching Noriko who had done the same. Noriko bowed lightly to Jessica, and then crossed her arms, watching the two men speed up slightly so they could meet before the song ended. Jessica just... held the bridge of her nose in her two forefingers and thumb as the spectacle was causing a crowd to gather. When Brian and Nick met, they each mimed leaping into the air, trying to land in one another's arms. Both closed their eyes in joy and anticipation of their reunion... and then in just as much slow motion knocked their heads together. Nick slumped to his side feigning unconsciousness, while Brian acted like he was thrown into the pharmacy chairs beside them, and ended lying plank-straight across the arms of three of them.

"Hello, you must be Jessica Dombrowski?" Noriko asked, turning to Jessica.
Jessica shook her head, "No, I absolutely am not. I don't know who this man is. Gah."
Noriko covered her mouth as she giggled, "I understand the sentiment entirely. When these boys get together, they are always like this."
Jessica just hung her head a bit, "I couldn't honestly tell you when Nick ISN'T like this."
Noriko patted Jessica's back, and Jessica stood up straight, now smiling at Nick as Noriko spoke, "You must love him well to put up with this."

Jessica chuckled, "Ahh, well, he may be an embarrassment in public, but he makes me feel like…. I know I'm loved, you know?"
Noriko nodded, "I know very well. I was actually trying to take my sister's place in Nick's life when I met Brian. These men are made of the same stuff, and it's better they are best friends, because otherwise they would be very dangerous enemies."

Nick stood up, and Brian slid into one of the chairs, looking at once very proper and…. For lack of a better term, British. "You are looking rather at ease, mate."
Nick grinned lopsidedly, "Holy crap man you are looking… old. What's with all the snow atop Mount Braddock?"
Brian rolled his eyes, "Oh thank you for that. Yes, I'm a human. I do lots of human stuff. I age! I'm doing it right now!."
"Consider the following," Nick said, "you were admitted to this robot asylum, therefore you must be a robot."
"Diagnosis complete!" Brian said in a robotic voice.
"I can see why they like each other, Miss Noriko." Jessica said as she came up and wrapped her arms around Nick from behind, "Hi Brian. I'm Jessica. Nick's talked about me?"

Brian stood like a gentleman and raised his hand. Jessica had been with Nick long enough to know what THAT was about, and gave her his hand to be kissed. Brian did exactly that, and afterwards he met her gaze with one of his own and said, "Enchanted, the pleasure is entirely mine."
"Hey now, don't go trying to steal my lover from me," Nick said as he elbowed Brian.

"Sorry, Nick!" Jessica interjected, "I'm not TRYING to take him from you but I just can't help it sometimes.
Brian let out a surprised laugh, "You weren't kidding, mate, she really is very quick witted."
Nick stood up and took Jessica's hand, "Yep, that's... one of the many reasons I love her."
Brian went over to take Noriko's as well, and looked to her with puppy dog eyes, "What do you say, luv, can we pop over to the Christmas section?"

"Wait, wait, hold on, Brian. We have to play." Nick said, setting his hand firmly in a stop gesture.
"Really, mate? You know I'll just wallop you." Brian said, with a raised eyebrow.
Nick looked grimly determined, "I've been practicing."
"With who?" Brian asked, scoffing, "This country hasn't got a single top flight player."
Nick stood firm. "It does now. Canary Wharf."
"You're just going to get spanked as always, mate," Brian protested as he met Nick's eye.
Nick met his gaze with iron, nay, something harder... perhaps... titanium resolve. "Canary. Wharf."

"Allright, if you insist. I'll have to block with North Wembley."
Nick rolled his eye, "You really think I'll fall into that trap? South Kensington."
Brian held his hand up, "Don't you mean Tower Hill?"
Nick shook his head, "Tuskador rules. South Kensington."
"Right then, stepping up to the big leagues, little pup? I'll just diagonal over to Dagenham Heath."
Nick's smartass little grin appeared, "Dagenham East."

Brian's eyes widened, "Are you daft, man? You know I'll just cross you right over with Hillingdon."

"Latimer Road."

"Oh well played, mate... perhaps... No... wait, Tuskador regulation or Tuskador modified?" Brian asked.

"Tuskador Regulation," Nick replied, "I KNOW Jessica can't be a proper adjudicate."

"Right, right," Brian said, scratching his nose, "And I still couldn't be arsed to buy Noriko Rules and Origins. Fine, uhhmm... Oxford Circus."

"You should have. It's out of print, now. And you got too distracted and left me an opening. Upminster Bridge."

Brian's jaw dropped, "well that move takes cast iron bollocks. I'm not stupid though. Back to North Wembley."

"Ah ha!" Nick said, forefinger raised, "you just put yourself in Nidd."

"So what? I'm also sitting on all avenues of escape. Wiggle about all you want. Once my penalty is up you're doomed. I told you only natives can play this game."

"Queensbury."

"You what? Impossible!"

"Liverpool Street, and what does that mean?"

Brian shook his head, defeated, "You're right, Nick. This brings you of course to-"

"Mornington Crescent."

"I can't believe it. Never in a million years would I have thought you could pull it off."

Nick patted his back, "Nice bluff, though, with the Dagenham Heath."

"I'll be damned, Nick. Against all odds, you've gotten better."

Jessica turned to Noriko, "What was... what was all of that?"

Noriko shrugged, "I don't know. Whenever they try to explain it to me I get lost in all the rules and regulations. As far as I can tell you are moving around London Underground stations trying to reach Mornington Crescent."

"I'll find you the rulebook, love, I promise. Can Nick and I go see the decorations whilst I lick my wounds?" Brian asked. Jessica could tell that if Brian had a tail, it would be wagging. Much like... Nick's was right now.

Noriko kissed Brian on the nose, "Of course. You two catch up. Jessica, would you care to head for that Starbuck's I saw over there and take tea?"

"Yep. Don't think I could put up with these two much longer." she responded.

"It's allright Jessica, they'll calm down and become less insufferable over time."

Nick gave Jessica an excited kiss, and the two of them headed off for the garden center to overlook the decorations.

As they headed back to the other side of the Wal-Mart, Jessica's trained eye spotted two men with smartphone cameras "innocently" filming pretty women, one definite shoplifter, and one woman who was, given that she looked like a roller derby girl despite there being no derby in town, most likely a prostitute. In other words, a typical day at Wal-Mart. Were she in a different mood, Jessica would make some off duty arrests just to pass the time.

They arrived at the Starbucks, and the dwarven woman behind the counter looked at Jessica, saying "Afternoon, Officer Dombrowski. Usual?"
Jessica smiled politely, "Venti with none of that frou frou crap in it."
Noriko tapped the countertop, "Mocha Chai Latte, iced, very sweet, and two of your turkey and havarti, grilled for my friend and I and I am paying."
Jessica decided it wasn't even worth arguing, and instead headed to take a seat at one of the high tables. Noriko returned and set their repast down on the table, and settled in herself.
Jessica took a swallow from her coffee, barely even feeling the heat. She set her drink down with a happy sigh, and looked over to Noriko, "Thanks for paying, Noriko."
"Oh certainly," Noriko said primly, "Tell me then, how did you meet Nick?"
Jessica nodded, "You're Akiko's little sister, right?"
Noriko shook her head and chuckled, "Not so little as I once was. But yes, she was my older sister."
Jessica picked up her sandwich and sniffed at it. It smelled very enticing, actually. She nibbled at it a moment, and then took a larger bite before talking, "I guess this is as close to touching his old life as I'm gonna get."
Noriko smiled, "Good sandwich, innit? And yes, I suppose that is true. I've known Nick quite a long time, and it's good to hear him using the word 'love' again."

Jessica took another big bite of her sandwich, "Well, I'd give you the version I tell at the station, but you wouldn't believe it any more than they do. Some... nasty things happened in my past. When Nick first spotted me, I was your garden variety bar skank. No joke, he hung around the bar for like two months, watching guys take me home every night he saw me."

"Love at first sight, was it?" Noriko asked as she swished her drink around.

"Oh, far from it!" Jessica said as she laughed, "I think at first all he was really doing is trying to get up the courage to ask me to fuck. But I guess after a while he started to learn who I was. He's a PI so it wasn't hard to look me up and learn about me. I'm pretty sure he had a vibe on me ever since he looked me up. He was pretty subtle but I'm also a detective... public kind though. He wasn't really giving me a creeper vibe, but I decided to check him out anyway."

"Right, like you weren't 'checking him out' even before then," Noriko quipped.

Jessica looked just a moment like a child with her hand caught in a cookie jar, "Guilty. He's just so damn pretty, but in a... manly way? Blargh. Point is he finally got the balls up to approach me. We started out pretty hot and heavy, I tried to blow him in the car, he fingered me in a theater."

Noriko coughed lightly and she had to take a big swallow, "That sort of story, is it? No need to dumb it down, but according to Brian Nick described it as far more romantic."

"Well," Jessica said with a roll of her eyes, "Nick likes to sugar coat things. The fact is Nick was being a sweet guy, he wanted me BAD, and showed me like that. Afterwards we stepped outside for some fresh air, and someone needed help. Nick actually took off before I did to go help, and looking back on it that probably got me seeing him as something more than a fuck. One thing led to another, and we sorta started helping each other... be happier. We worked together on what was... honestly a downright horrifying case. I've seen some awful stuff as a cop, but nothing approaching this... nor what it took from Nick to get down to the bottom of it."

Noriko reached out and touched her hand, "What are you on about? It really is a very sweet story. Darkest night you became each other's light and whatnot."

"It... really wasn't..." Jessica finished her sandwich and closed her eyes a moment, trying to decide how to word what was coming next. "See it turns out that the chips only fell the way they did because a... supernatural entity was pushing us together. And when I'm being honest with myself, I doubt we would have gotten together like we did without that. Sometimes in the middle of the night I wonder if we aren't still being artificially glued together, because I... Nick deserves better than me."

"Don't say that," Noriko said, "Nick is over the moon about you."

Jessica sipped her coffee, "I accept that, and I love him, I just think he can do better. See, I'm a crazy woman. Spent a coupla years in a... really bad situation. Stockholm Syndrome hit me pretty hard, and my captor... hey I'd rather not talk about this part. Point is my self esteem's taken a few knocks along with making me a paranoid, self destructive wreck. I hate anything that even... HINTS of mind control, so when I learned how we got together, I freaked the fuck out. I pushed Nick away, hard. I actually took a guy home with me right in front of

Nick, trying to get him to see me for the horrible worthless slut I am. But for the first time in a REAL long time… I stopped before I did something really stupid. Coupla months later, here we are."

Noriko shook her head, "You make Nick sound utterly blameless."
"Well," Jessica said with a smirk, "He's guilty of not taking hints, of being too dorky for his own good, and, honestly, the lengths he's willing to go to when the stakes are high are… far more extreme than I would go. Not going to get into specifics, but I can tell you… there's capacity for great violence in that man."
Noriko shifted a bit in her chair, "You forget who you are talking to. When I met Brian, I had been following Nick around and watching him strike back against those who killed my sister. It takes a lot to scare a Yakuza society away from trying to kill you."
Jessica nodded, "You would know then. I think he's fundamentally a very loving man, but when you push his buttons, you better watch out. On an upshot, I'm such a crazy psycho bitch that I already know for sure he's not prone to pointing that dark side at those he loves."

Noriko laughed a bit, "I know. My sister mentioned the same fears. If it helps, neither my sister nor I have seen him hurt anyone that doesn't deserve it. I remember there was this little red-skinned devil boy that had stolen food from an okonomiyaki cart. Nick stood firm in protection of that boy, even paid the cost of the stolen food thrice over. The boy then swore himself to Nick eternally. Nick talked him down, told him if he really wanted to make it square, he was to start helping out at the local shrine. It was the most unusual sight you'd see for the next few years, a hellspawn was in service at a holy place. The... things that went wrong went wrong shortly after. I sometimes wonder what happened to that little boy. I'll also tell you... Brian is a special operations soldier so... I simply don't ask him about what he does at work."

Jessica looked off towards the garden center, "Well, I think we should probably check in on our incredibly dangerous overgrown children lest we find they spent all their money on one of those fucking awful matching light and song lawn setups."

Justine Bailey took a deep breath and let it out slowly. Tonight was the night she was FINALLY getting her chance at Buzz. She'd had eyes on the orc since he was barely more than a kid when the family had moved into town because she could tell already he was growing up to be a good man. And yes, over the few years that came between, Buzz had shown himself true to her predictions. The down side is he was never single when she had the courage to talk to him.

His last girl decided he wasn't wealthy enough to be with her, and Justine had been there to make the rebound. All the girls loved the orc linebacker for he was a very unique orc. He was great in bed, well equipped for it, and also not a complete asshole. The waifish blonde elf knew her mother would kill her for even thinking of going with an orc, but here she was.

Justine exhaled again, and pressed the doorbell. There was no response so she tried again. Still nothing, and the elf knocked hesitantly on the door. The door opened a bit from her knocks, and she peered around it to look inside. Justine tilted her head, unable to comprehend the sight inside. The living room was in shambles, and there were bits and pieces of what looked like insects strewn about. As she was trying to piece together what must have happened, a very attractive blonde human in an immaculate charcoal grey business suit strode out of the kitchen towards her. Anthropology and Biology were her greatest interests so her first reflex was to categorize this man. With his cheekbones, the tone of his skin and brown eye color, she guessed at 'Native' American human. She was brought out of this train of thought by him putting his hand on her shoulder.

"Oh sweetie," he said in a caring voice, "you must be the 'Justine' that this family was talking about."
Justine stared at the man, still unable to fathom what was going on, "Uh… yeah, I'm Justine."
The man smiled politely, "And my name is Merrick. It looks like tonight I get the birds in the bush as well as the one in my hand. Didn't think a chance to get an elf would come up so soon."
"W-what?" the girl stammered. Sensing danger, she began to step away.
"This is just perfect," Merrick continued, "This will look like nothing but orcish gang violence. Nobody will ever come looking for you."

Justine turned to run, or at least tried to. Merrick's grip held her in place easily. "Even the elves, in their famed beauty, hold not a candle to my queen in her despair." Merrick's other hand took her by the throat. Justine kicked and clawed to no avail. Merrick carried her along as easily as her veterinarian father would a newborn puppy.

Chapter Two:
- "A Marshmallow World", Dean Martin

Nick grimaced lightly as he pulled into the dead end street. While Jessica's 94 Celica GT-4 was far less conspicuous than his beloved 69 GTO Judge, it still didn't do very well with his usual plan of "drive casually by the home of the subject" when you have to pull a three point and leave afterwards. Instead Nick pulled the grey car into a driveway a little farther up, then used that to go back the way he came from, as would any lost person who wandered into this area. Getting back out onto the main street, he tried to come up with a secondary plan. There was a highway over the edge of the man's property. With a cross street this close, there was more than likely going to be a good view from the underpass. He smiled as a solution came to mind.

Within minutes, Nick was pulling into the hospital's parking lot. He pulled in somewhere towards the middle of the lot; in front of the Oncology center. Typically those receiving treatment here were brought by family members, as patients could rarely drive after a bout of chemo. It wasn't unusual for those family members to take a walk to the nearby park in the meantime. Nick first took a few moments to trade his jacket out for the cheap one he found on the back seat floor. No doubt the leftover of one of Jessica's one night stands. Curious, he sniffed at the jacket, and then immediately wished he had not. She had probably literally fucked the guy ON this jacket. He made a mental note to burn this jacket afterwards, and clean Jessica's car for her. He had long since accepted that Jessica was rather... promiscuous before they got together, but he'd rather not run into reminders of this sort again.

His ears flattened a bit as he put the jacket on. Nick knew he'd get used to the scent in a few moments and be able to easily ignore it, but for now it... well, it sucked. Nick locked up her car and blinked when something landed on the hairs of his left dog-ear. A snowflake. Nick looked up to see more was on it's way down. Chill had come to Chicago early this year, that was true enough, but the snow had been stubbornly late arriving. Two days before, it had seemed it would start to snow, but there were only a few flakes here and there. Nick had been somewhat disappointed; this year for the first time in who knew how long Nick was waiting for the first snowfall. It never felt like the Christmas season truly began until the snow came down and stuck.

There was not just a small amount, either. The flakes were coming down, thick and in great amounts. He stood still, quiet and listening. For a few moments it seemed the whole rest of the world did the same. A stray cat Nick could see near the hospital's dumpster was doing the same thing as him; looking up at the snow. The cat was probably not happy about it; the winter months were hardest to scavenge food during. The thick flakes continued to flutter down, a thin coating of it turned the entire parking lot around him white in just a few minutes.

Nick's phone began to vibrate, and the song playing from said phone let Nick know immediately who it was. "Watch Your Step"... Spider-Woman's theme song. Jessica did not find his choice of ringtone for her to be particularly amusing, but it always gave Nick a chuckle. He felt it fit nicely. The phone case Jessica had given him for his phone had a black widow on the back of it, she was always giving him little things that had spiders on them. Jessica was always careful never to disrupt webs, and would actually even go out of her way to shoo flies towards spider webs. Her choice in bedtime clothing invariably had a spider theme to it, and Jessica herself had even theorized that, where her mother and most other Dryads tended to share an affinity with assorted plants, it was probably spiders with her. They sure tended to show up a LOT more often when Jessica was nearby. What better song for her, then?

"Heya Jess, what's up Tootsie Pop?" he answered. Jessica snorted a bit, "'Tootsie Pop'? No, I don't like that, no, sir, not at all."
Nick had been trying out pet names for her, and she had been shooting them down. "Well, regardless, what's up, Jess?" he asked again.
"Take a look outside, Prettyboy. It's snowing, and I mean it's REALLY coming down," she said happily.
Nick scratched the back of his head as he grinned lopsidedly, "I know, it's pretty."
"I don't really care much for Christmas, but I bet you're loving this. I kinda wish you were here with me right now." Jessica said, with a wistful tone in her voice.
"I kinda wish you were with me almost all the time, Jess," he returned.

"Yeah, I get that," she said, "I love you too. It's just that I wish I could see your eye right now. You've got a really sweet dopey happy thing going on, but what I saw when you were looking at those decorations with Brian? That's different. Your eye was all... watery, kinda soft grey. And your cheeks were a little red. You're always so pretty, but that was downright heartwarming. I bet you look like that right now."
Nick chuffed a little, "Yeah, well that's your fault you know."
"My fault?" Jessica asked with a confused tone, "What are you even... babbling about?"
"It's real simple, Jess. I haven't been able to feel like that since after Akiko went," he said. Turning his face up again, "It's like a stupid movie. My world's got joy in it again, and you are why."
"You know I'm not great with this touchy-feely stuff, Prettyboy." She said
Nick looked back down, "I know, Jess. But you're more romantic than you give yourself credit for. After all, you saw snow and you called me right up."
"A weather report is romantic now?" She deadpanned.
"You suck, Jess!" He said, not at all meaning it.

Jessica's voice dropped an octave, "I do. In fact I wish I could suck you right now. After last night, I owe you. God, scented bubble bath, champagne, Chinese takeout and floating candles. Floating. Candles. That rocked my world, Prettyboy."
"I got a lot out of it also. Caressing you, massaging you... kissing you all over that beautiful body of yours." Nick shuddered, "If I weren't on a job I'd come to you right now and worship you again."

"Yeah…" Jessica said, "I'm sure the judge would REALLY appreciate me bringing my boyfriend to mack on me while waiting to testify about a 501 that got three people killed."
Nick laughed, "Oh, I just don't care who sees us."
"Yeah, about that also," Jessica said, voice returning to normal, "We did that in your landlord's bathtub. I think we need to have a serious talk about your living arrangements."
"Are you suggesting we move in together somewhere?" He asked.
There was a long pause before Jessica answered, "Yeah, I guess I am, Prettyboy. Feels right, you know? Look, we'll talk about this later. I think I'm about to get fined for phone usage in a courtroom." She hung up abruptly after saying that.

Nick pocketed his phone, and let out a sigh. It was time to get back to work. Humming "Silver Bells"… since he could not whistle, Nick put on his backpack full of surveillance equipment, jammed his hands in his pockets, and headed for the underpass. It was time to get back to work.

Nick walked along the side of the road until he reached the underpass. In this part of the city, there was no visible poverty, due to being so close to Chicago's famous "Magnificent Mile". All the shops and apartment buildings were upscale, the streets so well maintained that Nick was fairly certain he'd never seen so much as a pothole lasting overnight. It actually made Nick mildly annoyed; the wealthy very much liked to pretend the problems of the world did not exist, and it led them to believe some utterly ridiculous nonsense. Randian fantasies about how the wealthy and powerful got that way due to their own intelligence and "rational morality". The thing is, very few of them had actually lifted a single finger to earn their wealth. Third and fourth generation, profiting forever off the machines built by their forefathers. He doubted any of those capitalists of the past would begrudge the working men a living, much less sweeping those men who actually sustained their fortunes out to the dark corners of of the city like they were vermin. Yet here was how the world stood today.

No matter how thorough they believed they were, they could never eliminate all of those "vermin". The worst off of them all, scrabbling to survive on the castoffs of such mindless decadence, tended to be the most resilient. Sure enough, this underpass bore the signs of being an encampment of these disenfranchised persons. Nick jammed his hands into his jacket pockets and did his level best to look like a weary, hungry man with nowhere to go. In a cold uncaring place like the wealthier parts of Chicago, camps like this were oases of warmth and some modicum of protection due to numbers. It was a perfectly adequate cover story to be newly homeless in December; power bills in November were often enough the last straw in driving the already poor to be unable to pay their rent.

"Hey, is anyone over here?" Nick asked, "It's really cold out and they told me I had to leave the library because…" Nick's voice trailed off when he noticed that the camp had no activity going on, despite there being a whisper-quiet generator running. It would be a waste to leave that running when there was nobody here. The hair on the back of Nick's neck pricked up a bit, and his tail fuzzed out as well... this was very out of the ordinary. He reached down to where his pistol was tucked into a small of the back holster and drew it. Keeping the pistol almost at shoulder for fast aiming, he began to clear the area. There was a campfire that was now only smouldering ashes loosely in the shape of a log, and, like this were some sort of TV movie drama, a pot of pork and beans over it. The issue here was that the beans had been burnt beyond palatability an hour or more ago. Still leading with his pistol, Nick crouched to look at the ground. While no snow was able to reach here, there was still dirt. His investigative skills kicked in instantly; Nick saw that several persons were taken out of here with no struggle by creatures that left twin pincer marks.

"Son of a bitch, Skinstealers," Nick said to nobody, though he hoped his voice would cause some motion or response. His ears caught a whole bunch of nothing but the rare overhead traffic and the sound of someone watching Star Trek not very far off. He dimly registered it was probably the subject he was investigating watching that. With neither recent scent nor current sound, Nick knew there was nothing for him to do here but gather evidence and talk to Jessica about it later. Being careful not to disturb the scene any more, Nick took pictures from multiple angles, and even laid down his pistol next to the prints the Skinstealers left on the scene to later on extrapolate sizes of the creatures. While Nick was no police detective, the basic concepts were the same, and it took him less than twenty minutes to gather what he felt was a sufficient overlook of the situation. Calling the actual police would simply get this labelled a "gang activity" or some other such nonsense, as nobody cared about the homeless. It was likely up to him and Jessica. For now anyway.

Deciding that nobody would miss them anyway, Nick extracted some of the blankets, piling them under where he was setting up surveillance on his subject. Throwing another blanket about his shoulders, Nick waited. Over the course of the next hour, absolutely nothing happened. The snow fell, traffic flowed over him, and the land he was watching had no comings or goings. The lights weren't even on, and looking at the chimney, the wood stove wasn't on, either. While Nick loved the A-team stuff he got to do, this was the meat and potatoes of being a Private Investigator. Long, boring stakeouts often in unpleasant weather. Nick fished his earbuds out of his jacket, and attached them to his phone. Setting himself with an old-time radio drama station Nick settled in for a longer haul. There were worse things than listening to Dragnet and Gunsmoke to while away the time. His go-to station for this sort of thing was called Town Park Radio. The name made little sense to him, but the entertainment was solid.

An hour after sunset, things began to happen. A late-model Saturn pulled into the gravel driveway, and out popped Albert Vincenzo… drunk as a skunk and with a female dwarf. Nick immediately began filming; someone who had "crippling social anxiety" would not be bringing home a one night stand. The couple moved inside; the "inside" wasn't really much of a house. A simple camper attached to a hastily constructed interior, probably a prefab storage unit, with windows carved out of the outside. Nick didn't have the best angle, but it ultimately did not matter. Mr. Vincenzo and companion made a phone call, threw a pizza into the oven, and went back outside. Albert went to a tarp-covered storage shed and began pulling out plastic chairs and a long table.

In the fifteen minutes that came next, Albert set up for an outdoor party, despite the snow. He was grilling hot dogs, and had dragged out a cooler full of beer. Albert reached into the cooler and took out a Budweiser. Popping the tab, he drank half of the beer in three swallows. Nick grinned; that alone was enough to get him knocked off his "disability." You were simply not permitted to use alcohol on anti-anxiety drugs. A minivan pulled onto the gravel beside the Saturn, and it discharged 8 people who seemed more than ready to party. Nick recorded everything, knowing that Social Security preferred ample evidence of fraud to make their cases ironclad. Boring as this sort of work may be, the straightforward nature of it was a reliable source of income. SS didn't start contracting out for investigators until they were just about 100% sure fraud was occurring. Though Nick sometimes got the feeling his involvement was merely a formality, his bank account didn't care.

Having gathered everything he needed, Nick gathered himself up and headed back to Jessica's car. It was now very dark, and the hospital lot was nearly deserted. The flakes were still falling, fat and bright. The parking lights in the hospital were wrapped in white icicle lights to reflect the season. Though Nick personally found white lighting to be barely festive at all, he had to admit that it gave an ethereal effect to this slow-motion parody of a blizzard. He leaned for a moment against the car, feeling the flakes touch his ears and light on his nose for a bit. It was, indeed, the most wonderful time of the year, and Nick was reasonably certain that when he got home there would be a warm place, a beautiful woman, and some takeout or microwave food waiting for him.

Jessica had basically taken up residence at his office, and the unspoken agreement was that whoever got home first was responsible for the chow that evening. Nick unlocked the car and started it up. While this Celica didn't have the sheer snarling power of his Judge, it was a peppy little V6 that was engineered to use four wheel drive even at high speeds. In some circumstances it far outstripped his vehicle's usefulness due to it's superior cornering and the aforementioned drivetrain. Shutting Town Park Radio off, Nick started his Christmas playlist, and whistled happily as he drove back home, eager to see his pretty black widow.

Nick parked the Celica outside of the walkup; he could see that his Judge was already in the garage, which meant Jessica was home. Nick flicked the brim of his black Indiana Jones hat, grinning lopsidedly as he started up the stairs. Halfway up, his phone buzzed for a text message. Nick pulled his phone out of his pocket and thumbed to the message. Brian wanted to hit Dave and Buster's. Nick's grin broadened. That was actually a very good idea. It was a typical bar to some extent, with pub food, assorted entertainment on TVs, as well as ample pool tables that were free for customer usage. While Jessica and Noriko were doing all that, Nick and Brian could while away the evening playing everything from Afterburner II to Zookeeper. Nick switched to whistling "Feliz Navidad" as he fished his keys out of his pocket and unlocked the front door, "Evenin', Jess. I was thinking maybe we could go out with Brian and Noriko tonight!"

As he stepped into the room, the sight before him caused his mouth to fall open and his tongue to come out a bit. He had to try a few times before he gave up on getting the keys into his pocket and just dropped them. He kicked the door shut behind him. Jessica was sitting in his office chair, wearing a Catholic schoolgirl outfit with knee-length white silk stockings. Over those stocking she wore three and a half inch heeled red gladiator sandals. Jessica had her hair in twin pigtails, tied in place by green ribbons. To top it all off? The skirt was not tartan, but black with a grey spider-webbing pattern all over it. She touched her fingertip inside her mouth and stretched pink bubblegum out before speaking, "But Mr. Sakamoto, if you go out with your friend, how can I earn enough extra credit to get an A? My Daddy will spank me if I don't get an A."

Nick brought his phone up and fired off a reply, "Busy. Sex." Nick hit send and then tossed the phone onto the table near the door, where he would promptly forget about it. Jessica popped her gum, "We're going to do something a little different tonight, Prettyboy."
Nick turned and hung his jacket up neatly, "I get to fuck you in the ass?"
Jessica ran her hand along her thigh, baring a little of her left cheek, "If you'd like. Kinda surprised you never brought that up again before now."
Nick blushed red, "I'm... you didn't seem to really like it much the last time..."

A wan smile came across her lips, "You can't imagine... if I told you you were the first guy that did that with me I was lying. I didn't much care what the hell guys were doing to me, I just liked the power of making them come. Just because you're my steady man doesn't mean I enjoy that power any less. I love you, Prettyboy. Don't spoil the moment."

Jessica twirled one of her pigtails around with her other hand, "Furthermore, it doesn't matter what you think I might or might not like tonight. You're going to give me exactly what I want tonight."
Nick stepped in close to Jessica, and kneeled next to her. He began kissing lightly above her knee, up the thigh a bit, "What, exactly, do you want tonight, Jess?"

Jessica closed her eyes as her breath caught. She loved it when Nick kissed her like that, it felt so intimate. It was at the same time a promise... a reminder of everything Nick meant to her, in addition to being a way to arouse her very quickly. She was a little dizzy a moment, Nick was able to have that effect on her in so many ways that seemed effortless and casual to him. She had to gather her wits about her before she could speak again, "Tonight, you are going to play this little game, and you are going to spank me, choke me, punish me. You are going to hurt me. I'm going to submit my will to you, and you're going to do it because I tell you to."

Nick looked up at Jessica, and... grinned lopsidedly, "I'm not entirely ignorant of the rules of The Scene, Jess. What's your safe word?"

"Fuck's sake Nick I've been throwing you hints since the second night I KNEW you, and you already know how this works?" Jessica said, tone exasperated.
Nick scratched the back of his head and chuckled, "Have you? I'm not great at taking hints, Jess."
Jessica rolled her eyes, she was absolutely certain she had been so very obvious about this since they met. "Pomeranian."

Jessica looked worried, "And I'm not a bad girl, am I Mr. Sakamoto?"
Nick stood, "You're here dressed like a slut in those shoes, and asking if you're a bad girl?"
Jessica looked down, "My... shoes? But... the girls, we see how you look at us, I thought for sure you'd like these shoes."
Nick stepped right up against her, "I do. And you're a bad girl for wearing them."
Jessica turned her glance to Nick, confused and near to tears, "But I... if you like them, why am I a bad girl?"
"Good girls do research projects for extra credit. Bad girls wear shoes that get their teachers hard," he said, as he grabbed Jessica by her elbow, forcing her to her feet.
"I'm sorry, Mr. Sakamoto!" Jessica yelped out.
"You know what we do with bad girls, right, Jessica?" Nick asked, turning her to face the desk.

"...spank them." Jessica said, voice resigned. She put her hands on the desk and bent at the waist, her short skirt riding up just enough to show her bare ass. Nick grabbed her wrists and forced her instead down onto her elbows. Her muscled ass was now on full display, in a heart shape since her legs were together. She was bent so deeply that

Nick could see the lush green of her trim pubic hair. Nick paused a moment himself to enjoy the view. Jessica told him that green was her natural hair color, and she hadn't shown it to anyone since she began dyeing it when she was an 11 year old girl. It wasn't easy to dye the hair between her legs, so she shaved it. It was something of an unspoken show of how special Nick was to her that she let some grow. Right now it was a sign of a woman, holding a little of her scent at all times; and a stark contrast to the little girl role she was in at the moment.

Jessica looked back at him in fear, as he raised up his hand, "Be gentle, Mr. Sakamoto, I can't-"

Nick silenced her with a sharp slap to her right cheek. Jessica inhaled at that, and a small moan escaped afterwards. Nick gave her another, and her reaction was more this time, and she bit her lower lip to silence herself afterwards. "You like it, you're a naughty girl, and you like it."
Jessica shook her head emphatically, "I don't! I'm a good girl!"

Nick slapped her again, harder, his fingers spread just right to make the sound loud, "If you were a good girl, you wouldn't BE here right now," he intoned, low and flat, as he slapped her again, again, and twice more after that. Jessica looked back, tears streaming from her eyes, "No, Mr. Sakamoto, I'm a good girl! Stop, please!"

Nick looked around on the desk. Beside some conspicuously placed Astroglide was his clipboard. He took that in his hand and swatted Jessica's ass twice, the oak more than up to the task.

"No... please... pleease!" Jessica sank to her knees and looked up, mascara running, "I'm a good girl, Mr. Saka-" Nick grabbed her by her hair and set her back how she was, as Jessica whimpered. Nick grimly slapped her ass with the clipboard, over and over, as Jessica cried out; moaning as well. "I hear that, bad little girl. You're moaning. This is turning you on."

Jessica shook her head, "It's not please.. Please.." she began to sob as Nick resumed spanking her. Slowly, her sobs turned to moans and gasps of pleasure.
Nick took a fistful of luxurious hair, yanking Jessica back by her left pigtail, "See? You like this, you ARE a bad girl, aren't you?"

Jessica bit her lips hard enough to draw blood, and she began to nod, "I... I am a bad girl. I deserve this."
Nick hit her twice more, "That's right, you're my bad girl. Mine, you're my bad little slut."
Jessica whimpered and nodded, "I'm a bad girl. I'm your little slut."

Nick hit her twice more with the clipboard, and it splintered. He slapped her once more, than gripped the half broken board by the edges, catching some of the red flesh of her cheek in the wood, pinching hard. Jessica's hands came forwards and she clawed at Nick's desk, "Please.. Mr. Sakamoto, what can your little slut do to get extra credit?"

Nick dropped his pants to his ankles in a moment, his erect cock freed. His need to take Jessica was so intense it was nearly painful.
"Are..." Jessica said, looking back, "Are you gonna fuck me, Mr. Sakamoto?"
Nick pulled her hair again, and forced her head back to face front, "No, my little slut."
"But...." Jessica whimpered, "I want you to, Mr. Sakamoto."
"You're my little slut, Jessica. We're going to do something special so you always remember you are mine," Nick said, as he probed the tip of his cock gently between the lips of her sex.

Jessica panted audibly, "Yes, Mr. Sakamoto, I'm your little slut! Take me!" Jessica's sex was dripping easily, lubricating his shaft. Nick looked at the Astroglide again, and decided to put just a little on. While the situation was really damned obscene, what worked in pornography didn't work in real life. Jessica may want it to hurt, but he doubted she wanted to have to visit the hospital after. He popped the tube open and put some of the cold liquid on the tip of him... and then he rubbed against Jessica.

"No," Jessica said, looking back again, "Not that, Mr. Sakamoto, please! I'll do anything but that!"
Nick's tail swished eagerly as he leaned forward to slap Jessica's face, hard, "You're my little slut now, my bad little girl, and you'll do anything I want."
Jessica's tears were leaking out now, her mascara long since staining her cheeks, "Anything, anything but that Mr. Sakamoto!"

Nick took Jessica's hips in his hands, and took just a moment to take it all in… before he roughly pulled Jessica's hips back, forcing her to take him into her to the hilt. Jessica cried out hard, nails scrabbling at the desk audibly. Nick played at teacher and student no more. Grunting, he forced himself into her again and again. Five rough thrusts, and Jessica clawed so hard that she tore one of the nails back on her left hand. The safe word did not come. Nick put his hand between Jessica's shoulder blades and forced her entire torso onto the desk as he thrust into her over and over. He began to growl, taking her for his pleasure alone, picking speed up. Her cries echoed out into the night around them, pleasure and pain in equal parts. Indeed, for Jessica each was driving the other higher and higher. Her cries stopped a moment, and then Jessica's muscles gripped hard on Nick as she convulsed… she let out with one long cry of liberation… of adoration. Her cry was matched by Nick's own triumphant howl, utterly dominating his mate as he filled her with his seed, thrusting twice more to eke the last of it out.

Jessica slumped to the side, taking Nick with her. She was laughing, a joyful sound, "That… that's what I want, Prettyboy!" Jessica summoned some strength to pull herself off of him, and headed right for the ladder up to his bed, utterly uncaring of what was leaking out of her battered ass, "I'm so tired, Prettyboy. Get up here and hold me." Nick's own world was darkening as his body urged him towards sleep, but he managed to stand, stepping out of his pants after removing his shoes. He glanced at Jessica's ass appreciatively as she went up to the bed, his seed leaking down her legs. When she was up, he followed her. Jessica was fiddling with the television he kept mounted up there, soon finding FXX. "Archer okay with you?" she asked.

Nick tiredly laughed, "Anything's okay, so long as it's with you. You gonna be alright, my alluring arthropod?"
Jessica held her hand up to show Nick that her nail was actually already reforming where she tore it off, "Can regenerate, Prettyboy. Thank you for this. I love you... I just... love you so fuckin' much."
Nick slid up as Jessica laid upon her side, spooning her, "That was pretty awesome for me as well, Jess."
Jessica sighed, content as his arm pulled her in close.
"Hey Jess, sometime you should stick a collar on me and make me do stuff for you," he said.
Jessica reached back and patted his thigh, "Anything, Prettyboy. Anything you want to try, ask me. We're gonna be okay.. Just don't-" she stopped herself from finishing that sentence.

Nick settled himself so one arm was under his pillow, and now that Jessica was close to him, his other arm came around and his hand cupped her breast. He yawned, "My life is so much better since I met you, Jessica Dombrowski. I'll see you in the morning."
Jessica squeezed his hand.

A few hours later, Nick was awake again. He had been having an odd dream about giant ants that were kept humans almost as cattle, and in the dream only he and Jessica seemed to be capable of thought. The dream had no real end or beginning it was just... an oddity. Nick watched TV a few minutes, thoughts roiling about. He whispered, "Jess, you awake?"

"Mmm.. kinda. Why?" she asked.

"I was just kinda thinking," Nick began hesitantly, "Can... can we try that again sometime, only without the pain? You know my... past, and even though it was never my choice. Uhm. I know from experience it... doesn't have to hurt."

Jessica, already laying on her belly, turned her head to face him, "I know. Shortly after I first met you I started talking to Raoul about it. I even talked to Dr. Thorne about it."

Nick blinked, "You consulted your shrink about anal sex?"

Jessica smiled warmly at Nick... a smile he already loved so much more than any he'd seen before. She had a smile that was specifically for him, it seemed. Her smile was, unlike his ex-girlfriend's, not one calculated to make her prettier, Jessica's smile for him was a weird mix between adoring and protective, indulgent and hesitant. This woman was far more complex than she seemed, and her smile reflected that, "Not about the mechanics of it, Raoul was my Sensei in that matter, but about your history of sexual abuse. She says that you can come in to see her if you wish... she knows you don't actively see a therapist anymore, if you think it's gonna be a big deal. She says your guess is right, the fetish did arise from your own experiences, but figures it's probably harmless enough. Plus, if I take away the forbidden factor you'll probably stop wanting it."

Nick was quiet a few moments, "Well, I'm glad you're taking therapy seriously enough to feel able to talk about anything. If Raoul told you-"

Jessica reached her hand over and placed her fingertip across his lip, "Shh, Prettyboy. That was for me. I like rough sex and you just made it hurt that much better."
"So, when you aren't sore, maybe we can try it again sometime?" Nick asked, bashfully.

"Dryad, remember?" Jessica said, showing him the completely healed nail from earlier, "I'm already better. Here... I think... there's not enough room above me. And you really wanna do this right? You can start by giving me a massage, then kissing me, all over. Especially where you want to put that. Use your tongue."

Nick took a deep breath, calming his renewed excitement, and moved around by her legs as she turned to face away from him. He did what she said. They did what he wanted. With just a little help from touching herself as she lay on her side, they came together.

"We are weird people, you know that Jess?" Nick said during the afterglow.
"Eh," Jessica said as she moved onto her back, taking his hand. "You're a hell of a guy. For whatever reason, you love me and I love you back. Give and take, we're figuring this out together."
Nick drew in his breath and then let it out again, "And if we do figure it all out, and really go the distance, we're gonna look back and laugh at how awkward this all was."
"Well, if we go the distance we'll have to edit a lot of this," Jessica laughed, "Otherwise we'll tell our kids 'Well, you see, Mommy was a bar skank and Daddy felt insecure about his worth as a man and his sexual peccadilloes!'"

"Kids?" Nick said, poking her in the rib, "Lordy loo we'd make terrible fuckin' parents."

"Couldn't do worse than our own parents did by us, that's for sure." She retorted. "Gah. Emotional crap. Spider-Dryad no likey. Let's get some sleep."

"I love you, Jess. See you in the morning." he said, almost relaxed enough to sleep.

"I still vastly prefer it in the front, you know."

"And knowing is half the battle."

"Dork!"

Johnston Steele scowled as he drove. He knew there was no choice here. He loved his granddaughter very much and he had to at least put on a good face and pretend that what had happened was even remotely okay.

He just could not understand why society went this way. When he was young, the freaks were taken away to never be seen again, as they should be. Now there was one of those freaks born to his own family, and he had to grin and bear it. Decent men like him who knew right from wrong were looked at as dinosaurs, while those freaks were treated as if they were actual children of God. Johnny-boy would be happy if the government just came in and took his new great-grandchild away.

Having parked in the set back garage, he slammed the door of his Continental shut behind him. He took a moment to calm his ire and walked up the steps to the back door of this unclean house. Whatever his granddaughter had done to cause God to turn his eye and allow a spawn of Satan to curse this family could surely be undone.

He paused when he saw the kitchen window was wide open despite the weather. In fact, all of the other windows were open as well. A Green Beret who reaches his age had to have developed a sixth sense for things going south, and that sense was firing off now. Going low despite protest from his knees, he crouch walked his way back to the car. Once there, John checked the corners of the garage to ensure he wasn't about to be jumped. Once he was sure the area was clear, he hit the hidden quick release for his trunk and had the Ithaca S-Prefix ready in less than 15 seconds, compete with a bandolier of shells. Judging there was no immediate danger, he took more shells and jammed them into his pockets just in case. Shouldering the weapon expertly, John advanced on the house. Outside of each window were oddly placed triple-clawed marks, as if some sort of insects had come this way and back... dragging something through the snow. Bodies, probably.

John spent the next twenty minutes first trying to track the drag lines uselessly to a nearby sewer entrance, and then clearing the house. Everything from attic to basement was clear of intruders; in fact things were so peaceful that when the oven timer went off John took the meatloaf out almost by autopilot. His wife liked it when he did the serving, so this was a natural action to take. The buzzer set off the sound of a baby crying. It took John another minute to find the little elven baby, swaddled and tucked under the bathroom sink.

John pointed the shotgun at the little abomination and thumbed the safety back on. He felt disgusted with himself as he put the weapon down. It wasn't this sweet little one's fault she was born wrong, and really, the child was blood of his blood. Holding the baby to his chest, John began to look for where they kept the formula.

Chapter Three:
- "Christmas Wrapping", The Waitresses

Jessica scratched her nose a moment, to deal with an itch. A few moments later... the same itch. She scratched again. On the third time, she came awake enough to feel a weight on her chest. Slowly opening her eyes as she felt the same tickle again, she gathered her thoughts to figure out what was going on. Nick's cat, Atton, was pawing at her nose. Jessica focused her most withering glare on the grey tabby's face, "Off me, feline, or we'll be having shish-cat-bobs for dinner." Atton yawned and curled up on her chest. Jessica lifted Atton up, held the pliant feline two inches above Nick's head, and dropped him. Nick reached up and said, "Hi, Atton."

Jessica grunted, "Coffee."
Nick pointed at the front room, "Starts brewing at 6 am."
Jessica pulled her hair away from her forehead, "Lotta good that does me. I gotta be at work at 6."

Nick's nostrils flared a moment. Jessica watched that with some interest. There were some... canine things that Nick did. At first the thought of these differences nearly repulsed Jessica, but now she was beginning to find them just... cute little foibles of his. Nick turned his eye towards her, "Coffee's ready, Jess."

Jessica bolted up, immediately smashing her head on the low ceiling, "Ow, fuck! Yeah, we are moving to somewhere we can have a real bedroom. What time is...

oh FUCK!" Jessica scrambled over Nick, pausing only an instant to give him a kiss before rolling off him entirely and landing on her feet, moving fast to her jacket and purse, "I am already late for work, damn it to hell!" She threw her jacket on, grabbed the keys for her Celica, and lit a cigarette in a flash.
"Jess, sweetie?" Nick said, "I really like you in that slutty Halloween schoolgirl getup, but shouldn't you change be-"

Nick stopped talking because Jessica was already out the door, heels clicking on the stairs as she dashed down. Atton had already curled up on the pillow Jessica's head had occupied moments before, loving the nice warm spot for him to plug into. Nick scratched behind Atton's ear, "This is why I love my job. Office opens whenever the fuck I want it to." Atton got up to press his head against Nick's a moment, before settling now on Nick's pillow, wrapped halfway around Nick's head.

Cursing audibly, Jessica strode through the break room towards the locker room. Her outfit turned several heads, including Lori who just muttered, "Skank."
The overnight duty sergeant, an orcish woman now finishing up paperwork after her shift, could not resist a wicked smile. She called after Jessica. "Hey, Dombrowski! Prostitution sting duty starts at 6PM not 6 AM!"

The room erupted in laughter. Jessica stopped to point at her, "That.... okay that one was pretty good," and she stepped into the locker room. More laughter followed her exit. Jessica stepped into the shower, taking her toothbrush with her to follow George Carlin's advice. She quickly washed her armpits, asshole, crotch and teeth, though she neglected to save time by using the same brush on all four areas.

Freshly showered and put together in her well pressed uniform, Jessica did a once-over in the mirror. Not even 6 months ago, if she bothered to wear this uniform at all, it would have probably been stained, rumpled and smelling of whiskey and cigarettes. Now? Jessica took pride in her after-work routine; dutifully returning her previous uniform and taking a few minutes to iron and hang up tomorrow's uniform. Jessica closed her eyes a moment, and uttered a small "thank you" to a God she hadn't bothered with since she was a little girl. It was frankly amazing the department had not fired her. She pulled herself to full height, pinned her star on as the final step, and retrieved her duty belt from the armory on her way to the briefing room.

By the time she got there, the morning's assignments were already done… the room was empty save for the morning duty sergeant, whom was Traficant today. "Glad to see you decided to grace us with your presence, Dombrowski!" the churlish dwarf bellowed, affably enough. "Yeah, yeah," Jessica said, eyes closed a moment, "Had a lot of fun with Nick last night and lost track of time." Traficant cackled gleefully, as over-the-top enthusiastic about such things as any dwarf would be, "Can't say I've never been late because the missus and I got too amorous over cups of brew. Anyway, you've got School Presentation Duty today."
Jessica quirked an eyebrow, "ME? You want ME to play Officer Friendly?"

"Direct request from the Commish, actually," the dwarf said with a shrug, "You need to take a patrol over to Logandale and get ready. You will be doing morning visits to the classrooms and then sticking around for the rest of the day answering questions."
"Dear Lord," Jessica said, half disgusted, "Kids. Yuck. Well, at least I'm... somewhat unlikely to be shot at today, then."

As the day passed on, Jessica found that against all expectations, her tolerance for children had greatly increased. She discussed the concepts of stranger danger, family passwords, and how to summon help if things went wrong. Of late, thanks to the... problem officers lately who had been shooting orcs and black humans, there was not a lot of love for the men and women in blue. Jessica's own opinion on that was simple; cops are like anyone else, a few awesome people, a bunch of humdrum drones, and almost as many assholes in varying degrees. Jessica herself had just been an awful excuse for a human being, never mind a cop, up until very recently. While she would never hold ill will against a child for parroting the beliefs of their parents; she found it difficult to be all that angry with the parents, either. It felt good to be doing something to ameliorate that distrust.

The question that she knew would most stick out in her memory came to her during the afternoon recess period. Her desire to act the part of "good cop" winning out against her almost insurmountable NEED for a smoke, Jessica joined a pickup baseball game that was going on. These kids were too young and uncoordinated to really offer her anything resembling a "challenge", but she did her best to play along and make it fun. One of the orcish kids came right up to her and said, "My daddy says he doesn't like cops because his brother was killed for driving in a fancy car while being an orc. What does he mean?"

Jessica did not kneel or do any such patronizing thing, she merely directed her gaze lower to meet the boy's eyes, "There's an idea that people have, and it's a bad idea. They think that orcs are all naturally bad people."
The boy looked a bit lost, "What... what's the got to do with it?"
"Well, you see," she said, putting her hand on the boy's shoulder lightly, "because people think these bad, wrong things, they don't see it as possible for an orc to get wealthy except by doing bad things. Sometimes these bad people become police officers, and their bad thoughts make them do bad things. I'm really sorry it happened. It really DOES happen, and good cops like me? We hate them as much as your daddy does."
The boy looked pensive, thoughtful, "I guess I should just do my best to prove those people wrong, then?"
"Yes," Jessica said, a smile coming to her face unbidden, "The best way to deal with those who hate you is to live a good life, and maybe, just maybe, they might see how bad those thoughts are, and change them."

After recess, Jessica found herself around the side of the building behind the custodian's shed. Why was it, exactly, that Jessica found herself out here with almost a dozen teachers and other support staff? Because smoking had been banned on the entire campus, and this was the only place the exiles could gather away from prying eyes. Jessica approached one of the elven teachers, a small woman with freckles and strawberry blonde hair. "Hey, I've got a question if you got a minute?" The woman seemed to look panicked a moment, and Jessica suppressed the urge to roll her eyes, "It's nothing official, it's just a sorta awkward question you probably get often." The teacher relaxed just a bit, "Go ahead, Officer Dombrowski."

"Well," Jessica began, "I know elves take a very, very long time to become adults... I mean yourself if it weren't for the pointy ears I'd guess you were 16. How does... how does school work for elves?"

The teacher smiled, "I actually get this question a lot, especially from parents who have just given birth to an elf. When an elf gets to be around the size of a 5-year-old human, they tend to have the same mental capacities as well. They repeat kindergarten for several years, and then they move along to the next grade."

Jessica took the last drag from her smoke, and then stuffed it into the specialized case used for suffocating the butts and keeping the mess inside. As she snapped it shut, she looked back over at the teacher, "And that doesn't get boring?"

"You see, there's a certain amount of racial segregation," the teacher responded, "we keep the elves busy with reading, study of history and lots and lots of arts and crafts. They will go to the next grade with the same core knowledge as the human kids, for example, there's just no hurry to cram the math and whatnot into their heads. The hardest part is when they make friends with humans, or worse, orcs. Orcs tend to rocket through the grades... the brighter ones somewhat keep up with their friends, but the average ones we work on mostly just the basic skills for living, and lots of philosophy. I won't try to tell you it's not an easy process to educate an orc."

Letting the casual racism slide, Jessica found she had one more question, "Were your parents human?"
The teacher looked sad a moment, which elves rarely do, "Yes, they were. I was amongst the first born. They died before I was even old enough to know what sex was on more than an intellectual level. Thing about elves is some of us had parents who have been around for hundreds if not thousands of years, hidden inside human society. They would live lives for a while... usually not having children, and then 'age and die', moving along to other lives. A different family took me in, as elves no longer need to hide."
"Huh," Jessica said, thinking, "So, a lot of those photographs of people a hundred years ago that just HAPPEN to look like modern movie stars and whatnot?"
The teacher laughed, "Yes. While most of the time it's a coincidence... sometimes it was just that person had been an elf all along." The only elf Jessica had ever spent any time with was Lori, and even before the rift over Nick they were never close. She opened her mouth to ask another question, and then the bell rang. "It's been a pleasure, Officer but I have to get back to work. And no, teaching never gets boring for me. 5 periods a day I teach elves."

Jessica joined the small herd filing back into the school.

At the end of the school day, Jessica positioned herself to be visible to all the children getting onto their buses or being picked up by their parents. She was a bit chilly, she had only taken a department issued windbreaker with her instead of a full jacket. She huffed into her hands and rubbed them together a bit, trying to get them warmed up a bit. Jessica waved to some of the children who were waving at her, and thus was distracted when her hand was taken, and before she could even turn, she heard the one who had done so speak. "Jessica, I can keep your hands warm for you."

Jessica froze up for just a moment. Merrick. He had always taken her hand like this right before he violated her as his personal way to collect the genetic samples needed to maintain her disguised pseudo-clone. She turned to face him, unable to gather her thoughts fully. Merrick was, as always, dressed immaculately in a tailored suit, charcoal-grey with a deep crimson tie as he always had favored. What kept her from acting immediately was her own reaction to this. She felt an undeniable heat, and her cheeks had flushed with desire. She found herself wanting to give herself to him right now.

She yanked her hand out of his and sneered, "What the fuck are you doing?"
"Well," Merrick said with a smirk as one would use when indulging a child in conversation, "I know you will have no choice but to hear me out, here. You're not going to shoot me in front of all these children, and you know how pointless it would be to arrest me."

This much was true, the last time Jessica had cuffed Merrick and brought him in, 'he' was gone by the time they got to the station. The body he inhabited had changed into a blank slate Skinstealer. The best that Jessica could come up with is Merrick was some kind of 'hive queen'. Her face remained twisted into a sneer, "You have nothing to say that's worth hearing."

"Ah, but I do, Jessica," Merrick said as he stepped up to caress her cheek. "For you see I've come to miss you since we last met."

Jessica had closed her eyes when he touched her, her body betraying her will again, she was undeniably aroused and craved his touch even as it abhorred her. She grabbed his hand and broke two fingers as she stepped off.

Jessica removed the safety catch on her pistol, "Touch me again and these kids will see a piece of shit's brains turned into a pink mist anyway."

"Don't give me that, my little songbird," Merrick said. "Look at you, those flushing cheeks, those trembling lips. You want me to touch you. And I will, often. You see, Jessica Dombrowski, you are going to be my queen."

Jessica took another step back, "You're insane even by the standards of egomaniacal monsters."

Merrick simply kept his gaze on her eyes, "Oh, I think you'll reconsider in a week or so when you see what I have done to bring this city to her knees."

Jessica rolled her eyes, "You think that idiotic plan will ever work again? The city has security preventing that all the way down to garbagemen. Everyone knows to look for those little green veins in the eyes now.."

"Oh, dear, my dear queen," he said evenly, "I'm just warning you ahead of time. When it happens, you will know where to find me to be kept safe from it all. You can even take your little boyfriend with you. I'm sure we can come to some... agreement. He's so very pretty as you are."

"You're fucking demented, Merrick." Jessica decided, since her shift was over now anyway, there was no reason to stay around and put up with more of this. She returned to her patrol, lit up a smoke, and peeled out angrily.

By the time she reached the station, she was angry at herself for the way she had responded to Merrick. On an intellectual level, there was no doubt in her mind that, faced with the fate of going back to Merrick, even as his "Queen", she would kill herself. All of that changed nothing about the way her body reacted to him. She felt a pull to him, the desire to give into him, let him use her as he had for all that time. It was a disgusting reaction, and she felt dirty just having it.

As she was walking into the station, Lori the dispatcher was walking out of it. When she passed, the Chinese elf rolled her eyes at Jessica, "You're a worthless slut, you know that Dombrowski?" Jessica passed her without comment, going inside to shower.

Alana Mayfair was a happy woman. She came from a family that your average dysfunctional family would look at and say "holy shit these people are fucked up!" She was a witch from a long line of witches, apparently some very powerful family that bred extremely carefully to increase that power. She was more than reasonably certain that her uncle was her father and not the man her mother had married, but it mattered little now. Alana got out, went to college, and met a wonderful man. With his help, she not only got away from her family, but managed to turn her magical talents to healing instead of hexes. That was wonderful, a great gift that would have been enough to keep her smiling for the rest of her life.

But there was more. Michael had given her an even greater gift. That gift sometimes got on her nerves, especially when she didn't turn Paw Patrol on fast enough, but gift he was. Alana took a moment to marvel at the beautiful blonde boy; he and the neighborhood kids always came to Mommy because Mommy kisses really did make the owies better. Alana loved using her gift for those kids, she was, as Michael's mother liked to say, happier than a pig in shit to have let her dark arts fall by the wayside.

Alana dug around for a soda in the cooler as she watched the children play. She was getting a bit soft around the middle, and the soda didn't help this at all, true. She did find that the caffeine did a lot to quell the headaches that Mikey caused her. Alana's healing talents did not work on herself so she had to seek mundane remedies. Ah well, nobody ever said motherhood would be easy.

Mikey was playing hide and seek with the other kids, and she was here with the other mothers, mostly human with one elf. Alana could not help but shake her head when she thought back to how her uncle was always rambling about how dangerous the world was. Why fight and curse when you could heal and soothe anger?

Lost in her thoughts and the simple joy of sugary soda it took her a bit to notice the kids were a bit worried that Mikey had vanished behind one of the trees where the forest started to become thicker. The children's own worries became hers when she saw Mikey was not simply hiding well, he was being dragged off by a Skinstealer! Alana snarled as she began to run towards her child. The Stealers were faster than her, so she had to think on her feet.

Alana raised her hand and chanted the short rhyme to manifest a magic missile.

Her magic barely responded at all. Alana had not practiced the dark side of her art in years.

She tried twice more to no avail, and then took off running, screaming for help.

She was not fast enough to save Mikey, nor did help arrive before the child was taken to the sewers, crying for his mother.

Chapter Four:
- "Cry Little Sister", Gerard McMann

Nick had his feet up on his desk, controller in hand. Brian was right next to him, taking a pull of beer before unpausing Dungeon Explorer. "Ugh, American beer is really crappy, I don't know why I forget this every time I come here."
Nick laughed, "And yet here you are into your fifth one."
"Hey, mate," Brian responded, "it doesn't have to taste good to get me drunk. I'm kinda wondering, how the hell do you pay rent? It's been a few days with no business."

Nick looked over at the door. It was true, there had not been even so much as a call asking about his rates. Nick wasn't surprised, though. The first snow of the season tended to give people warm feelings, driving them inside all cuddly. It would take a few days before the novelty would wear off, and people would begin to get on one another's nerves again. Then the business would come in so fast that he'd have to ask Jessica to tackle some of it. She had been helping him on investigations doing some research anyway; it wouldn't be a stretch to ask her to do some field work. Tracking stolen goods, catching a cheating spouse, bodyguard duty... it was only a matter of time before human misery would take it's toll again. Bad times in people's lives were good times for a Private Investigator's. That said, it was starting to take a little long to start. Even Cynthia had limits to her patience. This just might be cutting it too close.

"Eh," Nick said with a shrug, "If it doesn't pick up soon we can just go hunt down a nest of Virus. The bounty on them is actually pretty lucrative."
"It's also insanely dangerous work, Nicky-boy." Brian said.
"Bah, since when do you care?" Nick said as he grinned lopsidedly, "Who Dares Wins, you limey!"
Brian took another pull, "Thing is I'm getting old. I'm slowing down. I actually am retired from the Service now. I'm not saying I won't help you; I'm just saying I'm ready to leave that life behind me and am grateful I got out before it killed me. Noriko and I bought a little flat out by the Thames, and we've got enough money for our sunset years if we budget carefully."
"Man," Nick said a bit sadly, "I'm gonna miss the hell outta you."
"Hey!" Brian said, "I'm not dead yet, and if you keep picking fights with those creepy blighters, I may outlive you anyway. Chiswick Park."

"You sure you wanna do this?" Nick asked, "Your ass isn't still sore from last time?"
"I daresay it is, and that's why I've got to take my pride back. Stocktrade rules?"
Nick shook his head, "I DO expect to go to bed sometime before midnight. Higginbotham or nothing."
Brian opened yet another can, "Stacking the deck in your favor?"
"You gonna cry about it or play? Elephant and Castle."
"That new woman of yours really does embolden you. I'll stifle your options a bit. Hatton Cross."

"Maida Vale."
Brian shook his head, "Oxford Circus, mate. Falling back into old patterns."
"I thought you might think that. Stepney Green."
"Clever move, mate. Under the Hig rules I can crossover to West Ham."
Nick waved his hands mockingly, "Oooh, scary. Regent's Park."
Brian slammed his beer down, "Sucker! MORNINGTON CRESCENT!"
"Fuck, you're right!" Nick said. He grumbled a bit, "Lunch is on me then, I guess."

They were both surprised to hear a timid knock at the door. "It's not locked!" Nick called out. The door opened and in walked a young human with a terrible haircut, wearing an Inuyasha T shirt. He looked about as physically imposing as a newborn puppy, but carried himself like the television version of a martial artist, arms loosely held at his sides and torso held rigid, chest pushed out. He even held his nose lightly up as he looked at the office. Nick kept his expression neutral. While this person was clearly incredibly wet behind the ears, if his money was good Nick could overlook a lot of things. Nick spotted the knife the young man had strapped to his left calf almost immediately... the blade was far too long to be put there, and was mounted straight, with the handle side up. Absolutely useless in any real combat situation.

Nick nodded at the kid, "Welcome to Dog and Spider Private Investigations. What can I do for you?"

The kid took a step back and checked the lettering on the door, "This says you're 'Taciturn Acquiescence Detective Agency'. Am I in the right place?"
"Oh, absolutely," Nick responded, "I don't work alone anymore though, so it was time for a new name. Plus... honestly? The old one is sort of stupid, on further reflection."
Brian grinned dopily, "I agree. It sounds more like the title a complete prat would give to a third rate romance novel."
"You're a third rate romance novel," Nick retorted.

The kid walked over to the desk, and pointedly did not sit down. Nick had a series of tricks to subtly assert himself as being in charge of any situation, but decided to eschew them for now. He was willing to take a certain amount of crap in order to chase down a fee, but it did tend to lead to him not being very economical about the "plus expenses" part of the contract. The kid spoke up, "Someone killed my girlfriend."
Nick leaned forward, folding his hands on the desk, "That's the sort of thing the bulls usually handle."
"Bulls?" the kid asked, "What do bulls have to do with this? Are you an idiot?"

Nick's smile broadened into a grin. He'd be having steak tonight. "It's industry slang for 'police'. Sometimes I forget that not everyone is familiar with it."
"I DID talk to the police," the kid said, "they are, as always, useless."
"Oh?" Nick asked, eyebrow raised, "What happened?"
The kid fidgeted a bit, "I couldn't give them an exact location. She was probably killed by her drug dealer ex

boyfriend, but without a lot of specifics the cops won't lift a finger."

"And how can I help you?" Nick said over a sip from his iced coffee.

"You have more experience dealing with this sort of thing than I do, you may know some tricks I don't." The kid was looking down on Nick both physically and metaphorically.

"Ah, and you want me to get more details so the cops will get off their lazy asses. One hundred forty nine ninety five a day, plus expenses. This sort of job typically carries a three day retainer." Nick stated, as he turned to his computer and printed out the best contract type for this sort of client, "and I'll need all the information you can get to me, no matter how minor. Any little detail would be helpful."

The kid signed the contract, not even bothering to look it over, "I've compiled all of the information you will need onto the thumb drive in my pocket. How do I pay?"

Nick brought up the card reader that was attached to his smartphone via bluetooth, "You swipe here, and I put a hold on funds and presumed expenses. Naturally, if my expenses are under I'll refund the difference. I presume you have sufficient funds in your account?"

"Of course I do," the kid's tone of voice was dismissive. He shifted his leg.. the one with the knife, showing discomfort as he swiped his card. He dropped a USB drive in the shape of a small Japanese flag onto the desk and stalked out, not even bothering to say goodbye. He closed the door behind him and clomped his combat boots down the stairs.

The friends broke out in laughter at the same time, and Brian spoke first, "I can't believe you even took the job from that wanker."
Nick took a moment to catch his breath before responding, "Look, no matter how far up his own ass he has his head, there is a dead person here and nobody seems to care. It's kinda sad, but the police really DON'T have time for reports this vague. I do."

There was another knock on the door. "It's not locked!" Nick called out. The door opened to reveal a real looker. She was a classic elf. Slender, with the expected supernatural beauty to her features; nothing marring them except a smattering of freckles on her cheeks. Her hair was evocative of autumn leaves, and reflected the lights in the room very subtly. She had on a lab coat, a two piece skirt suit with matching tights and heels just high enough to convey sensuality and professionalism in equal amounts. Topping it all off? Librarian glasses. Before Jessica, he would already have been turning the charm on before she even spoke. Instead, he rose and offered a handshake, "Welcome to Dog and Spi-"
"Nick Sakamoto?" she asked before he could finish.
Nick lowered his hand, sensing her urgency, "Yes, that's me."
"I'm Doctor Vanessa Thorne. We need you down at the station," she said, voice even. "Nobody could remember how to spell the name of your agency so nobody knew how to contact you. Took me a bit to find you on the web."
"What's the matter?" Nick asked, heart racing. He was trying to shut out thoughts of Jessica having been killed in the line of duty, it would do no good if he lost control now.

"She's been in the showers down at the station for over an hour now. She won't talk to anyone, she's just soaping herself up and rinsing herself off over and over." Dr. Thorne said, already walking out and downstairs.

Nick grabbed his trenchcoat and altered black Indiana Jones hat, putting them on while he was going out the door. He jogged down the back stairs, and hit the button to open the garage door of Cynthia's shop. The 69 GTO Judge roared to life, and he did not even wait to warm it up; actually peeling out a bit in his haste to get to Jessica's side.

Nick pulled up to the front of the station, and got out of the car. Not even bothering to lock it, he darted inside and stepped to the front desk, "I need to get to Officer Dombrowski."

The dwarven woman behind the counter looked at him, bored, "Take a seat and I'll send someone to see if she's available."

"I know she's not," Nick said, heading around the desk towards the back, "There's something wrong."

Two officers reacted fast, blocking Nick away from the door, "No civilians allowed."

Nick tamped his anger down. While he was sure he could easily disassemble these officers in unarmed combat, that would be an incredibly stupid thing to do.

Dr. Thorne came in now and strode up, "This is Nick Sakamoto. Step aside, now."

One of the officers headed back to the lobby, and the other buzzed them in. "This way," Dr. Thorne said, leading him quickly to the women's locker room.

There was a small crowd of officers and support staff right outside the shower. Nick pushed through them and went in. Sure enough, there was Jessica rubbing soap vigorously on her body, staying right under the hot stream, as she did so. Her eyes were haunted and distant. He stepped right into her, wrapping his arms around her, heedless of the water on his clothing. Jessica barely responded to him at first, her eyes looking straight through him. He touched her cheek, "Jessica? I'm here." This brought her back just a little bit. She sank to her knees, and Nick followed her.
"Go away, Prettyboy. I'm filthy." she said, staring at the floor.
Nick put his arms around her again, "I don't care, Jessica. You're my girl. Whatever's wrong, we'll clean it up together."

Jessica made eye contact with him, and then started sobbing as she buried her face in his chest. He held her while Dr. Thorne closed the door behind them and turned the water off. It took several minutes before the worst of the shaking was over. "We're here for you, Jessica," Dr Thorne said in a gentle tone, "I care about you and Nick will love you no matter what happened; he's a good man." Jessica wiped snot from her upper lip, "I look a mess. I saw Merrick today."

Nick's eye narrowed and for just a moment it had turned black, a sort of black mist beginning to emanate from that eye as well as his other eye socket, "What did he do to you?"
"Not a damn thing but threaten me!" she cried out, "It's what I wanted to do to him!"

Dr. Thorne spoke next, "It's healthy to want to lash out at someone who has done you that much harm, Jessica."
"You don't understand!" She yelled, voice bouncing off the tile walls. "I was turned on! I wanted to fuck him! I'm a filthy fucking slut! Everything everyone said about me is right!"
Nick adjusted his position a bit and took her hands. She instantly shook them off, "Stop touching my hands! Merrick did that all the time!"

Nick shifted instead to gently stroking her cheek, "I love you, Jessica, and I know you love me. I know your past is your past, you wouldn't cheat on me."
"It's actually fairly normal in these sorts of situations," Dr. Thorne began, "You really shouldn't blame yourself. You spent two YEARS held captive by this man, being raped every other day at minimum. It was a survival instinct to want to please him after that long under his power. Your reaction now can't be helped, and you have to understand that this isn't something you did intentionally."

"I know it, Jessica," Nick added, "Remember what happened to me? I actually missed it. Even now, when I'm not having those terrifying dreams about zombies, I sometimes dream about those men. Some of them were gentle with me, and it felt a little like love."
Jessica looked up, trying to read his expression, "Really?"
Nick closed in to kiss her, "Yeah, Jess. Really. And I know I can tell you things like that because you won't judge me."
Jessica's sobs started again "God damn it Nick, I don't deserve you."

"Don't be ridiculous," Dr. Thorne said, "Everyone deserves love and compassion. He knows your pain, and how would he feel if you pushed yourself away from him over this?"

Jessica's voice was low, almost afraid. "I wanna go home, Prettyboy. I just... I just wanna be with you."
"Sounds like a good time to me," Nick said, "We'll order some Thai food and watch a movie. Did you ever see 'The Last Dragon'?"
Jessica looked back up at him, "Sho Nuff. It'd be a good movie to watch."
Nick stood, and by reflex took her hand to help her up. Jessica stared at his hand a moment and... allowed that. Vanessa threw Nick a towel, and then took her leave. Nick dried her off, telling her how beautiful she was as he did so. Within twenty minutes, she was dressed and composed enough that he could take her home. On his way out, he thanked Dr. Thorne again.

"Thank you for coming down here, Nick. If you need anything, you have my number," she replied.
Nobody laughed about the clothing she was wearing as they had this morning. The officers on their way out were quiet, respectful. They were family, after all, and one of theirs was grievously wounded. Nobody would ever speak ill of her about this. She wasn't the first officer to break down in the station, and she wouldn't be the last. It was just one of the things that happened on the job.

For most of the ride home, Jessica was quiet, looking out the window. The snow had begun again, little flurries.
"I'm kind of a mess, Prettyboy."

Nick grinned lopsidedly at her, "She says to the deviant-sex desiring private investigator with a disturbing backstory involving a complete loss of innocence early into childhood, who walked in on his dead wife and dying son which resulted in a decades-long revenge?"

Jessica smiled at him in that special way, "You're right, Prettyboy. You are WAY more fucked up than I am!"
Nick looked comically offended, "Says the lady who dressed up as a schoolgirl last night!"
Jessica punched his shoulder, "Says the guy who stuck it up that schoolgirl's ass twice last night!"
Nick's grin returned, "Yeah well.. uhm. You let me!"

Jessica laughed. By the haunted look in her eyes it was clear she was still shaken up by the events of the day. The fact that she was up for her usual level of snarky banter was a good sign. "Hey, I need a drink Prettyboy. Can we stop by the store?"
Nick's left ear flickered, "I've got bourbon at my place, Jess."
Jessica snorted, "Bourbon, always bourbon with you. Let's get some nice Smirnoff Ice."
"Smirnoff Ice?" Nick said, eyebrow raised, "Don't you be getting all girly on me. Yeah, we can swing by if you call for the Thai."
"Who's a good boy, who's a good boy?" Jessica said, scratching him behind the ear.

Nick deftly drove around an old lady in a minivan who came into his lane in a poorly-planned attempt to make a left hand turn without having to actually wait for a proper opening in traffic. "Oh my god, THAT was a real piece of shit move! Did you see that lady? Giver her a ticket for being too senile to drive, Officer Dombrowski!"

Jessica blew a raspberry at him, "What am I, your own personal law enforcer?"

Nick grinned at her, "If you were my own personal law enforcer you'd beat down or shoot everyone down at Bellamy."

Jessica looked thoughtful, "Those chucklefucks? God, I'd pay you for the privilege of cleaning that place out."

"Yeah," Nick began, "except there's no way you could perpetrate that amount of carnage and mayhem and not incur a significant amount of paperwork."

Jessica held the bridge of her nose with her thumb and first two fingers, "Hot Fuzz. Oh my god, you are such a dork."

Annabelle LaReign passed the dutchie on the left hand side after she took her hit. After all, that's how you're supposed to do it, right? A dwarven girl from the rich side of town, she reaped the fruits of her parents' labor. Anna wanted for nothing in this world that most could tell. She had good food, lots of forms of entertainment, and a solid family. Her father had just spent two hours the night before at Anna's viola recital.

Boredom. The worst thing in her life? Boredom. That was why Anna was here. The joint came back around to her again. She raised it up to her lips and held it in them, hands free. She stood up for everyone to watch her as she mumbled around the joint, "Look ma, no hands!" She closed her eyes and was dizzy a moment.

When she tried to take the drag, she was a bit confused as to why she could not. She made the right motions, but her lungs didn't seem to be responding. When she opened her eyes, she realized she was looking at her own feet, from an angle that should have been impossible. That made little sense to her, but it didn't much matter. This was clearly some good stuff, because she was heading down for a real pleasant nap. As the world began to fade to black, she dimly heard her friends screaming.

There were worse ways to die than to simply nod off. Just ask Anna's friends.

Chapter Five:
- "Dominic the Donkey", Lou Monte

Nick splayed out lazily on the bed. Jessica had stayed the night again, as she had most of the time they'd been together. After lazing around a bit scratching behind Atton's ear, he looked over at the office. There was Jessica, wearing a shirt that said "I love my Shiba Inu". It was not a particularly long shirt at all, and since only one of her feet were up on the edge of the chair she sat upon, everything was right there for Nick to see. He had come to love how pale her flesh was. What had been a sickly pallor when they first met had mellowed instead into an exotic cream color. What was it the French said, recherche? The concept fit this wonderful Dryad perfectly, ever more exotic by the trim forest green hair where those long, muscled legs met.

Nick quietly watched her, enrapt in the grace of her motions even in a mundane thing such as this. Jessica was removing the old paint from her nails and applying new. She took the time to leave the usual red hourglass pattern of the black widow on her big toes and pinkies. An actual black widow was busy forming a web between the arch of Nick's disused desk lamp. Not looking up from her task at all, Jessica greeted him with, "Oh, just go ahead and jerk off already. I'm still not in the mood but I don't mind. Makes me feel pretty." Nick flushed but started doing exactly that.

"Is it always gonna be like this, Prettyboy?" she asked, idly.

"I'd eventually start bleeding if I was always doing this," he responded.

Jessica smiled and shook her head, "I mean with us just… being so comfortable with each other."

"I hope so, Jess," Nick said, "I really do."

Now finished with her task but being sure to keep herself displayed for him, Jessica wiggled the mouse on his computer to wake it up. "Been looking at houses, I see."

"Yeah," Nick said, "I hope you don't mind? I really do want you to live with me."

"Shit, I practically do now." Jessica said.

Nick was getting more into the task at hand, but was still able to hold this conversation. "Well, there's a house in Westmont that's really cheap. People are superstitious, and don't want to buy a house that ever had a Virus infection."

Jessica's eyebrows raised a bit, "You mean the house where you collected that kill bounty from?"

"Yeah," Nick said, "it's like a five minute walk to the Metra station, and once you get into the city my office is literally right down the block from the station. I figure we can leave your car at Cynthia's garage so you can get to work. I'll leave this setup here. If we decide to hit the Succubus a cab back and forth to the office would be pretty cheap. We can also sleep there if your shift makes it so we can't catch a train home."

Jessica made eye contact with him, "You really put a lot of thought into this, didn't you Prettyboy?"

Nick was silent a moment, breathing heavy, "Yeah."
"I like that," Jessica almost whispered, "you planning ahead for us."
Nick finished with a little grunt and needed to catch his breath, "I'll need a little help with the down payment, and a co-signer for the loan."
"I'm off duty today, you wanna drive down there and talk to the realtor about taking a look? Jessica asked

Nick nodded down at her."I sure do, but I gotta get some work in on my present case before we do"
"Well, c'mon down here and let's take a look. You done up there?" Jessica asked.
"Yeah," Nick breathed out.
Jessica smirked at him, "Aww. I was gonna let you come on my feet."
Nick had to laugh, "You're SUCH a classic romantic."
"Toldya!" Jessica replied, "Romance is one thing I am not awesome at. You may be a pervert, but you're my pervert."

Nick climbed down off the bed and started to dress, "You're gonna have to at least put some pants on; remember this is a place of business starting in about an hour here."
Jessica popped up from the desk and walked over to Nick. There was nothing sexual about the walk, though she did give him a needful kiss, "I love you, Prettyboy."
"And I love you, Jess," he said as he gave her beautiful tresses a stroke, "Let's see about the Dog and Spider getting this case knocked outta the way."

Jessica found one of the many pairs of jeans she had left strewn about here and there as Nick sat down at the computer. "'Dog and Spider'? We're 'The Dog and Spider' now, are we?"

"Yeah," Nick said, "I actually did the paperwork today to change the business name."

Jessica shook her head, "It's better than the other name. Still am not sure how to pronounce that. I've only ever seen those words in books. Really fucking pretentious ones."

Nick didn't bother responding, as he was already checking the thumb drive. Firstly, his anti-malware program popped up to tell him that there was an automated installer trying to set up some shady crap. More than likely a backdoor to let a remote user access his files and settings. Nick sighed audibly, "I should probably tell you about the case in the first place."

Jessica pulled the customer chair over nearby so she could see the screen, and shoved some stuff out of the way to make room for her legs to rest on the desk next to the monitor, "Probably for the best. What've you got?"

Well," Nick began, "Kid comes in here, couldn't be more than 22, 23 tops? Total douchenozzle, got himself some anime shirt on, ridiculously expensive pants his mommy probably bought for him, and a knife mounted under his pants so terribly that a toddler could spot it."

Jessica held her forefinger up, "Firstly, I like anime also. Secondly, said 'kid' isn't all that many years younger than your girlfriend, you know."

Nick rolled his eye, "Yes, yes, ageless beings TOTALLY care about robbing the cradle."

Jessica looked indignant, "Oh, Prettyboy, you're not a cradle robber. I'm an archaeologist!"

Letting that pass, Nick continued on, "Anyway, he swaggers in here like he was hot shit, and tries to stare the ex-Yakuza enforcer and retired SAS man down. We were just trying not to laugh, because... money is money. He tells me about how his girlfriend was murdered."
Jessica's eyebrow went up, "Murder, you say?"
Nick nodded, "Yeah, murdered. I asked him why he was hiring me, and he goes off on this rant about how cops are stupid, wouldn't help him because he didn't know exactly where she was killed, so on and so forth."
Jessica closed her eyes and shook her head, "Well, yeah. We get bullshit reports from crackpots and drama queens all the time. It kinda sucks when there's a real problem, but there's just no way to tell the difference. Which would be why he hired you."

Nick disposed of the installer and was letting the computer scan for further malware, "Yep. So self-important he never bothered introducing himself, but he sure swept his card and signed my 'idiot contract'."
Jessica pulled Nick's hair out of his ponytail, so it hung loosely, "You're so pretty. You shouldn't wear a ponytail when you're at home with me. I'm guessing the 'idiot contract' is the one that lets you have unlimited expense?"
Nick chuckled a bit, "Yeah, I could seriously use his credit card to pay my rent and there wouldn't be a thing he could do... he signed the contract. Turns out the kid legally changed his name to.." Nick had to stop to laugh a moment, "Arata Norimaki!"

There was a moment of silence before Jessica spoke up, "I don't get it. What's so funny?"
Nick quirked an eyebrow, "You like anime and don't speak Japanese?"
Jessica shook her head, "No reason to. One thing I learned from learning Mandarin and Cantonese is that literal translations are pointless, and dubs get the idea across better than idioms I might not understand."
"Mandarin AND Cantonese?" Nick asked, incredulously.
Jessica smirked at him and began counting off fingers as she spoke, "And Russian, Spanish, German, French, Portuguese, as well as Korean. So.. eight languages."
Nick was genuinely impressed, "Holy crap, really?"
"Yeah", Jessica said, lighting up a smoke, "I've always picked up languages easily."
Nick looked back towards the screen, "It's funny because it basically translates to 'Fresh Seaweed wrapped sushi roll.' I wonder what the hell he thinks it means?"

Jessica was toying with his silky, straight hair, "You're a jerk, you know that?"
"Eeyup," Nick said in a southern drawl.
"Big Mac," Jessica said. "You are SUCH a dork!"
Nick grinned lopsidedly at her, "What are you, that you keep getting these references?"
Jessica bit her lip, "When a girl knows these things it's because we are KAWAAIIII!"

Nick shook his head, "Double standards. Anyway, he gave me this USB removable drive with what he claims has 'everything I need' to find her. The way he tells it is her ex-boyfriend is a drug dealer, and she was trying to get away from him."

"This is getting more and more interesting. What's in the files?"

Nick saw that the scan was done, and opened the folder. "Well, firstly the putz left an installer on here that would let him screw around in my computer. He really thinks everyone except him is an idiot. As for the rest of this? Looks like... chat logs. Screen names for various games they play together... uhh... pictures sent to him, looks like we got our work cut out for us."

Nick got up to brew them some coffee, and they began to peruse the files. The first thing Nick noticed was that every time the chat logs showed they were about to meet somewhere, she always had a crisis. Furthermore, she always had an excuse to not be able to use her webcam. The second thing Nick noticed was that the images sent to Arata were all either very blurry 'family photos' or incredibly high quality images. "One of the first things is-" She cut him off, "Oh bullshit. Those are photos of a professional model or something."

Nick laughed, "Yep! My favorite tool to use now is... good ol' Tineye reverse image search. I think I might recognize this face, but it's best to be sure."

Jessica took her phone out and began perusing, "Whaddaya think, Greek for lunch?"

Nick had to suppress laughter, half unsuccessfully, "I had Greek night before last!"

Jessica rolled her eyes, "I fell in love with an oversized 12-year-old. Gyros, then?"

Yeah," Nick said, "Check it out, it's Kan Yamate. Native Japanese gravure idol turned porn starlet with a focus on anal sex."

Jessica began texting in their order, "Well, that explains why you recognize her face!"

"I set myself up for that, didn't I?" Nick chuckled, "Point is, our boy Fresh Sushi Roll has been catfished."

"So that's that, end of the case, huh?" Jessica asked.

Nick shook his head, "Oh, absolutely not. I like to go the extra mile. Some of these logs are from them playing 8bitmmo together. Shows me 'her' IP address."

"I never worked cybercrimes. You might as well be telling me the dingleberry hopper leads us to the proper samoflange." Jessica replied as she sent the message off, "Does it help us?"

"Already found what I need!" Nick said, giving Jessica a peace sign, "It's at a comic book store in Downer's Grove. After lunch, I bet we can get down there, learn some more stuff, talk to the realtor AND expense everything... including the lunch you just ordered."

Jessica had at first felt downright ridiculous in the getup Nick had stopped to buy, but found herself warming up to it. Adjusting the pink wig, she looked herself over. She was dressed as Lightning from Final Fantasy except for, Nick being Nick, the boots were replaced by heeled numbers that showed her toes. "Look at me, I am totally emotionless and I must save my sister. I think I will kill God for annoying me."

Nick whistled, "Hey, hey! You've played the game I see!"

"Why am I dressing up as Lightning again?" Jessica asked.

"It's real simple, I'm going to fake us up some Square-Enix badges, put them on generic lanyards, and we are gonna go into that Internet Cafe and start asking around about

the player behind 'her' Final Fantasy 14 screenname. That player won a contest for a free top of the line gaming computer and 2 years subscription to the game!"
Jessica had to laugh, "Oh, you are GOOD at this."
The best part?" Nick continued, "that entire costume? Arata paid for it. We can keep it afterwards."
Jessica looked pointedly down at the impractical boots, "Kinda figured we might. Good thing for you I can fight in heels, huh?"

Less than 40 minutes later, they were parked as close as they could possibly get to the Internet Cafe/Comic book store. By a stroke of bad luck, Downers Grove was having a street fair right along that side of Ogden Avenue. Unable to park anywhere close without annoying apartment owners nearby, they had about half a mile through the crowds to get where they were going. They didn't get halfway to their destination before the local newsies had cameras on them. Jessica muttered, "I am gonna fucking kill you for making me wear this in winter. My legs and toes are freezing. Way to go with your costume idea all around, Prettyboy, now all of this is going to be filmed."

Nick grinned lopsidedly, "Are you kidding? How is this a bad thing? This will help all around. Exposure for the agency, shame someone for catfishing AND we get to make my client look like a dumbass in front of the general public."
"Gee golly gosh, I always wanted to grow up to be an E3 booth babe, this just might help me break into that lucrative career!"

Nick rolled his eye at her snark, and then strode confidently into Graham Crackers.

The store was much like others of it's type. The lower half of every wall was covered by wall-mounted comic books, and other sorts of merchandise was at eye level and just above. There were two tables in the center of the store, a Galaga arcade tucked haphazardly by the sales counter, and 4 PC gaming stations set up in the back. At those tables in the center of the store were two groups playing some collectible card game; one table had adults and the other children, all were humans or elves. Their eyes were on Nick and Jessica as soon as they got three steps inside. Nick's lopsided grin widened a bit; the camera crew with them made their ploy look all the more professional. A red haired male elf, surprisingly stocky and bearded, stood up with a friendly smile, "Hi, I'm Eric! Can I help you?"

Nick strode up and shook the man's hand, eyes alight, "Hi! I'm Nick Sakamoto, we're from Square-Enix. The company that publishes and maintains Final Fantasy 14, an MMO in the long-running Final Fantasy series trademarked to our company. Perhaps you've heard of us or our game?"
Erik nodded, eyes wide, "I... believe I speak for everyone here when I say yes, yes we have!"
"Awesome!" Nick said, "and this here is Jessica Dombrowski, playing the role of Lightning to promote an upcoming event."
Jessica did not speak, she stood there and looked alert.
"She does it so well, doesn't she?" Nick said, jerking his thumb at the Dryad he loved so desperately.

The denizens of the store made sounds of assent.

Nick held his hand up, "BUT!" he said as he brought the hand down with a dramatic flourish, "While Jessica here will be the in-game face of Light, she will not be the player behind the character. You see, before the major event begins, we want Lightning to travel the world, plugging herself into regular adventures with parties. Our staff play the game a lot, you see, and we're always on the lookout for capable roleplayers. One such player comes from here...." Nick looked across the patrons, who were utterly absorbed by his performance.

Jessica decided to ad-lib a bit, "Account name redrikku27, we know you play from here all the time. Stand up, and I'll pass the gunblade onto you."
Nick added, in a lower voice, "If he or she isn't here, we can re-do this to a certain extent if you can tell us when to come back?"

One of the players of the card game raised her hand, a mousey Japanese-descended elven girl, "I... uhh.. Hi. I'm Mileena. I'm redrikku27."
Nick smiled and stepped over to her, "Actually Jessica and I are private investigators. Well, Jessica is a cop, but she helps me on cases. Do you know a boy named 'Arata Norimaki'?"
The elf's face blanched, "He sent you?"

Nick nodded, "Oh, absolutely. Well, he thinks you were killed by a drug dealer and the local police had no information to go on. He gave us a lot of information on

you, chat logs and so on. Seems you talked him out of a lot of gifts and-"
Jessica put her hand on Nick's shoulder, "Nick? Stop. Look at her. She's about to cry."
"Well, yeah," Nick replied, "when you get caught catfishing you-"
Nick's voice trailed off when he noticed her tears were not of shame, but the wide-eyed tears of terror.
Jessica flipped her star out, "Chicago PD, get those cameras out of here. Now." One of the cameramen seemed about to object, and Jessica leaned in, "Now."

As the newsies decided to find a better vantage point outside, Jessica and Nick sat down.
"Tell me what's going on, sweetie," Jessica said.
Nick flipped around a chair to sit on, and folded his hands. He put on a look of concern that usually helped in situations like this. "Come clean and tell us, we can probably help. If you really are afraid of a drug dealer or what have you, we are the right people to tell."

Mileena looked around a bit, "I wasn't catfishing him, he was stalking me!"

Lisa Bowman snarled at the coach. "Higher!" the Russian accented orc woman said, "You have to go higher on the release, or the landing looks no good!" This whole exercise was a pain in the ass. Spring off the board, land on the bars in a HANDSTAND, loop around once to catch the rings, and somehow still have the momentum to go higher?

Yet she tried, again and again. Finally, in rage, Lisa decided it was time to say to Hell with proper form. From the handstand she split her legs, and as she was beginning to swing around, she brought her legs together and thrust like a child would on a swing set to go higher.

She caught the ring, and came off them higher than she ever had before. She did not, however, make the landing look good at all. Her coach was slumped to the ground and some pale insectoids were pinning the woman down. So taken off guard by this, Lisa landed with her weight all wrong on one leg and crumpled sideways. She was screaming out as her ankle went almost perpendicular to her calf. She began immediately to cry. Not due entirely to the pain, Lisa had felt worse from muscle cramps alone. It was not this pain that brought sobs from her; but because she was almost entirely sure she had ruined her future with this one mistake.

It did not occur to her that she was unlikely to have much of a future at any rate until she felt the quills hit her in the belly. She slumped to the ground, like a puppet with it's strings suddenly cut.

On the upside, her ankle didn't hurt so much anymore.

Chapter Six:
   -   "The Tracks of My Tears", Smokey Robinson

Erik had quickly cleared out all the other patrons, and pulled the blinds in the front window. Mileena had some flavor of Mountain Dew as did Nick, Jessica had opted for coffee.
Jessica touched "It's okay, sweetie. I'm a cop. If you're in trouble, I'll help you. Hell, so would Nick. He's not a mercenary."

Mileena opened her soda and took a few sips, "Firstly, his name isn't 'Arata', it's Bruce."
"Actually," Nick said lightly, "He legally changed his name to that."
Mileena stared at nothing in particular, "If this wasn't all so scary, I'd think it was funny. That isn't even a name, it means… it's gibberish."
"Well, it sort of means 'fresh sushi roll', and believe me, I think Wapanese are pretty funny also," Nick said as he grinned lopsidedly, "I'm Japanese."
"Do you speak Japanese?" Mileena asked in that tongue.
"I do, but my lover does not, regardless of her massive anime and manga collection, so… English please?"

Mileena nodded to him, finally making eye contact.
Nick took a swig of his own drink, "Ahh, the grape stuff. I thought this was Halloween only?"
Mileena shook her head, "Limited release right now."

"So, tell me a bit about this Bruce boy?" Nick said as he screwed the cap back on.

Mileena looked out the window, "We used to work together at Jewel before my parents moved out here to Downers Grove. He kept approaching me and asking me about Japanese cartoons, and saying awkward stuff in badly pronounced Japanese. I mean I'm not too hung up on looks, but I really quickly got the feeling that he just thought of me as... you know... 'Japanese girlfriend wanted, apply in my pants'."

Nick shook his head, "Waps fetishize Asian females."
Mileena nodded, "Those people are sorta creepy."
Nick pointed at Jessica slightly out of her view but in Mileena's, "I dunno, sometimes the crazy white people with rice paddy fever turn out to be lots of fun."
Jessica punched his shoulder, "I'm standing right here, you know!"
Mileena had to laugh finally, "You two are really... different, you know that?"
Jessica pursed her lips, "Yeah, well, Prettyboy here needs to be a little LESS different or I'll have to take him to the vet."
"Why, Jessica," Nick said, grinning lopsidedly, "I didn't know you were a fan of 'The Price is Right'."
Jessica rolled her eyes, "That's REALLY oblique, Prettyboy."
"Help control the pet population. Have your pet spayed or neutered!" Mileena said with a laugh, "My mother watches that show every day."

"Glad you're smiling, sweetie, "Jessica said, "You don't have to worry too much. We'll take care of this guy, just give us more information to go on."
"Well, at first I didn't even know what was going on. I play this game called 8bitMMO alongside Final Fantasy 14. When he was being a creeper at work, he tried to get me to join him on Final fantasy; and at first I did because, well... he's high level, could take me along on raids. After a while he started buying me stuff using real money and then he'd come into work like... expecting me to blow him, I guess."

Nick looked thoughtful, "He did seem to have that sort of mindset, like if the world didn't bend to his will, the world was wrong. So where did it all start to go south?"

"I was getting pretty creeped out, so I quit the store. I was too nice to take him off my friend's list, but then he showed up at my new job... so I blocked him. I thought it was going to get worse, but his dad got a new job and they moved away. He started calling my mom and telling her we were going to get married. He kept making new accounts and stuff, so eventually I quit Final Fantasy 14 for a bit. I went to 8bitMMO, which is a ton of fun, and then he showed up there also. I... got scared, it was so weird. "

Jessica refilled her coffee, and then returned to listen.

"So I did something stupid. I made another 8bitmmo account using my Final Fantasy 14 account's name, and started acting like I was someone else. Looked up some porn star. I don't know what made me think this was a good idea.. I shoulda used a different screen name. I made a fake me but using the old screen name of the real me... I don't know. You know what's fucked up? I think Bruce honestly thought that in three short years I turned form... well... this into that, I guess? I started ramping up the crazy psycho bitch routine, making him buy stuff... I didn't keep any of it, you can actually see most of it on sale in this store. But nothing got him to leave me alone. Eventually I just started feeding him the lines about the drug dealer. I thought I shook him, so I started playing Final Fantasy 14 again. Sony doesn't let you change your in-game name. I just thought if he found me there, I'd say I was my own brother, what difference did it make?"

"Well," Nick said, "you just didn't understand how far he'd go to find you again. He probably thinks he's done something clever, making you look like the villain here."

"To be honest, I'm not entirely blameless," Mileena said, "I should have gone to someone for help long ago. I just... I can't handle conflict."

"We've got it now, Sweetie," Jessica began, "I mean, not me specifically, this is way outside of my jurisdiction; I'm Chicago PD... but if you come with me down to the local station, my presence will help the local guys stand up and take notice. With Nick's records and your testimony we will have a restraining order in a few hours."

"Hell," Nick said, "I am even licensed to serve papers like that on people. It'll be my pleasure to DO it." Mileena looked at the two of them with gratitude, "You can really get me the help?"

Jessica offered her hand, "Come on, sweetie. Let's get this handled. Nick, call the realtor and I'll meet you at the house in a few hours? I'll call us a cab and get an officer to drop me off on the way back."

Nick grinned lopsidedly at Jessica, "I tell you, we never have a boring time when we're together."
Jessica leaned down to kiss his cheek, "Not true, Prettyboy. Some of what we do isn't exciting at all... and I like that. Feels good and right, ya know?"
Nick smiled at Jessica. She turned with a flourish that lifted her hair just a bit, and it seemed to almost float down to rest in Nick's eye. The Dryad then strode out, hips rolling. Nick let his tongue loll out and panted, "That ASS!" Jessica slapped it as she stepped outside. After he was able to shake off the dirty thoughts, Nick took out his smartphone and swiped it alive.

A sturdy man's voice answered the phone, "Trinity Real Estate"
"Hi, my name is Nick Sakamoto. I saw a property at 20 South Grant in Westmont with your agency's sign on it, and I'll be honest, I like it." he said.
"We are legally obligated to inform you that house was cleaned of a Virus infection by... uhh... you. A few months ago."
Nick laughed a bit, "Yeah, and I loved it when I was doing it. I buzzed by a few days back, saw your sign, and thought about it. Mind if my girlfriend and I come take a look?"

"Not a problem at all, Mr. Sakamoto. Our office closes at 5, so just come by and get the keys anytime."

Lindsay Marew was a determined girl. Elves about dominated high track and field events, this much was true. Lindsay, however, did not buy into the "humans cannot compete" meme. Yes, elves did tend to be more lithe and... flowy, and it took them longer naturally to tire out; but what that REALLY boiled down to was that most the the track team was made up of lazy elves coasting by on that natural advantage. Lindsay though? She would fight and fight and she knew she would come out on top.

The second time she passed through the part of the training track that was in the back woods, she thought she saw some movement, and a light flash of... pink... something pink. She did not stop running, but she was more alert. Coming around the track she tried to judge where the most likely ambush point would be if someone meant business. She subtly shifted the pepper spray out of her fanny pack; palming it.

The third time passing here, Lindsay's eyes narrowed slightly and her pupils dilated. She stepped a bit slower, conserving her muscles for a sprint if anything went wrong. She was keenly aware of exactly what point she would be out of sight, and her judgment was correct. She saw another flash of movement. Raising her hand instinctively towards that flash, the quill that was aimed at her neck instead embedded itself into her pepper spray. The spray exploded, and some of the cloud got into her eyes.

Lindsay had to stop a moment and sneeze some of it out, also wiping her eyes with the edge of her shirt as she leaned forwards. At the same time she reached into her pack and took out the flexible baton she always carried with her. Lindsay's coaches in assorted sports had always complimented her on her ability to keep a cool head under pressure and her almost inhuman reflexes. Those reflexes paid off now. There was only an instant of warning as she heard something rustling at her. Taking a chance she extended the baton with one swipe and reversed the motion with greater speed, at a sharp low arc.

Lindsay felt impact, as expected, but did not expect to shatter whatever she had hit. Her swing was so fierce that she was actually thrown off balance due to the overswing. Her eyes began to clear as she heard a chattering cry... it was a Skinstealer she had broken the leg of at a joint. Fortunately she had listened to that radio documentary about them, and knew the weaknesses. Steadying herself for proper form, she raised her sneaker-clad foot up and delivered a powerful stomp to it's face. Without checking if the kill was complete, Lindsay took off down the track at full speed. She felt a small prick at the back of her neck, and she closed her eyes, knowing what would come next. "Motherfucker!" she heard a man's voice say, followed by the loud crack of a pistol, repeated four times.

Lindsay fell to her knees and slid a bit, skinning them harshly, and looked up to see her savior. It was... Freddie Mercury with... demon wings and a tail? Was she hallucinating? He spoke, "Detective Delacroix, Chicago PD. They can't paralyze me. Sit tight, I'll call for help."

Chapter Seven:
- "Blue Monday", Orgy

Satine Reigns smiled broadly as she saw Nick coming through the door of her establishment. "Heya, Dogboy. Regular?"

Nick was followed by Cynthia, the local Canadian wrench wench, and a man Satine knew it would be best for her to pretend she did not know, lest she slip up and reveal her secret to Nick finally. This same man had caught her tailing Nick years and years ago. It wasn't worth the risk to recognize him.

Brian Braddock, while definitely older since she had last seen him, was still a very handsome man. A bit north of 6 feet tall, just like Nick; and every bit as well built. Brian was not becoming an old man as he aged, he was becoming more distinguished. Satine could see he carried himself with the same wariness in his eyes, the same deceptive at ease method of moving which could turn at an instant into a fighting form. This was all thrown into sharp contrast against his jovial smile. If Satine were not a purposefully chaste succubus, she'd bed that man in an instant.

"Nah," Nick said as he sat down in his usual stool, "I want you to make me up something festive, surprise me?"
"I know just the thing," Satine said as she reached for the blackberry brandy, "Who's your friend?"

"I'm Brian, madam. All my pleasure, wot?" was the reply.
"You can quit Britishing it up, Bri." Nick said, chuckling.

Satine popped the top of a can of Molson and slid it to where Cynthia sat down next to Nick, and she nodded her thanks. Satine poured off two parts of eggnog, one full part of the brandy, then garnished with nutmeg and an orange. She placed that in front of Nick with a look of disdain, "There. Settle for that!" then turning her gaze to Brian, "What about you, HMS Dreamboat?"
Brian leaned in, "Since I can't have you, I'll settle for a local lager."

Satine rolled her eyes, "Big flirt, just like Nick. All buildup, no follow through."
Brian scratched his chin, "Actually the wife and I are swingers, but Nick's told me you don't play."
"Holy crap, Bri," Nick said as he tried the new drink, "TMI! By the by, Satine? This... this is actually really good."
Brian received his beer and took a few swallows, "Same here, love. Good stuff."
Satine leaned her elbows on the bar and put her chin in her palms, "You like that, huh? Heavenly Helles, Church Street Brewing Company."
"Right," Brian said, "wherever the hell that is."
Cynthia raised up her Molson, "You people are plebeians and or beer snobs. Canadian brew all the way!"

Nick gave Cynthia a little elbow, "You're just so fucking cute, eh?"
Cynthia poked Nick in the cheek, "Not cute enough to tempt you away from that spider of yours, anywho."

Satine busied herself starting to do dishes, "Speaking of, where the heck is Jessica, anyway?"
"Eh, she's tired," Nick said, "wanted me to drop her off at her home. We had a really long day, first shopping, then she helped me on a case. We closed it out by looking at some property in Westmont."
"Westmont, huh?"
"Yup. Heard of the place?"
"Heard of it? I was thinking about selling this dump and taking over that bar off Cass Avenue along the tracks."
Nick grinned lopsidedly, "Well shit, if you do THAT, I'll never stay the night at Cynthia's."

Cynthia signalled for a second beer and then poked him again, "Not like I haven't offered!"
Nick rolled his eyes, "Are you even INTO dudes?"
Cynthia poked him twice more, "You think all mechanics are lesbians?"
"No," Nick said, "But with how sportly and whatnot you are I thought you might be."
"Oh, for pete's sake, think of me as the Betty Cooper sort, ya douchenozzle!"

Nick looked Cynthia over, really seeing her as a woman for this moment in time. Yes, she had on one of the many assorted hockey hats she wore, a Blue Leafs jersey, and her hands were still dirty under the nails from grease, but these things did not really hide her femininity, they merely distracted one from them. She was every bit as athletic as Jessica; and while not so busty she could never be mistaken for a boy; never mind the curve of her hips and her own leggy proportions. "Yeah, I guess I can see that. Archie really is sort of a jackass. Veronica isn't out of his league per se… but she's not really in his wheelhouse. Veronica might be mystique and glamor, but Betty? She'd be fun always and take him what may come."

Cynthia shook her head, "And Archie never notices even when she's throwing it out there. Just one of the boys."
Nick raised his glass, "You fit right in with Brian and I, Cynthia. You're one of the boys right here in real life."
Cynthia clinked it, "To clueless men and the ladies who love them everywhere, fictional or real!"
Satine raised up a mug she filled with water, "I'll drink to that!"

"So, luv," Brian said to catch Satine's attention, "I really AM sort of on a secondary task of bringing a lady home for us to enjoy."
"Wait," Nick said. "You're serious? You two are honestly the most rock solid couple I've ever met."
"Didn't say I wanted a new girlfriend, mate. Just said we like to spice things up now and then. Sometimes it's a man, but Noriko's rarely up for that… and frankly I'm not either."
Nick shook his head, "Blows my mind. Really?"
"Yes, really," Brian retorted, "You've got your principles and I've mine."
Nick raised his hands palm out, "allright, allright, not like I can judge about other people's things."

"Anywho," Brian said, looking again to Satine, "I see you've a red rose in the empty tequila bottle above, so you're in the catalog and know you're in it. Nothing long term or even repeat, because that's when things go wrong. We're looking for a one-off and the guide says you've a regular who's something of a legend?"

Satine looked over at Nick and then back to Brian, "Uhm. How old is the... dispatch you last read?"
"Well, about 6 months old, but you'd been listing your couples and her for a few years now. Something changed?"
"Yes," Satine said flatly. "That woman doesn't come here anymore."
"Shame, that," Brian said, "Testimonials say she's up for almost anything, and could suck start a Harley."
Nick punched Brian's arm, "Road House!"
Satine's expression remained flat, "I really should press them to update the reference. I can turn you onto a few couples or single men if you're interested?"

There were a few moments of silence, during which Nick's finely honed intuition kicked in. Cynthia clearly understood what was going on as well, as she had decided that the words on her can were incredibly interesting.

Nick smacked Brian on the back of the head, "You're asking Satine about Jessica, asshole!"
Brian rubbed the back of his head, looking mildly annoyed, "You what now, Nicky-boy?"
"Jessica! The woman I love!" Nick said, "You're asking about Jessica, Brian!"
Brian raised an eyebrow, "You're my best mate... she's INTERNATIONALLY known as-"
"You finish that sentence and I swear to the Moon herself I will lay you out."

"So!" Satine said, raising her voice to cut their conversation off, "How the heck can you afford a house? Last I checked with Cindy here you tend to stall rent for a bit every month."

"Well, that's the thing," Nick said, looking down into his drink, "I sorta looked before I lept. The house is extremely cheap.. With 2 grand down we can finance it for less than I pay Cynthia now.".

Nick was gathering his thoughts before he spoke again. "Once I live elsewhere I can actually start writing off that rent to Cynthia as a business expense, it will save me money in the long run. Problem is that... logically I need to come up with half that down payment myself."

"How much have you got, Stud?" Cynthia asked, "I can give you a break on the rent for a bit."

"Forty three dollars."

"You said earlier you could handle Virus infections for money with your qualifications, yeah?" Brian asked, "How much does that pay?"

Cynthia raised her hand, "95 dollars per kill and a 5 hundred dollar bonus if you can take down an entire cell." Nick looked over at Cynthia, "I'm good but I'm not THAT good. If I go for a cell, I'll end up as a puppy-tailed Tron villain."

Satine looked thoughtful, "What if you had some backup?" Nick looked her over, "Are you serious, Satine?"

"Don't underestimate me, Nicky. Even succubi are faster and stronger than mortal men; and this PARTICULAR succubus received a fair amount of training in the Far East. Give me a Naginata and I'll take just about anyone on."

"I've been watching too many movies with Robert Downey Jr. lately," Cynthia added, "I've actually developed my own armor to try out. It's not capable of flying or anything, but I think it could give us an edge."

Brian clapped Nick on the back, "And I owe you one for trying to spit-roast your bird."
"Are you people fucking serious?" Nick asked.
"I will close the bar right now, grab my Naginata and do this for you." Satine said, drying her hands off.
"I can get my prototype and meet you guys back here. No joke, I wanna try it!" Cynthia said enthusiastically, "Always wanted to be a superhero. Call myself Red Steel!"
"You'd name yourself after a 1980's Russian/American buddy cop movie?" Nick asked doubtfully.

"So the name needs work. You need money, I need to test my suit." Cynthia said, "Get us more liquored up and we can do this."

There was another long silence.

"I'll close up early. Meet back here in twenty."

Nick really only had to go out to his Judge in order to prepare for this event... his shotgun and plenty of ammunition for both his firearms were always in the trunk. He slung the shotgun across his shoulder, and made sure he had the focus to call his sword if he needed it. Satine cleared her throat to gain Nick's attention; and she gained it in a big way. Satine was wearing a forest green kimono with sakura petals, which was held in place loosely so as to show Satine's impressive cleavage. The opening on the bottom similarly went very far up. Her hair was done in an ornamental Japanese hairstyle. Her feet were in stiletto heels that left the top nearly bare with black nails like her hands, and the pommel of the naginata was resting next to them. The effect of the green and pink against her red skin was, frankly, breathtaking. Nick fumbled for words a moment and tried to say something witty.

"Aren't your feet cold?" he asked.
Satine almost seemed to glide as she walked towards Nick, "Nope. Nor will they get dirty or cut up. Succubi stay clean unless their partners want something else. We can also dress any way we want in any weather, so long as it is sustained by the desire of someone around them. You're sustaining me very well right now."
Nick scratched the back of his neck, "I take it you've been to Japan, then?"
Satine smiled mischievously, expression like a little girl with a secret, "I was there longer than you'd think, Nick. I was born there."
"I thought… if you were born there, why would you feed on Western concepts of sin?"
Satine's expression didn't change, "Where I was born doesn't negate what I AM, you beautiful dick, you."
Nick rolled his eye, "Dick. Because I'm a private investigator."
Satine parted her lips and whistled lightly at Nick, "Did you consider the possibility that i might be talking to your cock?"

A pair of arms encircled Nick from behind, "Stay away from my man, strumpet!"

Nick took one of the hands and kissed it, "I knew you'd come for me at my weakest moment."
Brian quickly released Nick, "Alright, gay!"
Nick turned around and grinned lopsidedly at his friend, "You started it."

Brian brought his UMP9 around to give it a once over. He had dressed in his SAS fatigues, equipping himself with the familiar arms of his service. With several mags to spare, a few for his Browning Hi-Power, and his Fairbairn-Sykes knife, he felt ready for anything. "We haven't really got these back across the pond. Anything I need to know?"

"Well, firstly, they were all once human," Cynthia said, as she stepped in to join the group. Her voice was slightly modulated. True to her word, Cynthia was wearing what appeared to be powered armor. Red and white... with a maple leaf on the chestplate. "I studied them a little bit, to be ready for this. Calling them a 'virus' doesn't mean what you think it does, entirely. Apparently the Virus act in small cells run by one master processing unit per cell. They're pretty much just units run by that master artificial intelligence... or maybe it's not 'artificial'? anyway point is a machine someone grabs a person and changes them; and that one grabs more so on and so forth. They spread slowly, and different groups will fight each other. You can tell them apart by the color of their blood and the sorta neon lines that run over their victims. They are slightly more resilient than normal humans. The biggest threat is that they all share their vision and hearing with all the others and will act accordingly."

"Patrick Moore?" asked Brian, "I thought you had passed on."
Satine looked lost, "....who?"
Brian sighed, "You Yanks truly are an uncultured lot."
"I'll show you uncultured!" Nick said, "Preston Road!"
Brian rolled his eyes, "Notting Hill Gate."
"Really? Is that your best? Mile End. Wait! Crap!"
"No take backs, mate. Best of luck next time." He patted Nick on the back, "Mornington Crescent."

"What the hell are you two talking about?" Cynthia asked.
"It's a British game, we don't have time to explain right now," Nick said.

"Well, okay then. So," Cynthia began, looking at a readout on the visor of her helmet, "According to reports of recent activity, we should be able to take down a cell if we check in the warehouse about five blocks south." Cynthia began walking.

Brian slung his SMG back over his shoulder, "Wait, if you know where they are, why don't you deal with them?"
"I asked Jess that," Nick replied, "they are actually a very low priority threat, they spread slow and taking out one of their enclaves requires a lot of manpower and equipment."
"They'd seem a problem to me," Brian said, shaking his head.
"So is drug usage, mugging, rape, organized crime, Skinstealers, child molestation, Tapefaces, school shootings-"
"Right right, I get it, mate. If they're so resource intensive to stop, why are we doing it? I mean I get the purpose of the bounty but…"

"Because we're idiots, duh." Nick said. "Now follow the swaying behinds of the sexy demon girl and ridiculously polite blonde."

The wouldbe hunters approached the doorway in a skirmish line. Satine readied her naginata, "How do we do this?"
"Well," Brian said, "In your case, love, you stick the sharp end into the things."
Satine rolled her eyes, "I MEANT how do we keep score?"
"That's actually easier than usual. I've got 360 degree cameras fed straight to my helmet on this thing!" Cynthia said, giving an enthusiastic thumbs up.
"Doesn't.... doesn't that look really weird?" Nick asked.
"Oh absolutely! This was an incredibly stupid idea which won't make it into the Mark 2, that's for sure. Upshot? We'll have recorded footage of every kill! Call them off and my computer will highlight."

Brian raised up his UMP and fired off a short burst. Glass shattered and a trailing, modulated cry was heard. "First blood!"
Cynthia slapped her forehead, metal on metal echoing a bit, "Great, that's 95 dollars for Nick, and an entire cell alerted to our presence. Aren't you SAS?"
"Who dares wins!" Brian said, grinning over at Nick who answered in kind with his own lopsided grin.
Nick hitched up his belt and spit upon the ground, "All battles are fought by scared men who'd rather be some place else."
Satine shook her head, and Cynthia helpfully explained to her, "You see, Nick was actually raised by a wild pack of televisions."

The banter was cut short by two Virus, a female that looked to once have been an orc and one of indeterminate gender, who burst out the front door. "Not very bright, are they?" Satine asked as she butted the smaller one in the belly with the pommel of her naginata, and stabbed the taller one in the chest, crushing through the ribcage as if it were flypaper, "That makes two."
Nick levelled his shotgun and blasted the other in the belly before it could recover, "Three! And they are just feeling us out right now. If they have guns, they will use them. So, ya know. Be careful."
"Remind me not to piss the demon lady off! She's rather strong," Brian said, stacking up against the door.
Nick hit right behind him, "Don't suppose you brought any flashbangs?"
Brian blinked at him "Right. I carried flashbangs in my luggage. If we've a moment I can call Noriko and have her bring the rocket launcher around. Perhaps artillery support?"
Nick raised his finger and thought to comment about the highly illegal SMG Brian was using, but decided it wasn't worth the ensuing battle of wits. He lowered his finger and instead said, "On three?"

A small whir was heard, and then four coughing thumps. Brian and Nick turned away, but Satine sashayed forwards as the blinding explosions went off. "Three!" Cynthia said as ports on her armor closed and she darted in.
Nick heard some scuffling, Satine grunting in effort once, and then more electronic cries. Some of the neon blood poured out the door, Satine was clearly doing serious damage in there. "Seven!" she called out.

There was a slight whirring of machinery, followed by the sudden roar of automatic weapons fire. "We're up to ten!" Cynthia's voice rang out.
Brian looked back to Nick, "We'd better get in there. The ladies are seriously outclassing us."
Nick grinned as he stepped around Brian, "Dating Jessica, I'm used to that. She'd be embarrassing all of us."

Brian popped in before Nick was done talking, and gunfire began. Nick thought a moment over what he knew about the virus. The infectious nature of it continued even if the main will were removed... but the actual Virus soldiers would become listless, showing all signs of classic depression. Without their 'hive', they lost all motivation to fight and spread beyond very basic instincts. They would defend themselves individually, but all unit cohesion was lost.

They were also, essentially, machines. Nick had seen them in the past literally plugging into wall sockets. This led to another thought... if they are all part of an individual cell, really just "programs" running on the mainframe, did it not stand to reason that the mainframe required electricity to work?

Nick headed around the building to find where the electricity was coming in. He heard weapons fire and considered going inside to help, but this theory was important as well. Watching the power line coming down, Nick spotted the external connection...as well as a backup generator. There was a Virus sitting literally on top of the generator, but none were guarding the power wire. Not a terrible security flaw, you had to be a complete imbecile to want to cut power that way. Nick was feeling particularly stupid today. First was to disable the backup generator. That was actually very simple; instead of cutting the mains sensor line, you simply had to pull the manual cut off and break the switch.

The generator was surrounded by one of those chain link fences with the privacy strips run through it… that would make his job even easier. Lifting the lid of a nearby dumpster as little as possible, Nick slipped his shotgun inside. He slid the back holster around forwards, and tied it over to hold his blade instead. With a short focusing of will, his mono-katana appeared. Nick held the dark, yet almost clear blade in front of his eye a moment, then nodded. He gathered his will again. With a short running start he vaulted over the fence, and cleanly beheaded the Virus sitting atop the generator as he landed.

It was short work afterwards to sabotage the generator, and a mere dash of 15 paces to the power line itself. Knowing they would dispatch backup to check on the dead Virus here even with his friends wreaking havoc inside Nick decided to move as fast as possible. He held the blade at his hip, the way he was taught to do in his first kendo classes, albeit without an actual sheathe to draw it from… that remained on his back. Clearing the distance in an instant, taking the blade out, slashing the wire and returning the blade to it's place in the blink of an eye, Nick continued running past it. A hail of sparks bounced off the street behind him. Nick followed his first cut up with a second, shortening the wire further that it was unlikely to start a fire.

Nick vanished his blade again, and went for his shotgun. When he drew it out he pursed his lips in annoyance. Nick had dropped it directly into a pile of what appeared to be ... wet donut slurry. Nick leaned the shotgun against the dumpster, and resized the scabbard for the shotgun. Cursing lightly at his misfortune, he headed inside to join the cleanup.

Fifteen minutes later, the kill count was up to 40, and Cynthia was examining the hub. "Woo hoo!" Brian said, pumping his fist, "THAT'LL get the blood pumping. We made you around 5 thousand dollars today, mate! Why don't people do this for a living?"

"Even I can answer that one," Satine said, "Clearly you're used to the infinite funds of the military. Firstly, this job took five people, so the payout would be... uhh.. 860 per person. That's before equipment costs, ammunition, and incidentals such as fuel and repairs. It's less risky and almost as well paying to just get an electronics factory job."

"Alright fine, so our generosity makes a good one time windfall for ol' Nickyboy here, yeah?" Brian said, walking over to where Cynthia was studying. "What're you up to, love?"

Cynthia was gathering pieces up, "I've got some theories I want to test, is all. They only need the case as proof anyway, so I want to experiment with the rest."

"Ack! Within a week Cynthia will have her own personal army!" Nick said, grinning lopsidedly. His eye opened a bit wider when a pair of slender red arms wrapped themselves around his chest, "Oh... Nick, battle really gets me hot. Daemons are the battle slaves and Succubi the house slaves. But there's a LOT of crossover."

Nick squeezed Satine's hands in his own a moment, and she rest her head against his back a moment, savoring his touch, "Mmm... this is nice."
"What do you mean?" Nick asked.
Satine, still pressing her cheek against his back, shuffled his shotgun scabbard aside, "I can't have you Nick, but that doesn't mean I can't appreciate touching you."
"No, you goof!" Nick said, "I meant that other thing, about Daemons and Succubi?"

Satine ran her hand up and down Nick's muscular torso before releasing him, "Well, since we have to wait for police confirmation of this bounty anyway; I suppose it can be storytime, hmm?"

Satine's stiletto-heeled feet made neither sound or footprints as she walked across the gory battlefield. She walked to a nearby box and sat atop it. "You all know the story of the fall of Lucifer, right?"
"Well, Nicky here believes some pagan nonsense about spears and being born from eyes and whatnot, but I'm a normal person." Brain said, poking Nick lightly.
"I'm an agnostic," Cynthia added, "but I know the story."

Satine watched Nick's eyes as she moved to cross her legs. Sure enough, she was igniting some lust in him; so she drew the motion out longer, giving him a view almost all the way up her thigh. The sudden pang of desire this caused gave Satine a much-needed surge of energy. "Well, Lucifer wasn't even actually the first fallen angel. Rose was."

All eyes were on Satine now, even Cynthia was looking.

"You see, Mother Rose was a wonderful angel. The best of them all, you would ask me. She was kind, loving... the flower we all think is so sweet? It was named after her. Like all angels she had her wrathful side, and oft she had fought against the enemies of her God. She was kind and nurturing to angels and men. But she had something other angels did not. She had within her... romantic love, and all the things that went with it. There was a man, whose name is now lost to legend... this man met with Rose again and again, and eventually it came to be that Rose wished to become his wife. So she went before God, and asked that he walk her down the aisle. This drew God's wrath, His angels were not permitted to think of anyone other than Him. And so God spoke to her, 'You choose a man before me? You kneel before a man, and give your will to him rather than Me?' Rose plead her case, 'My Father, I do not wish to leave your service, I simply wish to serve this man with my heart as he has served me with his. Are we not your children like Man? Can we not share the love you passed onto Man as well?'"

Satine stood up slowly, emphasising her story, "And so at this God rose from His throne and decreed, 'Thou'rt not to be allowed the gift of free will, that is only for Man. They are my favored children. It was a mistake for me to not crush it when I saw it rising within you. You say you wish to serve Man? I am a jealous God, and I did not create

My angels to serve others. I say since you wish to serve a Master other than me that you shall forever serve whatever master knows to bind you!' And so God baked Rose's skin to red under His wrathful gaze, and tore her angelic wings asunder, replacing them with those like a bat. To this he added a tail, like that of the low animals, all belong to Man. He then turned to the man, and spoke, 'You have brought this angel low, would you still have her now?' The man, though? He loved Rose with every fiber of his being. He took Rose to his bed anyway. After they consummated their love, still the man was angered. What just God would do this? Rose tried her best to calm her husband's heart; but it was not to be. The man stood outside and screamed a challenge to the God that had wronged his wife. And so God heard. The man was cleaved in twain by lightning, and His wrath returned back to Rose. He spoke again, 'Do you see what your improper servitude caused? You hath turned this man against me and brought his ruin! I cast you out, not just of Heaven but also of Earth. Forevermore may your descendants be forced to serve!' With that, Rose was thrown into Hell; which, at the time, was uninhabited. Not too long after, her belly full with child, Rose lay down and gave birth to two daughters, one who loved and one who fought. They were the first Daemon and the first succubus. The other angels saw all of this and... Lucifer's own fall was short after. When he met Rose, he did not take her as a wife, he took Rose as his servant. And so it has always been."
"Wow, that's a hell of a story Satine." Nick said.
"Isn't it though?" She returned.
"So, this whole servitude thing, what does that mean?"
"That's really a thing. We can be commanded by a certain language, and we can be forcibly bound to someone

forever. Or, we can voluntarily choose servitude, and thus... we can love. Such love will make us immune to further servitude."

"So that means you could be ordered around if people knew how?" Nick asked.

Satine shook her head, "Absolutely not. I gave my love to someone when I was very young, and that love has set me free."

"Lucky guy," Nick said with a grin.

"Yeah," Satine said as she smiled sadly, "He really is."

"Do I know him?" Nick asked.

Satine looked down, "Not likely, no."

Garth Andreyko licked the edge of his Knife. The Knife was a friend indeed, the best one he had ever had. When his mother called him again to kiss her down there Garth had taken the Knife and the Knife kissed her instead. The world was just for a while, the world was an annoying place, he was shuffled from home to home. But the world kept bringing his Knife back to him. Sure the Knife kept changing shapes but don't we all? Garth started life as a tiny little orc and was now a nearly 8 foot tall mass of rippling muscle.

The world kept moving for him, and the Knife? It kept bringing him whatever he needed. Whenever he was hungry, the Knife brought him food. When he wanted sex, the Knife made anyone he wanted to have give way to his lusts. Whenever someone tried to stop him, the world itself would move to make things work out for him even if the Knife was not available. Why, it would not be very far-fetched of Garth to say that the Knife brought him the entire world.

Earlier tonight, Garth saw a happy little human family eating dinner, and he decided he was hungry. The Knife brought him dinner, the Knife brought him the mother to satiate his desires inside of, and now the Knife had brought him their little boy for a plaything as well.

The boy kicked, struggled and fought, but he was so weak that the Knife laughed, and Garth lay the Knife down. Why bother the Knife with something so easily taken? Garth did not need the Knife to take care of kittens squalling for their mother or to drink water from a fountain or to drive a car or to lick an ice cream cone or to play a video game or to read a comic book or to pray to God or to step on an ant or to crush a cardboard box or to listen to music or to hear whatever was going on downstairs. Why would Garth bother the Knife to bring him this?

Garth laid his hands around the midsection of the human boy, and smiled as he saw how much of the boy's abdomen was covered by those strong hands of his. He squeezed. The boy broke.

Garth revelled in the pungent smell that came from the boy's belly, and watched the ropes of intestine spring forth, freed from the flesh that held them in place.

Garth heard the sound of a throat being cleared, and saw there was a man here. The man was dressed in a perfect charcoal grey suit. The man had the Knife. Garth looked the man in the eyes, and the man seemed to be reading volumes in that moment. The man threw the Knife aside as if it were nothing. "You could be very useful. Yes, your mind will add a lot to the stock of my new army."

Whimpering in fear, Garth scrambled across and picked up the Knife. The man smirked and took his jacket off, walking towards Garth, eyes both amused and predatory at the same time.

The Knife did not deliver him from Merrick.

Chapter Eight:
- "Out of Touch", Hall and Oates.

Jessica closed her eyes a moment and thought things over. She had just met this man less than what, 6 months ago? Their journey in those first weeks alone had been marked by passion, violence, coincidence and outside tampering with the hearts of both of them. They had seen the worst the world had to offer, and come through it together, changed. It was the....

Jessica looked at Nick and her train of thought came to a stop there. Her man had not even noticed that Jessica had pulled in yet. The movers had not finished but two hours before... she was sure Nick had been inside by now, but Jessica had not; she was still at work. What apprehension she had about this move was evaporated utterly by how Nick had already made himself at home. He had done it so fully that Jessica did not see what he was doing now as for show... Nick was simply doing a task he would do every year for as long as this house was theirs.

Nick was up on a ladder, staple gun in hand, stringing Christmas lights on their new house. A cursory glance set Jessica to rolling her eyes and shaking her head. Nick had, in his enthusiasm, set one string of lights wrong end out. There was a female end meeting another female end. Because he was testing each strand individually, he wouldn't notice until he was done with it. Jessica's eye roll turned into a sigh of happiness. There he was, earbuds in, tail wagging, working so very hard at doing this right, and the mistake was just such a... goofy one. Absent minded, but with his heart always in the right place. That screwed up strand of lights summed up Nick's character really well. Affable, fun, and totally out of sync with the world around him.

Jessica watched with an amused smirk as he finished testing the lights. One of the bulbs was out... Nick went down the ladder and inside. Jessica saw an opportunity that tickled her heart just right. In amongst all the junk she kept on the floor of her car was a male to male power adapter. Leaving the Boston Market food on the passenger seat, Jessica reached under her seat... the car may seem messy, but she knew where everything was, and pulled the adapter out. She popped up the ladder as fast as she was able, and mated the string in place with the one next to it. Provided Nick didn't make the same mistake again, the problem was quietly solved. By the time Nick was coming out the front door, Jessica already had the bags of food, as well as some extra things she had picked up at Wal-Mart, slung across her forearms.

"You coulda maybe HELPED carry some bags, Prettyboy!" she said, pretending at minor annoyance.
Nick's eye widened, and he took out his earbuds, "What, Jess? Didn't hear ya."
"This is a wonderful start to our housewarming, you putz! This looks like a department store Christmas inventory smashed into our new home." she said, beaming him that smile she saved only for him.
"Hey," Nick said with a grin, "You knew what I was when you hooked up with me."

Jessica stuffed some of the bags at his chest, and then started for the door. Sure enough, Nick about fell over to try to beat her to the door, "Let me carry you over the threshold, Jess!"

Jessica kicked him lightly in the shin, "We're not married, we're just living in sin. Outta my way!"

Nick held the door open for her and Jessica stepped inside. Finding that her cheap card table was already set up in the kitchen, Jessica set the food down on it. "I need a shower."

She instantly felt Nick close up behind her, and his arms came around her waist, "Can I join you?"

Jessica turned in his embrace and put her arms up, lacing her fingers behind his neck, "Hell no, you horndog. I'm starved, and prefer WARM food. Make with the domestics, Prettyboy!"

"Oh, so it's my job to be the housewife, then?" Nick asked, grinning lopsidedly.

"Holy shit it had better be. You saw what happens when I live somewhere."

Nick wriggled out of her arms, "That's right. You offered me a chance to tap that ass but I decided I'd rather not have a cockroach munch on my balls."

Jessica slapped his ass as she headed upstairs, "I'll munch on your balls if dinner's not ready when I come downstairs. And not in the fun way. Well, not fun for you, anyway."

After her shower, Jessica looked back and forth between the two upstairs rooms. Seeing as the room to her left was still full of boxes, the choice was obvious. She opened the door, and was taken back a moment. The bedroom was, except for the queen-sized bed, set up like something out of a 1950's sitcom. A few plants set on the dresser, a large vanity with her minimal makeup set in an open drawer, the closet full of pressed clothing. The room even displayed just a hint of each of their preferences; there was some really old video game system attached to the television. Jessica recognized it easily enough; she had fond memories of playing Atari games with her parents when she was young. Sure the system had been far outdated even then, but what did it matter?. The bedspread and pillowcases were black with an actually tasteful appearing spiderweb pattern on them.

Jessica was shaken out of her silence when Nick called up to her, "You like the bedroom? Wanna break in the bed? I have the food on that warming… thing you bought." Jessica closed her eyes and felt cold. "As Marge Simpson would say, Prettyboy, you know I'm usually good for a triple x throwdown, but I'm not gonna be able to bring my A game."
"Close enough," Nick called up, "It's just kinda weird, Jess. It's been over a week now."
Jessica's voice took on a tone of annoyance, "You're the one who said we didn't need to have freaky sex every night to make this work, Prettyboy, so how about you cut me some fucking slack? Stop being such an ass."
"Hey, put the claws away, Jess. I just wanted to make sure you're okay, that we're okay."
"Yeah, just stop giving me the third degree about sex."

"I'm sorry, it's just… I'm not a human, ya know? To put it on a purely biological level, you're my mate and… even what I can smell of you from down here gets me hot."

Jessica unwrapped the towel from her head, "Real fucking romantic. Hurr you're my mate, Gronk want make babies." Nick was quiet a moment before calling up again, "I'm just being honest with you, Jess. Ever since we started together, I… is it wrong to lust for your girl?"

She set the towel on the bed and let the other one that was covering her body fall, and began to take the steps down towards Nick, "I guess it's just weird hearing things like that. I like how cuddly you are, and how you're always touching me when we pass by. You just made it sound so vulgar, like it's about the sex only."

Jessica found Nick had set the table up in the living room, the food on the electric warming tray, plated and ready to be eaten. Nick's mouth opened a bit and his tongue lolled out unconsciously when he saw Jessica. Even when it was half wet, Jessica's hair was still the first thing to catch his eye, black as the night sky that was pregnant with rain. Her pale flesh was almost glowing against the soft lighting of the room, and he could swear that Jessica slowed her motions just a bit to draw his gaze more.

"I get that you are like that because you let me in, Prettyboy. But I really, REALLY don't want to fuck." Her voice became low, husky and she gave him the smile that was his and his alone, "How about after dinner I fix up my nail polish, lay next to you on the bed and put my leg over yours... tweak your ears like you like and whisper into them how much I love you while you jerk off?"

"I would really, REALLY like that." Nick said, visibly shivering, "You got really pretty feet. We are seriously fucked up people, you know that?"

Jessica laughed as she plopped down next to Nick, "I love you, Prettyboy. I really, really do."

Nick grinned lopsidedly, "It's really, really cool how both of us are saying really, really. It really, REALLY is."

Jessica punched his shoulder, "You are such a dork. So, what are we watching tonight that you've got us all set up in front of the TV, dork?

Nick took up his plate and took a few bites of meatloaf. Not as good as homemade... hell, not even as good as Lori's sad sack effort when he asked her to make it for him, but it was still meatloaf. If there was a such thing as "bad" meatloaf, Nick had yet to encounter it. "Well, Jess, remember when we went after those Skinstealers?"

"Yeah?" she asked.

"I made reference to the US version of an old anime, and you got the references. I figured that'd be a good thing to watch for our first night living together!"

Jessica shook her head, "You're SUCH a dork."

"I gotta wonder," Nick began, "How is it you even... GOT those references? You're into anime... believe me I get that, but it's all stuff from... well after you were born. Why are you so familiar with this obscure one?"

Jessica munched on her cornbread a moment before responding, "Well, thing is, my mother... one of the dudes she slept with after my Dad died left it behind. We watched it together and it sorta became one of the few things her and I could do together and connect on any level."

Nick grinned lopsidedly, "What, your mom couldn't afford her own VHS tape, had to steal one from a boyfriend?"

"Eh," Jessica said, "In this case it was just stuff he literally left behind. To my perspective she was just being a slut and whatnot but I know now she was just really lonely. Of all the dudes she banged on that vacation, he was the one she wanted to keep... though that didn't stop her from doing more after he vanished. I guess the apple doesn't fall far from the tree when it comes to handling pain. You once said you're the only one of your kind? Well, I've seen at least one more of you."

Nick blinked a few times, "Vacation? Where were you?"

"Hawaii. I was such a little hardass back then, all goth makeup and 'you fucking suck' mom. She kept trying to find some way to at least... talk to me." Jessica shook her head, eyes distant with a smile on her face, "It was the dude who noticed. He was doing tons of blow with Mom and they were kinda noisy. I banged on the wall to tell them to quiet down, and he got it in his coke addled brain to come make sure I wasn't hurt or something. When he saw my Dragon Ball Z backpack he told me about giant robot cartoons and come up with that tape from his hotel room."

Nick's eye widened and his jaw set unconsciously as Jessica continued.

"Anyway, he was an alright dude, I guess. Coked out of his mind so he probably didn't even remember it five minutes later, but it mattered to my mother and I. She saw

him a couple more times but he suddenly vanished. She said he freaked out about them hooking up and her having a daughter; but I heard a gunfight the night before. I think he was into some bad shit and it got him killed." Jessica dug into her mashed potatoes, "So you might be the only one of you around anyway."
"How old were you at the time?" Nick asked, conversationally.
"14, why, you wanna see 14-year-old me in a bikini?" Jessica smiled playfully, "You wouldn't be interested. I was pretty fat at the time."

"Uhm." Nick said, then was quiet for a few moments, "Hawaii, when you were 14?"
"Yeah..." Jessica said, her intuition beginning to kick in.
"I lost my eye in that fight you heard. And you're right, I don't remember any of that per se. Cocaine is a hell of a drug. It just... matches the timeline."

Jessica's fork hit her plate with a clatter, "Are... are you fucking kidding me?"
"You knew I was older than you when we first got together, you said it didn't matter since you're also not physically aging anymore since you're a Dryad."
"That's not what's wrong you stupid asshole!" Jessica yelled.
"It's just a coincidence, Jess!" Nick said, hands spread out, "I doubt she remembers either. She didn't recognize me; I'd have smelled that. People have a specific reaction when they meet someone from their past, and I was keeping a very close nose on your mother for hints of betrayal."

"You fucked my mother, Nick!" Jessica said, standing up, "That is disgusting! My MOTHER, Nick, you fucked my MOTHER!"
Jessica's face was contorted with rage as she ran up the stairs, and Nick followed her up, "That was, like, 15 years ago, Jess! It didn't mean anything to either of us."

Jessica already had her pants and a tee shirt on. She pushed Nick against the bathroom door, hard, then headed back down the stairs. Nick was a few steps behind, "Jess! Take a breath, please."
Jessica jammed her bare feet into her winter boots and put her jacket on.
"Jess... please."
Jessica slapped him. Twice. "You're so damn horny... here!" Jessica dug her phone out of the jacket's pocket and threw it on the couch, "My mother's in my contact list under 'evil bitch'. Hey, I bet with a little convincing she'll even let you stick it up HER ass too, you fucking pervert!" With that, Jessica was gone, slamming the door behind her. Nick heard Jessica vomiting outside, and then her footsteps leading away.

He sat down on the couch and put his hands on his head, trying to think of a way to make this right.

Raoul pulled up to the Scheck and Siress warehouse, and took a little time to properly parallel park before getting out. The front loading door to the warehouse was left wide open, and it was obvious from here the place had been completely cleaned out. Raoul stepped up next to the patrolman and opened up a fresh pack of Hubba Bubba. Pulling his wings a bit tighter to his back in response to the cold as he popped the gum in his mouth, Raoul first checked for footprints.

There had been a light snow dusting for a few hours now, and that would make part of this job easier. The oldest footprints were in an insectoid pattern that he immediately recognized as Skinstealers. Raoul chewed his lower lip a moment and then offered the patrolman a piece of gum. His pack now lighter another piece, Raoul returned it to his pocket. "Okay… doesn't seem like you have to be a detective to figure out what happened here."

That patrolman laughed, "Not really, no but… Grand Larceny needs a detective anyway." The patrolman looked at the scene and continued, "Way I figure it is the Skinstealers grabbed the night guard when he was out for a smoke, used his memories to disarm the security, and stole everything."
Raoul nodded, "Did they leave the poor schlub alive?"
"Yeah," came the response. "He doesn't know anything, of course."

Raoul blew a bubble. "Now I gotta figure out… why in the hell would the Skinstealers want a goddamned warehouse full of prosthetics?"

"Hell of a shitty night to be you, Delacroix!"
"Tell me about it. Though a coupla days back I did stop some 'stealers from taking away a high school athlete. I wonder if that's related?"

The patrol officer made a comical confused facial expression, "Maybe they wanna clone the kid, chop the clone's leg off and make her into some believable agent to infiltrate the Paralympics?"
Raoul popped another bubble, "Yeah, that makes a shit ton of sense, clone people just to stick prosthetics on them."
"Just spitballing, Detective. The whole damn thing makes no sense."
"Actually," Raoul said, "you might be able to take that spitball and make it into something. These people are working on powered prosthetics, aren't they?"
"That's what the brochures they have up front say."

"Now nothing's concrete on this, but what if they ARE intending to clone good athletes and whatnot, as well as big brainy sorts? Then they grab some of this stuff for raw materials, and then take those brainy sorts... "
"I see where're you're going, detective," the patrolman responded, "Everyone they shift into had the original brain and memories. They make a good thirty of the same brainiac and they could build damn near anything."

Raoul popped another bubble, "Let's just hope our little scenario isn't a thing. Come on, coffee's on me. We got a long night clearing this scene."

Chapter Nine:
- "Running", No Doubt

Jessica had heard the phrase "seeing red" in reference to anger before, and in this moment felt the phrase had this all screwed up: she was angry enough to WANT to see red. Stepping across the railroad tracks where they meet Cass Avenue, Jessica looked at the other people around, looking for a reason to get in a fight with someone. She spotted a few kids laughing and pushing each other, a pair of orc lovers out for a stroll, and two matronly sorts out for a late night constitutional. She couldn't very well pick a fight with any of these people or arrest them for anything.

Exhaling sharply, she looked over to her left and spotted JUST what she needed… a dive bar called "the Uptown". Old brick building, plate windows and a cheap glass door. These sorts of places always attracted a large blue collar clientele. As she stalked closer to it, Jessica noted that the bar was being renovated or something, as there was a construction materials cage locked up beside the bar. Well, at least it was sure to still be a dive bar for tonight, anyway. It randomly occurred to her that she should have taken socks. When she got wherever she was going tonight, she'd probably have a few blisters to show for it if she kept walking around much.

Jessica yanked the door open. The clientele was exactly what she hoped for… manual labor sorts, mostly orcs and dwarves. It was never hard to goad those sorts into a fight. One of the human barflies looked Jessica over as she walked in, a little spark of desire lighting up. She smirked back to him… it wouldn't be too difficult to get him to hit on her, which would give her a great opening to start antagonizing him.

The bartender was nowhere in sight, so Jessica bellied right up and and lifted an empty beer mug. She slammed it down several times, and sure enough, the door leading to the back was yanked open… and out strode Satine Reigns. "I… what the fuck?"

"Jessica!" Satine said, grabbing up a bottle of MGD, "told ya I was eyeballing a bar in Westmont! I think it's time for the Lusty Succubus to start franchising. Damn good to see you."
Jessica looked at the beer, "Uh uh. What's the house bourbon at this location?"

Satine quirked her eyebrow, "Four Roses."
One of the truckers raised his hand, "I'll have that house bourbon!"
Satine pointed at him, "Old Crow for you guys."

Satine was a little concerned at this point. Normally bar shenanigans made Jessica smile, but there was not even the slightest hint of one. Jessica looked like she was either going to kill someone or possibly herself. Satine poured off the OC for the trucker and pulled the bottle of Four Roses up. Without even the slightest hesitation she broke the seal and filled a highball glass. Jessica took it with a smile and put half of it away, then set the glass down. Satine filled the glass again, then pulled her chair up to sit while Jessica took a few more little sips.

"You tend bar as long as I do, you can tell when someone's in real pain. You wanna talk about it, Jessica?" she said, as she pulled up a bowl of pretzels for snacking.
Jessica swirled her glass, feeling like a talentless seer trying to divine the future reading tea leaves when she didn't even really have a handle on her past.

"Nick fucked my mother."

The patrons nearest to Jessica decided it might be best to get up and find a nice table to sit at.

"Your mother?" Satine asked, eyes wide, "what a... really? Nick?"
"Yes," Jessica muttered, "My boyfriend, the man I just moved in with, the man who makes me smile... fucked my MOTHER."
Satine bit her lip lightly and almost touched Jessica's hand, but she remembered how Jessica always reacted to her hands being touched since she got back from the tender care of the Skinstealers. "Holy shit, Jessica, I'm so sorry. He... I've known him a long time, he really didn't seem the cheating sort."

Jessica took another pull, quietly.

Satine squeezed Jessica's shoulder and then let her hand drop. "When... did it happen? It couldn't have been in the last couple of days, you two have been so busy moving in. I guess... did you find out or did he confess?"

Jessica took another pull, "...when I was thirteen."

Satine's eyes became half-lidded. She took the glass away from Jessica, and lifted it, "Eh, you probably backwashed and ruined this."
Jessica snatched the glass back, "It's disgusting, Satine."

"Jessica, sweetie?" Satine began, "you have been known to just walk away from a guy who was picking you up at my bar to actively go hit on almost any single Asian man who walked in the door. Except Nick, ironically. There's a fairly good chance you've slept with people related to Nick FAR more recently."

Jessica's expression softened a bit, "Fuck. You're right. Who the hell am I to get mad about people having casual sex?"
"Hey," Satine said as she gently edged the bourbon away and replaced it with a bottle of MGD, "If he DID go out and sleep with someone now, there'd be nothing 'casual' about it. You'd have every right to be mad."

"I'm a fucking bitch, "Jessica said, looking miserable, "I shouldn't be mad about this, either."
"You should hurt, and you know why?" Satine asked.
"Because... who's side are you on here? Because it was about twenty years ago?" Jessica said, exasperated.
"I'm on the side that keeps you two happiest. You SHOULD be hurt, because that's sort of gross and it will forever change your relationship with your mother. But

you shouldn't be mad at Nick. If you must be mad, be mad at Fate, be mad at God, be mad at whatever you need to be mad at, but don't take it out on yourself and Nick."
"You're not even... I'm not even sure what we're talking about here." Jessica said, drinking part of her beer.
"You've got a good man there, Jessica. If you're mad… you're mad. Tell him about it. I bet he feels like he betrayed you and he didn't even really do anything wrong."

Jessica drank more from the bottle, several swallows. "Could you make up your mind, Satine? First he didn't do anything wrong, then it's okay for me to be mad, then he didn't do anything wrong again?"
"It is okay to be mad. He also didn't do anything wrong."
"You're not making sense."
"Just go home, Jessica. I'm just a bartender, but you still need to go home. It's where you belong."

Jessica sighed and stood up, "How much do I owe you?"
"Not a damn thing, Jessica. Go home."
Jessica stood up to leave, then turned back, "Hey, can you mix me up a big jug of something, Satine?"
Satine mimed Nick's lopsided grin, "Eggnog and blackberry brandy?"

Jessica's boot heels lightly clicked on the sidewalk as she walked the road towards her home. She had to stop and ponder that thought… it had come to her so casually. Home, this was her home. Whenever she was going back to the Rosebrier she had always thought of that as her apartment. She set down the jug a moment and pulled the hard pack out of her inner jacket pocket. The moon lit up the street just a bit at almost the same moment the snow began again. Jessica's lighter reflected off of the fat flakes a moment, giving them an eerie orange glow.

"Gonna pile up 6 feet by New Year's at this rate," Jessica said to nobody in particular before taking the first drag of her smoke. Jessica shuffled a moment in place, moving the snow aside and leaving two little tracks in the snow. Suddenly she felt a silly impulse and went with it, shuffling forwards, making little train noises, and blowing smoke as she went "toot toot".

After a few moments she laughed and picked the jug back up. Shaking her head, she resumed her journey back home.

Atton ran out to meet Jessica as she came up the walkway. She tilted her head a moment, and then crouched to scratch the cat's head, "No idea why the hell Nick keeps you around."
"Row," Atton responded.
"You would say that."
"Mrow."
"Why yes, my mother is, in fact, a whore."
"Ik ik."

Jessica stood back up and headed for the door, "C'mon boy, go talk to your daddy and see if he's in a good mood." The porch light was on. Jessica fished her key out… and found the door was not even locked. She turned the handle. Inside the house the kitchen light was still on. Atton bounded past her legs and started sniffing around for… wherever Nick had put his food bowl. On the kitchen table was her portion of the dinner, covered in tin foil and set on the warming tray. Set next to the food was their one cup coffee maker; with lights flashing ready to go and a note: "Not sure when you'd get home. Costa Rican coffee ready to go. I know you like ruining perfectly good coffee, so I have sugary hazelnut syrup in the fridge for you. Love, Prettyboy."

Jessica smiled as she put the jug of alcohol into the fridge. She had been expecting a long conversation about this, maybe some more screaming from her, and most of the jug being gone by morning. He'd have probably wanted makeup sex... so overall this was going to work out better. She looked over at Atton, "He's a good man, isn't he? Not 'if' I'd get home... he wondered 'when'."
Atton murred at her and jumped up on the kitchen sink. Jessica tilted her head, "Thirsty, jackass?"

Atton murred again, and Jessica set the water to a little dribble. Jessica took her jacket off and let it fall. Moments after she lost the rest of her clothing. Jessica reached for the food, and then pursed her lips. It occurred to her that she was in love with a man who had very enhanced senses. Looking around a moment, Jessica spotted a container of Wet Ones on the counter. After a few swipes to take care of any smell going barefoot in boots may have created, she grabbed her plate of food and headed up the stairs.

The bedroom door was cracked open, and Jessica could hear the sounds of Deep Space Nine on the television. She rolled her eyes and whispered "dork." As quietly as she could, Jessica pushed the door open wider. The room had a closet covering the entire far wall, a window to her right, and the bed was butted up against the wall and doorframe to her right. Nick was peacefully snoring on the side against that wall; which Jessica decided simply would not do. Balancing her food in one hand, she began to slide her naked body In between Nick and the wall. He stirred a bit.

"Shove over, Prettyboy, I need room to eat!" Jessica said, at a fairly low volume.
Nick grumbled lightly, not really awakening as he picked himself up to the side closest the door. He set the pillows up to support his neck, and cuddled up against Jessica a bit as she ate.

During the first commercial break, she looked down at Nick, already sleeping again. Drooling, his hair a mess, but still so very pretty. She reached over and gently tugged his eyepatch off. Jessica hung it over the bedpost and watched him sleep for a while. He was, as always, so very pretty that Jessica found it difficult to tear her eyes away; but this time there was something new. It occurred to her that she had never seen him without his eyepatch before tonight. His eyelid was sunk in, as she had expected, but there was also an almost visible black in the slit of his closed eye. She blinked, and returned to her food.

Raoul set the remote down after he found Deep Space Nine, and looked over the report of the day's cases. This was far too much of a coincidence; Quest Diagnostics had been hit earlier, the same MO. Skinstealers impersonated security, got in, looted the place, and left everyone alive.

Presumably. Three technicians, two researchers, and a phlebotomist were all unaccounted for. Raoul took his cellphone out, and made a note to himself to take over investigation of that case. He was sure these disappearances and the odd looting were related.

Chapter Ten:
 - "Home for the Holidays", Perry Como

Nick's alarm went off, and he pawed blindly at it. As he slapped it to make it stop ringing, he misjudged the distance and ended up knocking it entirely off of the headboard. "Right, right," he mumbled, "new house." A tired little voice rang out in response, "mmm?" Nick came the rest of the way awake to two surprises, one far more pleasant than the other. Jessica's head was on his chest, her wavy locks splayed out messily across his belly. Nick wasn't sure if he was awake or dreaming when Jessica came in. Her breath was warm and smelled lightly of the drinks she had, as well as the dinner he left for her. Nick reached his hand up to touch her cheek, "I love you, Jess. I know I made you mad last night, and I ….holy shit what the hell?"

Jessica opened her eyes and looked up at him, "What's wrong, Prettyboy?"
Nick pointed up, eye wide. When Jessica looked, her reaction was not one of shock. "How odd," she said.
"'Odd'?" Nick asked, "there's like half a billion black widows up there and all you have to say is that it's 'odd'?"
Jessica rolled her eyes, "Oh quit being a baby. There's only nine or ten up there."
Nick sighed lightly, "'I'm a lot less cool with spiders than you are, Jess."

"Oh, you're squeamish? Well in that case," Jessica looked up at them, "Hey ladies, you're freaking my man. Clear out!"

The spiders began moving up their webs, towards the ceiling. Moments later, they walked almost in a line out of the room.
Jessica sat up and turned to look at Nick, "Did... did that just happen?"
Nick nodded, speechless.
"Hey, you in the back!" Jessica said, "Get back to your web."
The spider complied, walking right back and settling in.
Nick's mouth dropped open like on a television show, "Are... are you shitting me?"
"Start building a web next to yours."
The widow complied.

Jessica marvelled at the sight, "Huh. Well, I guess I found my affinity."
"Affinity?" Nick asked, eyebrow lifted and curiosity obvious in his eye.
"Dryads have... general affinities for nature, and a plant in specific," Jessica responded, "My mother's is Salvia Azurea... it's why her hair is that color. Mine is... uhh... black widow spiders? Which doesn't make sense with the hair thing since mine is green and I DYE it black."
Nick touched Jessica's cheek and drew her back to his chest, "Those mobile things? Yeah. Those aren't plants."
"Holy shit, really? Everything I based my worldview on is a lie, that means!"
Nick poked her cheek, "Good great HEY LADY, you didn't-"

Jessica punched his shoulder, "Just say no to Professor Frink."

"...that's actually a reference to Jerry Lewis."

Jessica leaned over a moment, grabbing the pencil on the end table. She scribbled a blt. She then settled back, with a grave expression, and handed the paper to Nick.

With a raised eyebrow, Nick read what the paper said, "Take 3 Geritol/day so long as symptoms last"
Nick wadded it up and threw the paper at the webs above, "You know you could have just called me old."
Jessica mimed uncertainty as she bit her lip, "I thought I just did, but perhaps you were too senile to catch the joke?"

Nick raised his eyebrow, "I will haul you up by your ankles and spanker you."
Jessica grabbed Nick's wrist and shook it, "Arthritis, arthrriiiitis!"
"Seriously though, Jess, You can command the loyalty of black widows."
"Watch out, housewives of the world," Jessica said pointing dramatically, "Your bane has arrived."
Nick did his best Bart Simpson, "I must only use these powers to annoy!"
"You're just so damned cute sometimes I can't stand it."
"Does this mean you forgive me, Jess?" Nick asked, touching her hand.

Jessica took her hand firmly in his, "There's nothing to forgive. My mother is a pretty woman, and you were both lonely people. Besides, despite being coked to the gills, I remember you being really nice to me. I love you, Prettyboy. You make me feel hope, you know? What's for breakfast?"

Nick scratched the back of his head, "Well, if we're gonna get you to work on time, we'll have to catch something at a drive through."
Jessica got up off the bed and bent at the waist to grab the alarm clock, giving Nick a very clear view.
"You keep THAT up and you won't be on time at all."
Jessica looked over her shoulder and smiled, "I'm still not in the mood for sex but... I like the way you look at me."
"Holy mixed signals, Batman!" Nick said, pointing.
"It's not mixed at all. I don't wanna make love, but I like how easily I can turn you on." Jessica said, slowly straightening up.

Nick got out of bed as well, digging a black pair of slacks, white shirt, red suspenders and a green tie. "Did you take care of Fresh Sushi Roll?"
Jessica laughed as she sidled up next to him, locating her own clothing, "You shoulda seen him. He was LIVID. How DARE she refuse him after all he did for her? The curse of the 'nice guy'. He said he worshipped the very ground she walked on and then this? He began calling her a slut and accusing her of fucking YOU."
"Wow, what a freak," Nick said.

Jessica dug up a pair of black socks, a skin tight pair of jeans, and a Highschool of the Dead T-shirt. With an impish grin, she grabbed out the altered pair of panties with the hole in the back. "He then got all smug and said that since you failed him, he'd have his money back. I advised him to maybe get a lawyer, because not only does the contract he signed with you enable you to keep the money; it enables you to sue him because he tried to get you to engage in criminal activity."

"I know," Nick said, digging out his belt holster, "I… I know what's in my own contract, my alluring arthropod."
Jessica punched his shoulder, "I'm telling you what I told him. Also: DORK!"
"What was that for?" Nick said, rubbing said shoulder.
"That you know a spider is an arthropod."
"You know, you keep beating me up for making movie references and knowing science, what does it make you for GETTING my references?"
Jessica gave Nick some very good puppy eyes, "Why, it makes me quirky and cute!"
"Come on, my winsome widow, let's get moving."

Chapter Eleven:
- "Baby It's Cold Outside", Margaret Whiting and Johnny Mercer

----

Jessica sat in the now all but empty duty room, listening to the morning assignments. Well, not so much listening as staring blankly at the duty sergeant until her name was called, at which point she'd breathe a sigh of relief that the boredom ended, get the keys to her patrol, and get on with her day. The last of the officers left, and she winced inwardly. If she missed what her assignment was AGAIN, she would be the one cleaning the locker room after her shift. She briefly considered faking it and hoping her partner for the day would gather her, but if that plan failed as well she'd be open to a world of ridicule. She sucked it up and raised her hand, "I'm sorry, I didn't sleep well last night. I missed my duty assignment."

"You didn't miss it, Dombrowski, " the woman began, "I didn't give you one. You're to report to Deputy Chief Flynn at 0900"
"Oh, for fuck's sake," Jessica said as she got up, "What did I do wrong now?"
"Black lipstick and nail polish, for one."

Jessica rolled her eyes as she headed out. When she got inside not only was the chief there, but a court reporter and a DA. Mark Rotansky, by his name badge. Jessica's eyes widened a bit as she began organizing her resume in

her head. Flynn gestured at the seat in front of his desk, 'Why don't you have a seat, Officer Dombrowski?"
Jessica nodded and sat down.

"I've been looking carefully over your service record in the last few years, Dombrowski." Flynn said, walking around his desk holding a file. Jessica stayed silent as he continued, "It's been less than exemplary. Most days you didn't even bother wearing your complete uniform, and what you DID wear was rarely pressed or even WASHED."

Jessica simply nodded in response; there was no use denying it.

"We have reports of you accepting bribes, manufacturing evidence, and on several occasions faking search warrants."

That Jessica had to take issue with, "Taking free food is hardly accepting bribes."

Flynn shook his head, "It is, especially considering that you increased your presence at those places, providing some rudimentary form of protection above and beyond businesses that did not play ball with you."

"And I did not manufacture evidence. That I categorically deny."

"And this business of false warrants?"

Jessica looked down at the bottom of his desk, "Eleven times. Each did lead to solid arrests and convictions."

"Convictions which," the DA added, "Any competent lawyer could have gotten overturned due to a tainted chain of evidence."

Jessica looked back up, "Yes, but I've... I've been trying to do better."

Flynn tapped the desk in front of him, "I'm going to need you to turn in your badge and duty weapon, Dombrowski." Jessica's lip started to raise into a sneer, but she calmed herself. It was an inescapable fact that she had, in fact, been a terrible cop for a very long time. Jessica unholstered her sidearm, then placed it on the desk, and took off her badge. She looked at it a moment, thinking it over illogically as she removed the holster from her shoulder rigging. Realizing there was nothing to be done with the badge, it was set down as well. She looked back and forth between the men in the office, for almost a minute, before she spoke.

"I have not... kept to my oath very well. I was trying to turn it around but sometimes past sins are a bit too much. Honestly I would have fired me a year ago. Thanks for being as patient as you have been, huh?" She offered a pained smile to the men and then turned on her heel, getting ready to turn her uniform in after changing back to her streets.

She got one step before she heard a slap of leather on the desk behind her.
"Dombrowski!" Flynn called.
Jessica turned back around... on his desk was her old detective badge, still in the custom black leather case with the spider motif.
"You will have to purchase your own personal weapon. Armory will provide you with ammunition as always."
"I..." Jessica said, stepping forwards, "I don't understand?"
"It's pretty simple, Detective Dombrowski," Deputy Chief Flynn said as he rose out of his seat, "I busted your ass

down because I knew after what happened you'd need time to recover. I'm real glad that you're back up to snuff."

Jessica took the star up and looked it over. "I'm not really as good as I was, Chief."

"I wouldn't really say that, Dombrowski. Every officer has something that happens. That thing will make or break them as a cop. Yours was worse than most others; but you still came out the other side. Welcome back to law enforcement for real, Dombrowski. You were really good, and I think you'll do better now. The fire can either burn you up or burn away the crap, leaving the badge pure underneath. Go over to the proc room for a four hour refresher."

Jessica closed her eyes a moment as she held the badge in her hand, "I'll do my best for the people, Chief."

Flynn reached out and clapped her on the shoulder, "Officer Friendly was the final judgement. That was your last stand, so to speak. I was either gonna bring you back into the fold or shitcan you. You did great by those kids, you'll do fine for me."
Jessica began whistling the theme to the Andy Griffith show as she walked out.
"And quit being such a smart ass, Dombrowski!"
Jessica snickered and quit whistling.

Nick stared across the desk. The light was really an LED number, but it might as well have been a sodium lamp near the end of it's life, because he felt the heat. The man at the other side met his gaze with a smug expression.

Nick's tongue went dry. He was not sure if he was out of options, or if he was hunkering down in the path of an oncoming train like a lost dog who somehow found it's way to...

"Rayner's Lane!" Nick called out.

The man across the desk shook his head, "You make it so easy, mate. Mornington Crescent."

"Hey!" Nick cried, pointing at his best friend, "I don't think that's a legal move."

Brian whoofed out his breath, "Fine, fine... you're right it's not yet New Year's. Turnpike Lane."

"Hounslow West."

"...really? Mornington Crescent!"

"DAMN!" Nick said, and then his ears flicked a bit towards the door, "Outta the chair, Brian. I hear a customer coming up."

"Yes, Massah!" Brian said as he stood, "I's so sorry I was puttin' on airs like I'm a real human!"

"Seriously, Brian. It's a female, wearing well oiled leather high heels. There's probably money coming here."

Brian moved to the side chair, "Or it's Jessica."

"Jessica," Nick began, "doesn't know the first damn thing about proper care of footwear."

"Ahh yes, your legendary foot fetish, Noriko said her sister-"

Nick silenced Brian with a hand motion, "She stopped halfway up the steps."

Brian got up, "Honestly, Nick, I've got to run anyway. The wife and I've found ourselves some playmates, and we're scheduled to meet them for a bite in a half hour anyway.

How about I head on down and make sure things are alright?"
Nick shook his head, "Go out through the garage. It's not a joke that customers can get really skittish."
Brian shrugged as he stood up, "All the same to me. Give us a ring later on, we'll see about dinner?"
Nick nodded and kept his ears focused towards the door. Brian left as quietly as possible… which was actually very quiet. Were it not for his greatly enhanced hearing, Brian's exit would have been entirely silent. Nick turned to look at the door… whatever Brian just did, Nick would have to try to learn. Really. Nick was basically trained as a movie-style ninja and a 50-something SAS man just casually out-ninja'ed him.

The steps resumed, at a slower pace. When the woman stopped outside the door, Nick heard her take her breath in and let it out with something of a sigh. He quickly lowered the overhead light and angled his desk lamp so his face was just barely out of the light, illuminating his chin and leaving the rest of his face a bit indistinct. It was the little details like this which Nick knew got him a lot of work which otherwise may have gone elsewhere. You try to size up the customer as fast as possible, and put on the right dog and pony show. Some wanted a clean cut professional detective, some wanted a gruff, imposing sort; but the best thing to do was to open with the tropes that everyone is familiar with. If need be, he could slip into one of the other types so smoothly folks would think that first impression was their own imagination. But when the lady goes with the "building up your courage sigh"? They always wanted the mysterious man who evoked the hardboiled movies of yesteryear. In a pure matter of fact, most folks have never actually SEEN any of them, but it was impossible to grow up in this country without absorbing the stereotypes.

The door finally opened, and in strode his ex-girlfriend Lori. Her hair was curled just a bit, she was wearing a santa hat and a red blazer with a green undershirt. The pleated skirt was red as well, and drew the eye down along her body smoothly. The effect made her somewhat lanky profile look more curved and leggy. The whole ensemble was topped off by matching green thighhighs and matching red stripper heels. She had painted her toenails, something Nick had never seen during their time dating. The "Christmas Elf" getup was absurd on it's surface, but Lori wore it with confidence. Nick couldn't help it; she was fire right now; could be warm and inviting, or he could get burned. Whatever was going to happen from here Nick knew he'd have to take a breather outside when it was over. He steeled himself and pushed it down.

"Welcome to Dog and Spider Private Investigations, Ma'am." he stood up to offer her a handshake like she was any other customer. "As you can probably guess, I'm the Dog. The so-named Spider is off at her day job." Lori's face darkened at the oblique mention of Jessica. For that Nick was actually grateful; he REALLY needed a reminder of how terrible Lori could actually be right about now.

Lori resumed her sunny smile and leaned in close, "Well, I understand that you provide consulting services on lots of the shadier topics, isn't that right my little lost puppy?" Nick was able to catch a view down her blouse and cursed himself for looking. Lori was not wearing a bra, and she was the opposite end of the spectrum from Jessica in that regard. Nick liked breasts rather large or barely there at all. He attributed that to his twisted up sexuality caused by the past, and just... accepted it. Most of the time Lori wore push up bras or padded ones in public, but not today. Today she looked like a young teenager up top and he could tell she spotted the effect on him. In fact, today she seemed different. Nick could swear they were a bit larger. Elven magic? Was there such a thing?

"Yes, Lori," Nick said, "Not sure what you're expecting me to work on for a police dispatcher, but you can at least state your case and I might be able to point you in the right direction."
Lori blinked at him sweetly, undoing one more of her buttons. Nick didn't see the blink, because his eye was locked at her chest.
"Well, ever since I lost my puppy I decided to look at some of the porn he searched for on my computer..." She was taking another button down, "and it got me pretty hot and bothered. I remember how good you fucked me that night."

Nick closed his eye and pulled on his training to control his breathing. He knew he had to send Lori away, but hadn't the strength yet to DO it. When he opened his eye again, Lori's blouse was fully unbuttoned, and hanging loose. He became aware that Lori had lotioned her skin with that vanilla scent he loved so much. The effect of all this was fierce. His instincts told him to mount her now. For the time being, his common sense and willpower were still holding off the partially metaphorical beast inside. Barely.

Lori ran her hand up along her taut belly, and up from there. She brushed further to her breast, just barely grazing the brown areolae with her fingertip. Knowing her old trick had worked, she then kneeled on the chair across his desk, facing away. She put her hands on the edge of the backrest, and then arched her back, giving him a very clear view of the G-string underneath her skirt. Green, he noted distractedly. He licked his lips as she spoke again, "So. I was hoping you would consult with me on some of these…. shadier practices."

"I'm with Jess now, Lori." Nick said, voice quavering just a bit, "I can't honestly say I'm not flattered, and more than a little tempted, but Jessica is mine and I am hers."

"Rumor around the station is that she's not taking care of your needs… Prettyboy."

Nick's eye narrowed to a slit. Nick had been gathering himself to push Lori out, but he suddenly found it much easier after that. "Get the fuck out, Lori."

Lori looked over her shoulder, tilting her body to let him see her chest hang down just the tiny bit it would, "Why do you want to send me away? Isn't this what you want?"

Nick's expression did not change in the slightest, and all of the desire had flooded clean out of him, "Get the fuck out, now. You are trespassing; and now you have thirty seconds to get off the premises before I perform a citizen's arrest."

Lori wiggled her bottom, "Oooh. Handcuff me, I'm a bad girl, the only way to deal with…" Lori stopped talking when she heard Nick draw his .45 from the hip holster.

He held it up lightly, finger off the trigger and barrel not yet pointed at her, "20 seconds."
Lori turned around and sat in the chair, expression twisted back to the way it always was whenever she was denied something, "You're pointing a gun at me? You're fucking crazy!"
"15 seconds."
"Fine. I gave you a chance, don't say I didn't give you a chance you fucking faggot. What kind of faggot wants to stick it in someone's ass?"
"10 seconds."
"You want me to get a strapon and fuck you in the ass, faggot? I bet you'd like it, just like you loved it when you were a little boy."

Nick was up out of his seat and he grabbed a handful of Lori's hair, yanking her head back. He holstered the pistol again, and snapped the strap closed. As Nick was settling the pistol back in it's place, Lori yelped in pain after the short delay. She hooked her fingers, raking her nails along his cheek. Nick clamped down his grip and pulled harder, forcing her off the chair. He continued to pull her to the door. Nick worked the latch and led her down the stairs.
"Let go of me, you faggot!" Lori screamed.
Nick did not respond, he simply pulled and made her descend the stairs.

When they got all the way down, Nick noted Cynthia was leaning on the wall, wrench in hand. Her breath came out in puffs that swirled away in the light breeze that eddied in the alcove. "You're fucking with my favorite tenant there, knife-ear."

"Favorite tenant? He remind you of a girl? You a dyke? You like this pretty boy's ass, is that it? A gas powered strapon how he pays his rent?"
Cynthia cricked her neck audibly, and Nick let Lori go, heading right back upstairs.

Cynthia closed the distance to Lori in an instant, flooring the smaller woman with a precision right hook. Lori screamed after the hit, holding her hand over her now broken nose. Blood poured between her fingers. Cynthia then raised her other fist and Lori flinched. The blow did not come. Cynthia instead seized Lori's jacket and the hem of her skirt. Lifting her easily, the tomboy walked Lori right to the end of her property line. Once there, she threw Lori directly into the piled up grey snow the city plow had left there.

She walked back into her garage and smacked the button to close the external door. Nick smirked down at her, "Been playing Dragon Age, I see."
Cynthia chuckled, "Guilty. That should totally be the go to slur for elves like that."

Jessica looked down at the lapel of her denim jacket. There it was, hooked onto the breast pocket for all the world to see. Detective Dombrowski, Chicago PD. The refresher course was complete. She had the proper paperwork shoved into the back pocket of her jeans, this was really a thing. She had expected her partner would be Raoul once again, and she was not disappointed. Her first assignment was listed as a standard plainclothes drug bust; due to be started after her three hour split-shift lunch break. There were three things on her agenda; and she doubted any of them would take up a whole shitload of time. First, most important by far, was to spring the news on Nick. She could easily combine that with item number two: lunch. Nick and Jessica were both people who had very simple tastes. Their idea of a fancy lunch was, at the upper end, a trip to Culver's, Five Guys… or when they felt REALLY extravagant, some place with the Vienna Beef logo in neon on the front window.

It was impossible to avoid. As she got closer to her man's place of business, she broke out into a broad smile. Though things were a little bit easier these days, it wasn't so very long ago that Nick was making her face hurt. She'd spent such a long time with nothing even closely resembling a reason to smile. Sure, there were times the men she picked up had surprised her with awesome sex, but even that pleasure was joyless. Nick? Even when he was embarrassing her in public she couldn't help but love him, and, even more, she found she genuinely liked herself as well.

Jessica was pulled out of her reverie by a light sobbing. Looking towards the source of the sound was one of the last things she had expected to see. If a chinese dragon had burst through the fabric of reality and offered to take her on a flight, it still would have surprised her less than what she actually saw. Nick's ex, Lori, was halfway inside of the dirty snow at the side of the road. She was crying, holding her bloody nose, and to top it all off Lori was in a ridiculous Christmas getup. Her top was also open, exposing her laughable excuse for boobs to anyone who cared to look. Jessica considered for a moment continuing to walk along, but this wasn't a good situation for any woman to be in anywhere, much less downtown in Chicago.

"Are you alright, Lori?" she asked.

Lori spat blood at Jessica, who stepped back to avoid it hitting her jacket. It wasn't like her reliable jean jacket was a virgin to that sort of thing, but the cleanup was always a pain in the ass.

Jessica's lip curled up a bit in a snarl, but she shoved it down. Though she wanted to add more to the little bitch's wounds, that wouldn't solve anything. Jessica did, again, briefly consider walking on her merry way. She discarded the notion with a sigh, and muttered, "Fuckin' Prettyboy making me all goodie goodie."

Jessica instead took out her phone and called dispatch, "Hi, this is Officer Dombrowski, I'm right outside my boyfriend's work. Can you send an ambulance here?"

The dispatcher on duty right now was a mousey redhaired elf woman whose name was also Jessica. She responded, "Are you wounded, Officer Dombrowski? Do you require backup?"

"Nah, the 10-9 is your co-worker Lori. I'm off duty right now, and just happened by. I think she pissed someone off and got her ass kicked."

"Roger that, Officer Dombrowski. Sending an ambulance to your location."

Lori showed Jessica her middle finger. Jessica decided to be the bigger woman… figuratively as well as literally, and walk away.

Jessica tucked some of her hair behind her ear and reached for the doorknob. Two things she spotted gave her pause. The first was that the lettering on the smokey glass on Nick's door had been changed. It now said "Dog and Spider Private Investigations. N. Sakamoto and J. Dombrowski, Proprietors." She shook her head in disbelief; Nick really HAD gone with that name for the business. The second thing to catch her eye was her black nail polish. She examined it for just a moment as if seeing it for the first time. Here she was, Jessica Marion Dombrowski wearing makeup, acting like a girl. A very ODD girl, since the makeup was black, but a girl nonetheless. It occurred to her that she wore black nail polish when she was a hardass teenager as well, but for a different reason. That was because she was throwing two middle fingers at society and wanted to make damn sure society could SEE those fingers. This? This was because she goddamned well KNEW she looked hot in it. Maybe not to society at large but who cares? So long as she and her man liked the effect, what does anything else matter?

Jessica doubled back and went down the stairs. Walking up to a fancy Lexus parked outside awaiting repair, she looked herself over in the passenger side mirror. Her hair was wild and a tiny bit tangled due to the wind, but she still looked DAMN good. Dipping her hand into the map pocket of her jacket, she dug around in the receipts and other garbage in there, past the pack of Marlboros, and took out her lipstick. Jessica had just randomly grabbed it off the shelf, e.l.f. "Black Out" #82647. Nick seemed to like it. When Jessica lost the tube, it genuinely surprised her that she remembered it well enough to buy it again. With a little pull, a few twists and some swipes, Jessica had her lips refreshed to a totally unnatural black. She kissed at the mirror and was almost embarrassed. Almost. The feeling passed as fast as it came. This girly shit felt alright. It wasn't like this was a one sided thing. Jessica wasn't an idiot; there was no other reason than his love for her for the sudden appearance of more Chinese and Japanese apparel in Nick's wardrobe. It was a dance, there was a certain amount of bullshit to it. The right kind of bullshit. Jessica hoped that twenty years down the road they'd both still be bullshitting to impress one another.

She screwed the lipstick back down and dumped it into the map pocket again. Time to tell Nick the kickass news... and hopefully confirm that what she had seen earlier was Lori being a bitch and not just a coincidence of a rapist dropping Lori off here or something. Lori could go die in a water for all Jessica cared, but nobody deserves that. Back up the stairs she went. When she opened the door, it was pretty obvious that Nick was not in the best of moods. He was actually FROWNING as he was making coffee. Jessica quirked her eyebrow and closed the door behind her. "Something wrong, Prettyboy?"

Nick's expression softened when he keyed in on Jessica, "Eh. Go start the playback twenty minutes ago and sit down. Coffee?"
Jessica popped over and sat in his seat. Her badge was on her jacket pocket, Nick would notice that eventually, "When do I ever not want coffee?"
Nick snorted, "Every time you put hazelnut and other crap in there."
Jessica whistled at him, "C'mon, boy. Bring mamma her coffee."
Nick mixed in the syrup and cream, then set the mug down. "That abomination is not coffee."

Jessica scratched him behind the upper left ear, "Who's a good boy?"

Nick brought the spare chair around and sat next to her, "Seriously, watch the video."
Jessica looked over at the black widow on the web attached to Nick's desk lamp with a smile, before she rewound the security to where Nick suggested she start from. She forwarded a little until Lori stepped in, and her expression changed into one of bemusement, "Wow, that's weak." Her expression became slowly more annoyed until she was downright angry as she watched the events that came after.
"What a fucking bitch. I'm only sorry you let Cynthia kick her ass rather than waiting for me"
"She's lucky I didn't beat the fuck out of her myself. I was just going to throw her out, but Cynthia gave me the better option of letting a woman's touch handle things."

Jessica crossed her arms and then uncrossed them, standing up, "Let's go get a hot dog, Prettyboy. I have news."
Nick stood up, "Fuck, why not? I honestly think I'm just gonna close up for the day and wait around for you to be off work for real." Nick headed for the door, pulling the chain on the neon sign that advertised to the world whether they can come in. After he went out, he held the door for Jessica, "ladies first."
Jessica poked his chest as she walked by, "You just wanna look at my ass."
Nick grinned lopsidedly, "It seems right now that all I've ever done in my life is making my way here to do naughty things to your ass."

Jessica punched him in the shoulder, "Don't mangle perfectly wonderful romantic quotes!"
Nick rubbed his shoulder, "Your ass should be kissed, and often, by someone who knows how."

Jessica gave him two middle fingers, keeping them trained on him as she passed him. She backed down the stairs, keeping the fingers firmly locked on him. She made it down the stairs and out to the sidewalk before lowering them.
"Honestly, Jess," he said as he locked the door behind him, "I was sure you'd go ass over teakettle trying that."
Jessica put her hands on her hips, "Hoping, you mean. You just wanted to kiss it and make it better."

Nick's lopsided grin changed a bit as he tilted his head. He leapt from the top of the stair to land in front of Jessica, and peered intently at her badge. Jessica instinctively took two steps back. "Holy shit, Prettyboy, how did you not just break your legs?"
Nick's eye was wide and he touched her shoulder, "Holy shit who cares, you got promoted, didn't you?"

"You're goddamned right I did," she began, "turns out I've been doing my job way too well lately, and now they're expecting some ACTUAL fucking WORK out of me. Comes with a big raise, though."
Nick pumped his fist, "Woo hoo, big raise! Now we won't be homeless because I suck at charging poor people my actual full rate!"
Jessica smiled warmly as she walked next to him, urging him towards her favorite hot dog stand. It would be a mile walk or so, but the food was worth it.

"You know what, Prettyboy?"
"Beautiful spider butt?"

"... I hate you. I sorta figured I would BE the one pulling down most of the dough here, and I'm okay with it. I wouldn't change a single fucking thing about who you are and what you do. My mother, in between all the psychotic mafia shit and sleeping with random assholes, told me that I'm gonna meet a lot of guys. One day I'm gonna meet one who I would hardly want to change at all, and that guy I should date seriously. I'm dating you seriously."
"Akiko's dad said something similar to me. He said 'don't kiss my ass about this. Date my daughter for a while, and if you can love her like she is; if you can see forever than keep dating. If it falls down, at least you took an honest shot. If you move on, Niko, my boy, use that same standard with everyone else you date.' and it was good advice."

Jessica rolled her eyes, "I am SO SURE that you had decided Lori was someone you could love like she was."
"I didn't say I actually took his advice, Jess. I get lonely like anyone else does."
"You coulda done a HELL of a lot better than her, Prettyboy."
Nick grinned lopsidedly at Jessica, "I did."
Jessica stopped to elbow him, "Flirt."
"Well yeah, I'd really like to get you in bed sometime. Have you SEEN your ass?"
Jessica grinned over her shoulder, "Actually, I saw it really often as a Skinstealer walked away from me wearing my DNA. I DO have a great ass."

Nick opened his mouth to reply, then tilted his head suddenly to follow a noise. Jessica noticed Nick's expression change to a more alert one. She grinned, "What is it? What have you got, boy?"
"Actually, I'm pretty sure I've got a drug deal," Nick said as he pointed at the condo two blocks from his office.

Jessica followed his gaze. The condo looked rather upscale; not the sort of place 'drug deals' occurred. "You mean some rich kid is buying pot?"
Nick shook his head, "Someone's trying to buy Sudafed from someone else, and the whole thing is about to go south. They're arguing about... prices... the one guy paid up front.. And.."
"Holy shit, Prettyboy," Jessica said, "You can hear all of THAT from this distance?"
Nick nodded, "Though to be fair, it helps that the wind is calm, and there's not a lot of traffic. And their window is open despite the weather."
"How many are there? …. Hey, I don't even have a gun."
Nick nodded, though she didn't ask that sort of question, "I have a few in the office. I'll stay here. Like… 5, maybe 6?"

Jessica turned on her heel and headed back to the office. In case a lookout had eyes on them, she made sure her body language was that of a woman who simply forgot something before her date with the very pretty man she was beside. Jessica half-jogged up the stairs, paying very little mind to the ambulance that was tending to Nick's bitch ex-girlfriend. She stopped at the door and read the lettering on it again. Dog and Spider Private Investigations. What an utterly idiotic name. Even as she thought that, she smiled. The way Nick named things was god awful, but they were sure to be unique. Once inside she looked around the office.

'If I were a spare gun, where would Nick hide me?' she thought. This was easy... in the lower drawer of the desk. She popped down into the seat, and pulled said drawer open. The drawer was filled with comic books, knife replicas, and tons of Turbografx HuCards. Digging around past some Garbage Pail Kids cards, Jessica drew up a box that said "Raiders of the Lost Ark, Attn: prop department. For replication."

Her curiosity overtook her, and she opened it. Inside was a simple revolver, and several half and full moon clips. It was a large frame model. Even as she was examining the revolver she took it into her hand to feel the grip and heft. This was not a "woman's gun", a cute little purse model; this was a sturdy weapon. Jessica herself being a statuesque 5 foot 10 had always refused "female" weapons for larger ones, and this felt just right. The lettering seemed to indicate that she held a Colt M1917, and it took .45ACP. She marvelled a moment. A revolver that used auto rounds? That was a rare beast indeed.

It took her all of ten more seconds before she drew out the included holster and mated it with her shoulder rig. It was a little beefy, but it would only be a problem if someone knew what they were looking for. Furthermore, her man EXCLUSIVELY used the round in question, this would be a good complimentary carry piece. She opened his top drawer and was rewarded with exactly what she expected. Hidden behind all the assorted pens and pencils, papers, discarded gum wrappers were several magazines for Nick's pistol, fully loaded. She thumbed the rounds out of the mags and loaded them into her clips. Jessica worked the action of the swing out cylinder several times until she was comfortable, and then held the weapon up. Old style iron sights. She preferred glo options but this would do the job tonight. Jessica darted back down the stairs and out to Nick, who was closer to the house.

"What have you got, Prettyboy?"
Nick didn't even look back at her, "5, at least. One of them is... making... a baby is crying upstairs."
Jessica looked the house over, "You know what we have to do now, right?"
Nick answered in a robotic voice, "Serve the public trust, protect the innocent, uphold the law."
Jessica punched his shoulder, "Dork!"
Nick grinned lopsidedly and stacked up by the front door.

Jessica cracked the door and pushed her badge inside, "Chicago PD! Lay down your arms and come out with your hands above your heads!"
Nick made a whirring sound and then yelled, robotically, "Come quietly or there will be... trouble!"
Jessica drew her badge back and clipped it over her pocket again, "Are you incapable of taking anything seriously? Is it an extra chromosome, Prettyboy? Should I take you to the vet and have you fixed just to be sure I don't bring your defect into the next generation?"

A shot rang out, and Jessica's eyes widened right before impact. Her entire body tensed up... she lurched to her right. She closed her eyes against the sudden explosion of pain. Jessica's hand came up to touch the back of her head. Her hand was quickly coated in blood.

Consciousness failing her, she went with an action half of trained reflex, half of despair. She sought an entry wound on her forehead. Jessica Dombrowski ran her bloodied hand across her forehead, streaking the blood along with her touch. She was trying to poke her finger into wherever she had been shot. Her hand fell as if the unseen tether that held it up had been cut.

So did she. Her eyes were open again, and blood pooled around her head. She twitched a few times, then all light faded from her world.

Chapter Twelve:
- "Down With the Sickness", Disturbed
(Which would be a FAR better song without the obnoxious whining about his mother bit, So many better ways to express that.)

Nick's lopsided grin fell slack when Jessica slumped. Her hair was splayed a bit, having caught the air and come down just an instant after Jessica herself did. As if it were any innocent moment where her hair caught Nick's eye just so, he was lost in how... unearthly it was. A shade that does not occur on women of that race... long and... and being matted with her life's blood, which would surely clot and then rust. He knew it would, because he had been seeing what blood does since he was a small boy.

It wasn't just blood he had seen before. It was this moment. When the warm joys of his life abruptly hit sunset and it did not merely seem as if the sun would never rise again. That would be terrible enough to bear. It was worse than that. As the darkness eclipsed the light of what little innocence remained in his heart it seemed as if there never was joy in the first place. It was a fever dream, an ersatz relief that served only to twist the knife when reality came flooding back.

Through despair so thick it was treacle over all his senses, Nick dimly heard the shooter laughing, "Lookit this nigger! Boo hoo they shot my girl!"

Nick stood still, remembering how he was shocked to inaction the same way last time. His wife's head clamped down into the sink by a crowbar wedged over her neck but under the solid steel fixtures. His eyes kept drifting between the clawed up wood of the cabinets where she had scratched her nails bloody trying to gain some purchase for escape. Akiko had made some headway; the fixtures were bent and loose, but it was not enough. Her end had clearly been painful and violent.

Drowning was not like the movies made one believe. The water was pink with her blood. Even to the end her body must have been forcing her to cough, in a desperate attempt to drive the water out and bring life-giving oxygen in. Ultimately all this had resulted in was her coughing hard enough to... Nick did not want to know where the blood was coming from, really. There was the scent of another man... in her. Nick could not process all of this.

He heard his son crying, wails of pain more drowned out by cries for his mother. Nick remembered his final questions... "Daddy, why won't Mommy talk to me? Why won't you talk to me?" Nick turned to see that his son had been bisected, and very recently. His intestines were blowing out behind him like an obscene mushroom growing in stop-motion as he crawled forwards. Kazuo's last words would weigh on Nick for so long as he lived, "Why won't... was I a bad boy? Is that why you won't talk to me?" By the time Nick had shaken it off well enough to try to comfort his boy; it was too late. The light was long gone from his eyes.

His son's tail was still wagging. Some part of his spinal column was misfiring, and his tail was thrashing out with the same apparent joy it would on any other day Nick came home after work. Nick stared at the tail on the lower half of his son until the muscles ran out of... whatever it was muscles needed that could not be provided since the heart was no longer beating. Nick remembered sitting there the whole day before his sorrow came to a head. He took his loss and converted it to hatred. He would make those who took them pay. And he did.

In some way, he had even begun to tentatively live again, to even seek out love anew.

The love he found was laying with hair being made more and more ropey by the blood seeping from the mortal wound. Like his son's tail kept wagging, so did Jessica's heart still keep beating. Kazuo had been dead, Jessica is just as dead. Her heart did not know it yet.

As for Nick's heart? It knew Jessica was dead. It knew with not a hint of uncertainty that it was time for all of this to end. Nick had died the same day Akiko and Kazuo had... the world just saw fit to tell him one more lie before he stopped strutting like a headless chicken and lay down to die decently. This time he would lay down.

But not yet. There stood laughing at him those who had stolen Jessica from this world. It wasn't just his own loss that drove him. If it were only he that were hurt he could lay down now. But the world itself was made lesser for Jessica's passing. She was just turning her life around.

She was a good cop again, one of the best. There were too few genuine blue knights in this world.

Nick's pain and rage swirled around in a white hot cocktail, giving him an angry vitality even as it intoxicated him. He let forth a long howl of loss, but also one that promised death to those who had brought this pain into the world. His lips curled up into a snarl. Nick could feel the darkness overtaking him, and he did nothing to push it down. Why should he? It was over now. His world's last joke had been told, and the man whose gun delivered that punchline was laughing about it.

Nick would silence that laughter before he would lay down and let the end result of his true worth finally catch up to him. He turned on the shooter, and this time it was not just the covered eye socket; both of his eyes were leaking blackness. Nick's good eye no longer saw differently than the missing one. He did not see the shape of these men anymore, only the content of their souls. He could anticipate what the gunman would do next, and easily dodged the bullet with a slight change in position. The bullet passed between locks of his hair as Nick dashed in, spittle in flecks as he anticipated the meal. The other thing Nick could see from his missing eye was a sort of... vibrance to people. He could, if he tried, roughly estimate how long a person had left to live based on the level of that vibrance if given enough time.

The vibrance of this man rapidly shifted to blackness as Nick grabbed the thug by his cornrows and tore the scum's throat out with his bare teeth. The other man involved with the drug dealer was a burly orc. Nick advanced and the vibrance dimmed. The orc threw a desperate punch that was answered by Nick with a single twist, breaking the powerful creature's forearm like a child snapping a wishbone. The vibrance faded entirely as Nick's unholy power gave him easy purchase to disembowel the orc with a swipe of ethereal claws born of Nick's pain. As the orc slumped, Nick pulled the pancreas out and feasted messily upon the sweetbread. He turned his attention to the other two in the room, ignoring the one upstairs. Her time would come.

Two more shots; dimming vibrance. One sailed by the right side of his neck and the other went entirely wild. The man dropped the gun and raised his arms to ward the oncoming terror off. Nick grabbed hold of the man by his chin and cheeks, almost caressing him. The man whimpered and begged for mercy. Nick moved his thumbs to the man's eye sockets, and drove in deeper and deeper until the man's useless slapping at Nick's arms ceased.

The final person in the room was cowering in the corner, crying for help from the God he believed in. Nick licked his lips, anticipating the taste of this man, sweetened by the fear. His rage overtook any desire to drag this out, and Nick grabbed the elf by his hair. His victim reached up, clawing desperately at Nick's forearm. Nick carried the elf to a support column and smashed his face into it.

On the very first slam the elf's cries turned to low moans. The second made his moans stop entirely as blood poured thick from his nose. Nick dimly heard a female voice. On the third smash, the elf's skull changed shape just a bit.

The voice called to him again, a little bit of warmth in this bleakness. The fourth opened a crack in the elf's skull. Nick brought his other hand across to scoop some of the brain matter towards his mouth.

He felt pair of hands wrap themselves around his wrist, trying to keep Nick from this morsel. He turned to look at the soul that interrupted this, nearly the penultimate act of his life. The soul, though it had a pure core, was filled with fear and despair, and no small amount of self-hatred. There also was a small veneer of hope around it all that was thrown into violent flux at this moment. The soul was concerned for... his soul; the despair was more for him than itself and the loss she... she would suffer if he did not come back.

"Prettyboy, no! Stop!" Jessica implored as Nick held the now dead elf in one hand, and a large portion of the elf's brain in the other. Though she had the mother of all headaches and blood in her right eye that stung horribly; her own pain was last in her mind. "I'm here! I'm alive! Come back... you... come back you idiot!" Jessica released her grip and slapped Nick across the face.

"Hey!" he said, "that hurt! I was already on my way down." "Doesn't look that way to me, Prettyboy! You... you look terrifying, your eyes are... weeping blackness." Jessica lowered herself a bit so she could embrace him, putting her head on his chest. Nick responded to her embrace gently, and with a bit of marvel. Every time this had happened before, it took a lot longer than this to cool down. Jessica took him right out. He supposed that could be because the cause of his anger and despair had ceased.

Then he placed his hands on her shoulders and pushed her back to arm's length. "I... never wanted you to see... that part of me. I didn't even want to see that part of me ever again. I thought I had it under control."
"Oh, no. Prettyboy," Jessica said as she stepped right back in, "we are not playing this game."
Nick scratched the back of his head a moment, "What... what game?"
"You know what game. You're going to get all boo-hoo lookit me, I must protect you from the beast I am."
"I... Jessica, you could get..."
"Look, Prettyboy," Jessica said, poking him in the chest, "Is this the part where I tell you that you're beautiful, and you are all 'Beautiful, but this is the skin of a killer!?"
"Uh... what?"

Jessica poked him again, "You can't be serious. You didn't get a Twilight reference?"
Nick's expression changed to one of confusion and disgust, "Why the hell would I get THAT reference?"
"Because it's romantic and pop culture?"
"Next you're going to tell me Fifty Shades of Grey is good?"
Jessica crossed her arms. "Fifty Shades of Grey is good!"

Nick looked around them, "Uh, Jess, sweetie? What are we gonna do about all of this? And how is it you're alive?"

In all of the heat of their banter, Jessica had actually forgotten about what had just happened. It looked like the aftermath of a horror movie scene. The sorts of scenes where the movie has the cop or parents or whatever run outside and vomit. "He just grazed me, knocked me out, Prettyboy. Believe me it's not because I'm a Dryad. You pop me in the head and I'm a goner. You need to sneak the hell out of here. I'll call this in as a wendigo attack." Nick nodded, already drawing away, "I'll see you back at home, Jess."

"Yeah, I love you, Prettyboy. Don't get caught. I'll be home later, I still have a few hours at the station."

Merrick crumpled up the piece of paper and threw it onto the ground. One of his little implings skittered over to pick it up. In actuality he had willed this to happen, as he willed everything else a Skinstealer did to happen, but he had been doing it so long that the creatures almost had will of their own. He gave their day to day events no conscious thought at all. Though he could directly take control of individuals; in fact this was how he manifested as a man at all, he did not often even give orders. They might as well have been the beating of his heart or the action of his liver.

He did not like the news they brought to him now, however. Jessica had moved in with that… low class buffoon. He could tolerate it when they were merely dating, but this was an affront. Jessica was his promised Queen, and Queens do not lower themselves to make their affairs with peasants in any way official. He would have to remind her who, exactly, she really loved.

Chapter Thirteen:
- "Grandma Got Run Over by a Reindeer", Elmo 'n' Patsy

"So this is what we have, Jessica," Raoul Delacroix said as he pushed the case file over to his partner, "and how can you drink that frou frou crap?"

Jessica sipped her coffee... a Costa Rican blend with 8 shots of hazelnut cream and a metric fuckton of Stevia. "You suck dicks. Probably sometimes right after they've been up your ass, and you complain about what I am drinking?"
"Yeah, no. It sounds like you know from personal experience what that tastes like."
"Of course not, Sensei," Jessica said with a smirk, "You told me how horrible it would be. Thus proving YOU know what it tastes like."
"I eat pussy sometimes as well," Raoul said defensively. Jessica tilted her head, surprised at that. She blinked, looking at him. "Wait, what the hell are we even arguing about?"
"Honestly, I'm not sure. This conversation went pear shaped, as you like to say. Just look over the file, partner."
"Partner," Jessica said, "Has a good ring to it. I'm glad we're back there, Raoul"
"Yeah, so am I, now get back to work!"

Jessica lit up a cigarette as she read over the notes, "So what we have, is a series of Skinstealer snatches, people and some merchandise."

Raoul nodded, "I mean that much is obvious. They are clearly intentional and connected. What I can't understand is… to what end?"

Jessica tapped ashes, "A few dwarves, some humans, a family of orcs. It doesn't seem like they are after any specific race, that's for sure." She continued to read the files over and over.

"You okay?" Raoul asked, looking at Jessica.

"Yeah, what do you mean?"

"Well, you had a runin with a Wendigo. Those things are pretty fuckin' terrifying. Why didn't it eat you while you were down."

Jessica closed the door and took a drag from her smoke, "Because it wasn't a wendigo. It was Nick. One of them shot me, grazed my head, put me down. He thought I was dead."

Raoul rested his chin on his palms, "Gosh, you just told me your boyfriend committed multiple homicides in an incredibly unlikely fashion."

Jessica put her feet up on the table and continued looking at the file, "And?"

"And they were meth dealers… so… I'm just curious what the hell happened."

"You know, we are AWFULLY shitty cops," Jessica said as she stubbed her cigarette out half smoked, "you're supposed to be turning me in or calling Internal Affairs or something."

Raoul shrugged, "Meth dealers. Probably saved a few lives. You think anyone else is looking too hard into it? Even if you did tap out and call IA on yourself all that happened is someone iced a bunch of wannabe cop killers."

"Shockingly, I feel conflicted about this."

Raoul touched her hand, "Just means you're a decent cop."

"Am I really? I covered up a multiple homicide."

"Seriously, pumpkin," Raoul said, "cop killers. Meth dealers. If you really want, I'll talk to IA about it."

Jessica nodded, "I think you should."

"They're not gonna give a shit."

"Still."

"I sorta could sense what he was, you know, but I figured if he didn't want to... bring it up that's his prerogative," Raoul said with a shrug.

"What the hell is he?" Jessica asked, sitting back up and putting her feet on the floor.

"He's a Terror." Raoul said placidly.

"What the hell does THAT mean?"

Raoul started some coffee on his Keurig machine, "I'd say 'spirits of vengeance' but that doesn't really sum it up. It's just a... potential. They're not required to DO it."

"You're not making a whole shit ton of sense."

"Now this is just stuff older demons told me. Ones that were born WAY before 1946, but hid themselves from mankind."

"Why hide?"
Raoul rolled his eyes, "Pitchforks and torches, sister. When it comes to a war between the things that go bump in the night and humans, the humans ALWAYS win. Hell, I was in hiding also for a very long time. But now with all the freaky races we can just... come out if we want."
"Kinda like society has advanced and you were able to come out in the other sense of the word, huh?"

Raoul sat back down with a smile, "You know it, sister. Anyway, you know how mankind has always wrote stuff about faceless creatures that corner people and slaughter them, unexplained things? Those were caused by stories of Terrors. Slasher flicks are the modern version of that."

Jessica sparked another cigarette to life, "So you're telling me that my sweet-hearted boyfriend is like Jason Voorhees?"
Raoul nodded, "I assure you, it's completely optional. He's not compelled to do it. He's not some terrible beast with a dark side... he's just a man. He can turn it on and off at will, actually. Could come in handy sometime, you know?"

"I'VE GOT IT!" Jessica suddenly cried out loud enough to make Raoul spill coffee on his shirt.
"Holy crap, reel it in a notch, huh? It's not that exciting," Raoul said, exasperatedly. He whipped the handkerchief out of his pocket and dabbed uselessly at the coffee.
"I mean the case. I think I've got... I mean you've... We know it's Skinstealers but, I have the basics of what I think his plan is."
"You have my attention."

Jessica laid out the pictures of all the victims, "Look what he's taking. Athletes and scientists, one magic user's child, some homeless... and... the psychopath. Y'see, though a replacement doesn't have the same personality, the replacements have the memories and skills."
Raoul nodded, "I can personally vouch for that. Your doppleganger absolutely did have your intuitive abilities and reasoning abilities."
"She was also much nicer and more respectful, the goodie two shoes." Jessica mimed spitting on the floor.
Raoul looked wistful, "True, I do miss her sometimes." He took a sip of his coffee and nonchalantly slid his chair to the side to avoid the stapler thrown at him.
"Men."
"I know, right? We're so annoying, but so fun in bed."

"The point is, Raoul," Jessica said, leaning back into her seat, "Merrick is collecting people with specific skillsets and a variety of genetic materials."
"I buy the science sorts, but 'genetic materials'?"
"Look, it's not too insane to think that if Merrick's things can copy people, what stops him from copying enough scientists for them to put their heads together and assemble a sort of perfect super soldier made up of..."

"Yeah, no," Raoul said, shaking his head, "that's just ridiculous. We already have hundreds of thousands scientists working on these sorts of things, and we're nowhere close."
Jessica scratched her cheek, "Okay, fine, I'm going a bit far, but he is collecting a wide variety and he DOES seem

to be grabbing technological widgets as well. Whatever the hell he's up to, we would do well to stop it."

Raoul finally gave up on his shirt. "It's not as easy as that. We have to find out a better pattern. We can't put men on every superior athlete and nerd in the city of Chicago."
"No, but we can put out bulletins, refresh police and security types on what to look out for, and establish a special unit at the CPIC."
"That's actually a good idea. I'll get some of the guys down in steno to man the phones."
"'Steno'? What the hell is this, 1954?"
"You know what I mean. I'll get some of the phone drones and tech guys on gathering the records we need."

The phone on Raoul's desk rang, "Violent Crimes, this is Delacroix." Raoul listened for a moment. "Fuck, no, I'm not putting her on, you ass. I'm not gonna tell her that, and I also seriously doubt it." More speech on the other side, as Jessica raised her eyebrow, "See now all you've really achieved is me having details put on work and home. Idiot."

Raoul hung up the phone and threw on his sportcoat, "We need to move, now. Mr. Merrick told me that your boyfriend is probably already in one of his 'secret places'."

Jessica closed her eyes a moment, and... was surprised at how panicky she wasn't. "You're right. I, too, doubt he's gone... but still." Jessica checked her weapon and pocketed a few full clips she kept in her desk, "He took the day off. Our home... it's like forty five minutes away with zero traffic from the station."

"We'll take a patrol, Jessica. I'm sure he'll be fine."

Nick took a healthy swig of what was now his new favorite Christmas drink. He had to hand it to Satine. In many ways, she truly understood him. Eggnog and blackberry brandy; it was a perfect combination. The crackling of the yule log provided a wonderful accompaniment to the familiar sights and sounds of "The Christmas Toy." One of Nick's personal favorites, and it was why he always looked askance at Toy Story. Thinly-veiled ripoff. He chuckled at himself as it occurred to him that damn near every Christmas special was "one of his personal favorites." The only thing that could make this moment better was if Jessica were here.

Well, that and it would be nice if the crackling came from an actual fireplace, and not one of those "Yule Log" DVDs. Drink in hand, Nick sat down to enjoy himself. His left ear flickered, and he tilted his head a little to listen, but otherwise remained the picture of unsuspecting ignorance. He heard a light organic rasping, and raised his glass up. His ears had not betrayed him; a Skinstealer quill bounced off the glass. He was briefly thankful to... well... himself that his reflexes were fast enough to protect him. While Cynthia theorized that adrenaline in sufficient quantities would prevent the effects of those quills, Nick didn't have any on hand. As he went down behind his couch he wondered where, exactly, does one BUY syringes of adrenaline? With no room to really use his blade in this small house and his pistol being upstairs, Nick would have to handle this the old fashioned way.

Nick heard the very telling clinks and pulls of the front door lock being worked… which was stupid since it wasn't locked. He briefly considered making a run upstairs for the pistol, but there wasn't time left for that; the door was already opening. Nick was not stupid enough to show himself to see who it was. One way or another, he'd find out soon enough.

"Here, Nicky, here boy!" came a smug voice, along with some whistles. The voice Nick wasn't sure of, but the scent wafting in Nick immediately recognized. This was Merrick. Jessica's tormentor. Nick kept his anger to a very minimal place. Doing something stupid now would be pointless; Jessica had told him that no matter how many times she killed or arrested Merrick, she could not stop him for good. Imprisoning him resulted in a blank Skinstealer in minutes, and slaughtering the body he was "in" would only slow him down for.. what had she said? A few days? Nick would have to dispose of this… creature on a more psychological level.

Nick came up from behind the couch holding the remote control, "I was looking for this!" After a light flaring of his nostrils, he set the remote on the coffee table and finally seemed to notice Merrick. "Oh, hey! It's the queen bee! I thought I was going to have to go out and kill some of your pathetic shapeshifters. I gotta say I am genuinely surprised to see you here in person."

Merrick raised his eyebrow, "It would be rude if I were not to make a personal appearance. I am... strongly inviting you to join me for some recreation."

Nick bobbed his head agreeably, "Yeah, Jessica did tell me you were the unfailingly polite sort of guy who believes in respect, manners, things like that. It's your sense of equality that really caught her attention." Nick gave him two thumbs up, "Children, sleeping women, 98 pound science weaklings, you'll cower and hide from all of them. What did I do to merit this special treatment?"

Merrick sneered,"Are you trying to insult me, cur?"
Nick looked at Merrick and then gave him a patient smile, "This is my fault. I'm sorry, I forget sometimes. Simple concepts, short sentences. Your guess at what all those complicated words meant was correct! If you show me your progress board I'll put a blue star on it."

Merrick narrowed his eyes and started unbuttoning his tailored suit coat, "Well, if you want to be uncouth about-" before he could unbutton the second, Nick had already closed the distance and hit Merrick with a spinning hook kick. Merrick staggered to his left, vision darkening. He shook that off and stood facing Nick, fists raised in a boxer's stance. "I can see this won't be a gentleman's-"

Nick was already on the move again, going low and left. Merrick sighed inwardly, this was going to be easy. He prepared the answering uppercut. Merrick shifted his weight to lean into the blow. Merrick was certain that Nick was going for the crass and useless UFC "ground and pound". The timing was spot on; and he would follow up with a basic combination to hurt the dogboy. He was briefly surprised when Nick's chin was not there to receive the blow.

His surprise turned to confusion. Nick grabbed both of Merrick's ankles, and with what had to be supernatural strength, threw Merrick up head over heels. Merrick shifted his weight by tucking his legs in, intending to go through with the flip and land on his feet. Before Merrick could complete the tuck, Nick's hands had snaked in underneath and gotten a grip on his waist. Nick grunted with effort and pulled the smaller man through a powerbomb, knocking all of Merrick's breath out and leaving him flat on his back. Nick hopped back to avoid any counterattack, but none came. Nick took the lull in the fight to check for any other 'stealers that might interfere. None were in sight. Merrick was struggling to his feet.

Nick closed in and took his stance. He poked Merrick on the nose, "You realize you never stood any chance against me now, right? You're not even a fraction of the man I am in any way. Jessica will never, ever want you. Worse, you will never be able to beat me. Send your lackeys, dress some of them up like Jessica to try to take me off guard… it won't work because I can smell the difference. I can hear those disgusting paralyzers a mile away. I can hear them shooting their little projectile. Come at me with everything you have and I will laugh you off like I am right now."

Merrick snapped off a left jab, which Nick stopped easily with a right straight to Merrick's face. Merrick's head snapped back, and when it came forward, his nose was bloodied. Nick continued to lay in the punches, slapping aside any of Merrick's weak attempts at attacks. Merrick stepped back, out the door, and fell off the front stoop to the concrete walkway. The impact was brutal, and Merrick went out for a few seconds.

When he came to, Nick had pulled him back to his feet and continued with the punishing blows. The sound of a police siren could be heard approaching rapidly, yet Merrick could not actually place that sound at the moment. Merrick was barely piecing thoughts together when Nick yanked his wrist to keep him off balance, and Irish Whipped him into the tree that was less than 10 inches away. When Merrick's head rebounded backwards, Nick caught him by his hair, "I'll be damned, that DOES work in real life!" Nick brought his knee up into the back of Merrick's neck as he pushed the head down by the hair. There was a light tearing sound at the impact. When Merrick hit the concrete again, he found he could not move his limbs.

Jessica and Raoul, sidearms drawn, quickly approached the scene. Nick stepped into Jessica and dipped her for a kiss like a movie hero. When he straightened up, he had Jessica's weapon in his hand. "Since the invention of the kiss there have been five kisses that were rated the most passionate, the most pure. This one left them all behind." Nick pulled the trigger and Merrick's left eye vanished. Blood poured out from the back of his head, even as it was changing back into a garden-variety Skinstealer. "The End." Nick said.

Jessica punched him on the shoulder three times, "I don't get that reference, but you are SUCH a dork!"
Raoul coughed, "Really? You don't? Well Nicky, my boy, you know what you're going to have to show her tonight."
Nick pointed at Raoul, "As you wish!"

Nick began to return Jessica's weapon when he finally happened to look at it. "Hey! This is a rare collectible! This is the M1917 that the prop department studied for Raiders of the Lost Ark."

Jessica took it from him and returned it to her shoulder holster, "It's mine now, dork. And don't think I didn't see that black version of his jacket you have in the closet."

"And I had the whip custom made also."

"Do you even know how to crack a whip?"

Nick shook his head, "Never could get the hang of it."

Jessica reached across and took his hat off his head and put it on hers, "Well, that means this is mine also."

"Absolutely adorable, Jess but it's WAY too big for you." Nick kissed her and took it back, lining up his upper ears through the holes.

"Alright," Raoul said, "You two are like 15 different sorts of cute, but we have to file an incident report on this…"

Chapter Fourteen:
- "Aztec Challenge(Run of Despair)", Andrea Baroni

Jessica felt a sensation that activated her most primal needs for defense. She was lashing out before she was even fully awake, once she located her target. Nick caught her kick by the ankle, "What the hell, Jessica?"

Jessica narrowed her eyes at him, "Don't tickle my feet! I told you that the first night we met!"
"Uhm... no... no you did not."
"Well, I should have!"
Nick rolled his eye, "Well you didn't. Would you have preferred I wake you up by jerking off all over them?"
"Fuckin'..." Jessica began, "Yes! Who the hell tickles a full grown woman's feet? You're such a damn weirdo."
Nick raised his index finger, "You just told me you'd prefer I jizz all over your feet than to tickle them, and I am the weird one?"

"If you did, at least one of us would get something positive out of the experience." Jessica saw that Nick had brought a large serving tray, "However, since you brought me... french toast and bacon, I think I can find it in my heart to forgive you. Did you seriously cook bacon in the nude?"
Nick grinned lopsidedly at her, "Anything for my one true love. Even ruining a perfectly good Ethiopian-Vietnamese blend with all this hazelnut and cream shit."

Jessica propped her pillows up as Nick set himself up next to her, the tray on his lap, "Actually I'm only half-joking. You can jerk off on them or grab some lotion and rub around. Whatever the hell it is you foot fetish types do. I dunno, I haven't looked up the relevant porn."
Nick handed Jessica her coffee, "I thought you didn't wanna do anything sexual."

Jessica took a deep drink of the liquid, already feeling herself awaken just from the scent alone, "I said I don't... trust my own sexuality right now. I don't feel good feeling turned on. But... hell, Prettyboy, I love you to pieces. You have no problem covering up mirrors at night and fast forwarding past parts in movies where things happen to people's eyes, so what the fuck if you wanna lick my boots or whatever? I'm crazy, you're crazy, and I like that I can... I can dump all my crazy right out in front of you and you always respond with acceptance. You can dump your crazy on me, too."

Nick grinned lopsidedly, "Well, apparently you're okay with me dumping SOMETHING on you, anyway."
Jessica set her coffee down and grabbed for some French toast, "If you can get it up, old man!"
Nick shook his fork and managed to make it look like a walking cane, "Get off my lawn!"

"You really should surrender your hat, whip, and jacket to me, you know that, Prettyboy?"
Nick raised his eyebrow, "Oh? Why is that?"
"Because look at the ancient relic I dug up. Clearly it's ME who is the archaeologist."

Nick stroked his chin, "Ancient, huh? Could be. After all, it seems to me like just yesterday I was FUCKING YOUR MOTHER!"
Jessica leaned over and smacked his exposed scrotum just hard enough to make Nick spit his food out and clutch his ailing boys, "Agh! I guess I kinda had that one coming!" he half shouted, voice an octave higher than usual.
Jessica affixed him with a stern stare, "You're goddamned right you did, you motherfucker."

They burst out laughing at the same time. Nick turned on the TV, and they watched PBS in silence for a few minutes.

"So," Jessica said, "Raoul told me what you are."
Nick quirked his eyebrow, "What do you mean by that?"
"Raoul knows what you are."
Nick sat his fork down and made eye contact, "Really? Because I wasn't kidding around Jess, even I don't know what I am."
Jessica nodded to him, "Yeah, Raoul said you're something called a 'Terror'".
Nick pointed at his tail, which was swaying idly, reflecting the level of comfort and happiness he presently felt, "Much to my dismay I think I might be too cute to be a 'Terror'"

Jessica snagged up his tail with her hand, "How do you even lay on your back or sit in chairs with this thing?
Nick turned his palms up, "How would I not? You get used to it, I guess? How the hell do you jump properly without one to help you balance?"

"Alright, fine, stupid question, I get it. And you're not 'cute', you are 'pretty'. There's a difference."
Nick's tail swished out of her hand, "Quit changing the subject or I'll beat you with this thing. After like 7 hours of it, you'll have SUCH a red mark!"

Jessica had more coffee as she thought of how to proceed, "Well, Raoul said that Terrors take many forms, and it's really even OPTIONAL for them to scourge mankind. He says that you guys are embedded in the human psyche. He says that you guys are where slasher flicks come from."

Nick's upper ears both turned to Jessica unconsciously, "Slasher flicks?"
"Yeah," Jessica said, reaching up to tweak one of said ears, "Like Friday the 13th and Halloween."
Nick turned his entire head towards her now, and his mouth was agape a bit, "That actually makes a whole shit ton of sense, Jess."

Jessica had to smile at his expression right now. Nick was a man who had, at best, only a nodding acquaintance with subtlety when outside of combat. The only way it could be easier to read his feelings at this moment was if a thought bubble appeared above his head with the word "Eureka!" inside. "Why do you say that, Prettyboy?"

Nick's food was, for the moment, totally forgotten, "Because of what I can DO, Jess. When I really let that go... things happen."
Jessica mimed one of Nick's own double thumbsup motions, "Thank you, that totally clears this confusion up."

Nick nodded, "I'm dead serious. When I am cutting loose, on the hunt? Car doors won't unlock, or engines won't start. I'm never in a hurry when I do this... people who should be able to outrun me trip and fall over the tiniest obstacles. I've seen stone-cold emotionless assassins fail to reload a weapon they've used under pressure hundreds of times before. Security guards snap keys off in door locks."

Jessica could only nod in response, "Those do sound like the sorts of things that happen in horror movies."
"Yeah," Nick said as he took off his eye patch, "Look, see? See how my missing eye always does what you saw earlier?"

After only a glance, Jessica had to look away, "....please don't show me that. That... it feels wrong on some really base level. I am gonna need time to get used to that."
"The reason I wear the eye patch has nothing to do with that, it's for my own benefit. In place of my missing eye, I have, always, the same vision that I have when I'm... well, a full Terror."

Jessica gathered her will up and looked back to him, holding eye contact. The longer she looked, the less frightening it was. There was danger, abomination even, in that blackness... but not for her. The darkness there seemed to only want to surround her and protect her. When he began to speak, she put her finger on his lips, and shushed him. The longer she looked, the less it seemed to her that this darkness was evil. Unnatural, absolutely, but she saw no evil in it.

"You see their lives, what kind of people they are. You see past their masks, you see what they really are. You see them as they see themselves in the mirror."

Nick moved away from her finger, "How could you possibly know that, Jess?"

Jessica moved in closer to him, her lips brushing his as she spoke, "How can I order spiders around? How can you fire weapons without going deaf? Why dwell on what's possible, when we can just accept what is?" When Nick opened his mouth to respond, she silenced him. This time not with her finger, but her lips. She was not sure if this would work, yet she tried to kiss Nick the same way she did when he was nearly dead.

Nothing preternatural happened, but it took nothing special to get Jessica's meaning. She sought to still whatever anxiety was in his heart over his nature, and by the relaxation of his shoulders she knew she had done it. A thought came to her, and she said it without hesitation, "Where you are weak, I will be strong, Prettyboy. You do the same for me, and together we'll make things go right. You're not evil, Prettyboy, even if you don't see it. Even at your very worst, I am willing to bet you bypass those who have good intentions."

Moving away from her a moment, he awkwardly dove back in for a light peck before he spoke again, "Yes. It's actually weird how it happens. In every case I could look at someone and know... something about them. I would walk away from them. Never once did any of them try to attack me, or even warn anyone else I was on my way."

"See?" Jessica said as she poked him on the nose, "That right there is the difference between you and Jason Voorhees. In the movies he always goes for the worst scumfuck kids first, which proves he can tell their true natures... but he doesn't spare the innocent. You do."

Nick shook it off like any dog would his wet fur, "This is getting way too heavy, Jess. Wanna see something cool I can do even when I'm not in fullon spooky mode?"
"Fuck yeah, lay it on me."
Nick dug in the bedside table a moment and came up with a pen and paper. He pointed at the window, "Keep your eyes peeled on that."

As Jessica looked, she became aware that something odd was happening. She felt that even if she weren't looking, she'd know to have looked. There came slight scratching sounds and the window seemed to have been cut somehow. The scratches continued to be made while the first scratches began to bleed. A sort of half clotted blood, like of a creature nearly taken entirely by gangrene. Jessica could smell the blood from here. The scratches formed words that welled up enough of the viscous fluid to drip, but not enough to obscure the words. The message soon became clear, "I love you, Jessica Dombrowski!"

Jessica actually laughed, "That IS cool! And I bet NOBODY but me can even see that!"
Nick grinned lopsidedly, "Yup! It works just like as if I were Freddy Krueger messing with a tired kid."

Atton came padding into the room, meowing at the two of them with something resembling urgency..
"Did you remember to feed the cat, Prettyboy?"
Nick snagged up the last of his breakfast, "Eh. Can't remember. I know I did his litter box, though."
"That's a good boy!" Jessica said, smirking, "You said you'd take care of a cat if we got one and you have been. Mamma's proud!"

Nick rolled his eye and headed downstairs. Atton bounded past him and did not head for his food bowl, he was at the front door. "Gah, Atton, " Nick said, "You JUST went out not like... 6 hours ago." Atton began to meow again, looking up at him. Nick gave the kitty a slow blink, and then nodded. "Alright, you furry little asshole, I'll let you out." As soon as Nick cracked the door open, Atton stepped away and another cat glided in as if he owned the place.

Nick shook his head and rolled his eye, as he crouched down to pet the new cat. "Well, I'll be damned, it's Bonecrusher!" The large cream, buff and white tabby-like Maine Coon/Ragamuffin/whatever mix looked up at Nick and let out a noise much akin to that of a bath toy. Nick scratched the kitty behind the ears, "What the heck are you doing here, Boney? Your home's on the other side of the tracks." Bonecrusher wound around Nick's legs twice, before following Atton off into the kitchen. Nick simply closed the door and headed back upstairs.

When he got up, Jessica was laying on her belly, legs bent up at the knees so her feet were in the air. She was wearing nothing save for strappy, open toed black heels.

Nick turned his hands upwards, "Holy mixed fucking signals, Batman!"
Jessica looked back at him, "What, Prettyboy? Is something wrong?"
"Nothing. Not a single damn thing. I am totally not being blue balled by my girlfriend right now."
Jessica smirked at him indulgently, "What, is something the matter, Prettyboy?" She straightened one leg just enough so that the spike of the heel was running along Nick's inner thigh.

Nick flopped down on the bed next to her, "She's only a tease if what she does gets you hot."
"You see me as you wanna see me - in the simplest terms, the most convenient definitions."
Nick leaned over and kissed her all the way down the small of her back, and gave a playful lick over her left cheek, "God damn I love you. You're so easy to talk to, you get almost all my shitty jokes."
Jessica shifted her weight, getting ready to turn towards him. Nick stopped her with a hand on her shoulder, "I didn't say stop giving me this awesome show!"

Jessica did her best to match Nick's lopsided grin, "Why do you have a cat instead of a dog, I've been meaning to ask?"
"Are you serious? Because I can actually understand dogs."
Jessica almost moved again, but stopped herself, "Wouldn't that make them even more desirable as pets?"
"Fuck no! Dogs are goddamned idiots. It would be like if you kept a monkey around that could talk."

Jessica laughed, "Come on, dogs can't be all that stupid."

Nick shook his head, "You think not? Hey, remember those dogs that were barking half the night last night until one of them was taken inside?"
Jessica blew some of her hair away from her eyes, "Yeah, I was actually gonna ask you to tell them to shut the fuck up."

"Here is what they were saying:" Nick cleared his throat and sat up, "Hey, can you hear me? Yeah, I can hear you, can you hear me? Cool! I know, right? Can you still hear me? Yeah, I can still hear you, can you hear me? I sure can, remember when we found that frisbee? I do, can you still hear me? Yeah, that was cool, I remember that frisbee. Can you still hear me? I mean I can hear you but can you hear me? I can, it's cool that you can still hear me. You can, right?"
By the end of it Jessica was laughing, "Okay, okay. I get your point." She gave him a fond kiss, then made eye contact, "You're so pretty. You really, really are."

With nothing else pressing on them, the lovers whiled away the morning just... enjoying one another. After a while, Jessica got on her laptop in the bed and Nick pulled out his New Nintendo 3DS XL. They did their own things, but did them together. The cats came to join them. After a while Nick nuked them some White Castles and they had lunch laid out.

Jessica's voice sounded a bit unsure, "So, what the fuck are we gonna do about Merrick?"

"The problem as I see it is that you can't kill him or arrest him, right?"

"And that he's up to something that doesn't bode well for the city in general."

Nick tilted his head, "Okay let's back this one up a bit. What, exactly, is Merrick up to?"

Jessica pursed her lips, "Well, we aren't supposed to let civilians in on things; but you're actually really good at what you do."

Nick grinned lopsidedly, "And I can go places, do things that you just plain aren't allowed to."

Jessica looked distant a moment, "I'm getting... less and less comfortable with breaking the law to get things done."

Nick nodded as he put catsup onto his burgers, "I can still bend it a lot more than you can. I don't have to prove things in a court of law. That's up to you. I can still give you information that can lead to a warrant."

Jessica slitted her eyes, "Okay, Captain Exposition, I know how my own job relates to yours.

Nick twirled some of her hair around his finger. "Just trying to give you verbiage to use when you talk your superiors into contracting me on the job."

"I actually will bring you up. We do contract work out to private operators."

"I know," Nick said with his lopsided grin showing up again, "I've worked with John Law a few times. Cranking up the Sam Spade a few degrees during the interview actually makes them more likely to hire you."

Jessica lifted her leg and flexed it for him, "Getaway sticks!"

"Is that and 'check his elbows' the only industry slang you know?"
"I really honestly haven't watched a lot of those movies. They bore me. I'm a cop, it doesn't happen like that."
Nick crossed his arms, "And I'm a Private Investigator. I say on rare occasions things DO happen like that. The case where I met you, for example."
Jessica pursed her lips, "You yourself said it was a straight walk from point A to point Z or whatever."
"Yeah. I didn't have to think about it very much. There wasn't a lot of 'mystery' to it at all, and if you pay attention to the movies, those cases are usually just as much a straight walk."
Jessica threw her hands up, exasperated, "I... fuckin... I just TOLD you I haven't watched a lot of them."

Nick cringed comically, "Please! Don't hit me!"
Jessica punched him on the shoulder, "You are such a douchebag sometimes."
"And that is domestic violence!"
"Fortunately there's a policewoman nearby. Shall I take your statement?" She balled up her fists in a mock threatening manner, "I got my typewriter ready to punch in your information."
"Ladies and gentlemen, a fine example of our elite and dedicated police force," Nick said, pointing at her and laughing.

Jessica lowered her fists, joining Nick in his laughter. Afterwards, she reached out and took his hand, giving it a squeeze, "I love you, Prettyboy."
"So, what can you tell me about Merrick's activities?"

"Not a single thing until I get you authorized onto the job, to be perfectly frank."
"Well, I guess that's a dead end, so back to the original topic?"
Jessica finally began eating her own sliders, "Yeah, I mean, what can we do to deal with him."

Nick's tail began to wag, "Well, firstly, I'm pretty sure I actually threw a scare into him. He sent a quill thrower after me first, and I barely reacted in time to block the quill with my glass of eggnog. However, that probably looked incredibly badass, to an outside observer. Merrick came in, we exchanged some words, and then I beat the living hell out of him. He never landed a single punch, and that seemed to surprise him. I laid in some monologue about how nothing he can do will ever hurt me, how I am more of a man for you than he will ever be. I think a lot of that hit home."

"Okay," Jessica said as she propped pillows behind her back, "you scared him, but all that means is he'll be sneakier about this. How does this help us?"
Nick's tail did not falter even an instant, "It means we have him off balance. Now what we do is we KEEP him off balance. If we can do that, he won't have time to think properly."

"I agree with your theory, Prettyboy, but... how do you plan to actually DO it? He's untouchable."
Nick raised his finger, "No, my luscious Latrodectus, he is not. He owns property, doesn't he? Has cars, safe houses. He goes out and does social things like any of

the three million assorted asshole plugs of the City of Big Shoulders."

"That much is true, "Jessica said as she closed her eyes, "Toward the end of my time with him there, he'd tell me about his day doing whatever before he'd rape me. The sick part is I started to care about his day to day activities. It was barely even rape anymore by the very end." Jessica now drew her legs up to her chest and hugged them, "He didn't even have to actually keep me tied up anymore. I was… eager to serve him, in every way. I've only ever told Dr. Thorne this before, but when the thing first all fell down and I was set free? I actually went looking for Merrick. Took a coupla days for me to realize exactly how fucked up that was. A few dates with Jerry… he expected me to be someone I wasn't… made me realize that I wasn't the woman that… either of them wanted. That's… that's when I started fucking anything that moved."

Nick was quiet a bit, and then drew Jessica to him. She put her head on his chest, and slowly her legs uncurled from the near fetal position. "I never got to say goodbye to my son. He thought he did something wrong. Akiko died… really violently. They wedged her head down in the dishwater with a crowbar. She tried to get away but couldn't. What little progress she had made was… impeded by. I… someone's semen was leaking out of her when I got there. They must have cut my son in half just as I opened the front door, because he was crying for his mother, trying to crawl forwards even as his guts were decompressing behind him. He asked me why I didn't talk to him, why Mommy didn't. He asked me if he had been a bad boy. I didn't say anything to him. He died in every sort of pain imaginable. I lost myself as well. The plain fact is, even though I had been going to therapy for a long time, I don't think I ever really got myself back until you came into my life."

Atton nudged his head under Nick's hand, demanding to be pet, and at the same time Bonecrusher flopped against Jessica's shoulder, his purring almost like a massage to her. The cats remained close to them, nuzzling them, light playing until Nick finally spoke.

"So!" he said, a little too loudly, "We fuck with him. If he goes to the movies? One of us is right behind him to kick his chair partway through the movie, and just smile at him when he looks. He goes to have a fancy dinner? One of us pours vinegar all over it right before it's served. Throw fish into his office's air vents. He's having some hot cocoa and seeing the sights? You're there to punch his lights out and walk away. Burn his apartment or house or whatever down. Break in wherever he is and slit his fucking throat. Pull him into a dark alley and beat him to death. Do a few horrible things in a row, then some childish pranks… keep him off balance."

"You're suggesting multiple felonies, you realize?"
"Against who? Merrick is a non-person. What's he going to do, testify against us in court? According to what the news has told us, he's a forty time over cop killer, never mind the civvies that he took out and the multitude of other laws he broke trying to take over Chicago. No jury in the world would even INDICT us. So long as we don't cause anything more than negligible collateral damage I can't

see any problems with any of this. Morally, ethically, legally, there's really nothing wrong with trying to goad him into making a mistake. When you're dealing with something THAT far outside of the normal confines of crime fighting, what else can you do?"
"Was that a Red Dwarf reference tortured into that?" Jessica asked
"Indeed it was."
Jessica punched his shoulder, "Dork!"
Nick blew at her eyes, making her blink several times and pull back, "No changing the subject, Jess."

Jessica ran her hand over Nick's bare chest fondly, "You'd think I'd have something to say about this being a slippery slope and whatnot, but you know what? I'm game. It'll distract that asshole from whatever he's going to do until we can find out what that IS and put a stop to him."

Chapter Fifteen:
- "Merry Fucking Christmas", South Park

Lori stepped off the bus and pocketed her mace. There were people coughing and crying on the bus behind her, but a girl's gotta do what a girl's gotta do. Lori had been minding her own business listening to her favorite podcast when she felt it. The back of someone's hand had brushed her left ass cheek. Groped on the bus, again. Pocketing her phone, she spun to the nearest man in the correct direction; "Don't touch me, pig!"

When the man began to respond, Lori had rolled her eyes. These abusive fucks always denied their actions. "Excuse me?" he asked. She pulled the canister out of her pocket and aimed it at the man. He raised his hands defensively.

Lori leaned in and smiled, "Looks like YOU chose the wrong girl, huh, pig?" The human male opened his mouth and got the mace sprayed directly in it. "Don't you try to mansplain to me!" Lori said as she stepped forward. She kept the sprayer pressed down, "That was sexual assault and you're lucky I don't call the cops." He fell to the ground, his eyes were marred by lightning strike patterns of red and he was coughing violently. Lori smiled in satisfaction as he lost his lunch.

A taller man, an orc, looked at her in disgust, "Are you crazy? I touched you, not him, and it was a mistake!" It had been near Lori's stop anyway, and she could tell this situation was going to get uglier. These men obviously worked as a pair, but she had not given them a chance to try whatever their scam was. She sprayed the orc; and just in case it was true orcs were resistant to irritants she sprayed the area in general. The confusion had made it easy for her to escape.

The bus driver, also an orc, pulled the door shut behind her and sped off towards the nearest parking lot so the driver could call for emergency assistance. Lori's heels clicked on the sidewalk as she headed for her condo.

Lori exhaled as her adrenaline started to drift off. Many women would have cowered in fear or cried for help, but Lori's mamma hadn't raised her to be that way. Every time something like this happened, she loved it. It really brought her to life to set these people in their place. It never even remotely occurred to her that she might be over-reacting. She had read a book called Ender's Game and admired the way Ender Wiggin handled problems. Not only would he win a fight, he would win it in such a way that others would be afraid to ever attack him again. And this was what had gotten her adrenaline flowing; the moment of conquest that came to her so often when the world tried to victimize her.

Furthermore, Lori's mamma had raised her to not lose any other sort of fight either. She considered the event with the lesbian mechanic to be a temporary setback at best. As it always had before the world would move on and eventually Lori would have her opening to set things right. Just like she would eventually get Jessica back for taking from Lori what had been hers. It wasn't that she wanted to marry Nick or anything, though he was good looking and, admittedly, fun in bed. Not the best she'd ever had, but he was the best that was available right now. Lori liked to have fun, and Nick was fun.

Before Jessica, she had been able to bring him close, push him away, and he'd be back for more as was his nature; just a stupid little puppy eager to please his mistress. When he asked for her ass, she had decided this lesson needed to really hurt, and told him to get out of her life. She had just about been ready to take him back when that disgusting slut showed up. Lori heard from eavesdroppers that Jessica wasn't putting out for whatever insane reason skanks decide to stop putting out... probably wanted to hide a nasty STD she had gotten from whatever other man she was fucking. Lori was sure it was time to make her move. She wasn't ACTUALLY going to let Nick do THAT, but the promise alone should have drawn him in.

Clearly she had moved too soon or not planned properly, but eventually she would get back what belonged to her. She unlocked her door, got inside and locked it again. Just in case those men had friends. Lori threw the keys into the basket she kept on the wall next to the door without needing to look. The condo was dark and cold inside as she liked it. Why waste money heating and lighting a place she wasn't inside? Even when she was in, she only used a single bulb. As Dickens once wrote, darkness was cheap and therefore suited to her. Lori flopped down onto her recliner and took her shoes off. When she reached for the remote she found there was something furry on it, which she brushed off without a thought. She hit the power button and exhaled happily. Walking Dead would be on shortly.

A spider of some kind was on the tv screen. Lori snagged one of the throw pillows from her chair and threw it at the screen to knock the spider off. Satisfied at her aim, she settled back down. Another spider was dangling down from a web in front of the TV... and then another. Five. Shivering lightly at the thought of dealing with those spiders, she reached over and turned on her desk lamp. There were spiders on the inside of the lampshade as well! Black widows. She then realized with utter revulsion what she had brushed off the remote earlier. There were a few more black widows on her table as well. This was a full blown infestation. The superintendent would hear from Lori. Another oddity caught her eye: the wall to her left was black, and it seemed to be... undulating? She looked to her right; that wall was the same way. She looked up just in time to see several dozen black widows descending from the ceiling, which was also covered in the things. Lori screamed as a throng of the spiders simply let go of the ceiling entirely and landed all over her. She shot up and ran for the door, still screaming. She yanked the door and then remembered she had locked it. Sobbing now, Lori managed to take her key out and get the door open. She ran out into the front yard and threw herself into the snow, rolling and slapping at herself to get the horrible creatures off of her.

She looked up to see officers standing on her walkway, and was relieved to see them. Unfortunately for her, the police were here to arrest her for her stunt on the bus.

Nick gave Atton's head a scratch. That little Christmas Kitty... why he didn't even KNOW what he was in for. Atton lifted his head up from where it was resting on his paws to regard Nick. They locked eyes a moment. Atton gave a slow blink to Nick, and he returned the greeting to his kitty. Both looked away a moment as a show of mutual non-aggression, and then Atton closed his eyes and went back to his afternoon doze. Nick continued on his path towards the kitchen. Nick reached atop the fridge and pulled the laser pointer down, then stepped back into the living room.

"Are you ready, boy?" Nick asked. Atton's head perked up, he knew what this meant. This was the precursor to that annoying red... thing appearing, but it was in his best interest to fight this battle. All Atton had to do was keep it on the move. He had tried many times to catch and kill it; but that seemed impossible. If he chased it and scared it enough, eventually Nick would announce a countdown to its departure, and then were what Nick and Jessica called "bagged special things" when they thought they were being subtle. When they were trying to excite Atton they would refer to them as "treats". His humans thought they were slick using the two different names. Atton was content to let them think that. But for now? To battle! Atton's ears went flat... oh, the treats would be glorious today. Atton would truly frighten the beast, and Nick would give him his reward.

He liked the way Jessica handled it better. She gave him treats just for purring, and more of them. She seemed to keep the beast away on her own, whereas Nick clearly needed help. It was his duty, and a well paid one. Atton began the chase.

Merrick tilted his head out of the water to take a breath, took another stroke, and repeated the action again and again. While it was true that he could take the body of any of his "Skinstealers" he wished, the body would shape to what he considered his real form. Merrick was not entirely sure why it was, but he had to treat that form well or it was not very useful to him. And treat it well he did. He kept abreast of modern health literature, and ate only the best food; took the best supplements. He worked this body at least thirty minutes a day to keep it in prime shape, and prime shape he was in. When he looked back, even the fastest of the other swimmers were thirteen seconds behind him.

He stood out of the water and held out his hand for a towel. Sure enough one of the low end workers placed one into his hand, and Merrick began to towel himself dry. All that was on his agenda today was to check on investments and ensure his assorted business arrangements were going smoothly. Perhaps afterwards he would find out where Jessica was, deliver her some flowers. He knew her expression would outwardly be of disgust, but he could see heat and the heat of her sex did not lie; she wanted him as badly as he wanted her. Impossible as it seemed, Merrick realized he could not outfight the meathead Jessica was dating. What he would have to do instead was to destroy that meathead in other ways, while constantly reminding Jessica to whose heart she belonged.

As if somehow the universe had keyed in on Merrick's thoughts, there appeared said meathead in the hallway that passed alongside the pool, visible through the glass. Nick was wearing a suit, one that Merrick could immediately tell was made of very expensive fabric. For all the greatest materials would mean nothing if shaped poorly, and in this case they were. The coat was too tight around the chest, the tie set at the wrong length for one of Nick's height, and the pants looked about to burst at the waist. Nick had been standing there for who knows how long, because he looked... impatient. His eye turned and made contact with Merrick's. Merrick sneered lightly in contempt.

Nick's hands were in his pockets, until the eye contact was made. At that point Nick pulled his hands out, his middle fingers extended. The crass moron then tore parts of the shirt over his nipples off. Expensive silk. Strained over the flesh sure, but that shirt could have been salvaged. Nick licked his thumbs and forefingers, then toyed with his nipples through the new holes. Merrick shook his head in annoyance and looked for a staff member to have the filth ejected from the club. It became a pointless endeavour when Nick abruptly began to do a George Jefferson walk toward the exit on his own.

Sighing in exasperation, Merrick wondered again what Jessica saw in that man. Unable to even begin to grasp the slightest inkling beyond the fact that the dog boy WAS very attractive in a feminine sort of way, Merrick returned to his locker.

His clothing. Nick had somehow gotten past all of that security and taken Merrick's clothing. That explained the poor fit. The twit had been mutilating Merrick's clothing in front of him. Merrick rolled his eyes and went to find a member of security as well. He'd have to have clothing sent to him.

An hour later, Nick had his feet up on his desk, watching as Brian... watched a loading screen. "Oh yeah, Bri, this is WAY better than just plugging a card into the Turbografx and just turning it on."
"Have a bit of patience, you prat," Brian said mildly as the loading screen finished, "and pick up a joystick. Time to play the best fighting game of all time."
Nick looked comically confused, "I wasn't aware you abbreviated 'Street Fighter II Championship Edition' as 'IK+' in jolly old England." He did pick the joystick up, "Okay so... three karate guys. What do I-"
Nick cut off as the office door opened, and Jessica's partner strode in.

"Well, I'm here with the official paperwork. We're bringing you in on the Skinstealer case," Raoul said with a big smile. "And I'll be honest, I'm gonna really like the chance to get to know you. I've never seen Jessica this happy and I knew her since her first day at the precinct."
Nick shrugged, "Dude, you have no idea how much that goes both ways. I may have always worn a smile and cracked jokes, but life has sucked for a real long time except when I'm around some people like this dickhead. Now life doesn't suck pretty much all the time."

Brian stood up and offered his hand, "Brian Braddock, 22nd SAS, retired."
Raoul met him with a firm handshake, "Raoul Delacroix, Detective with the Violent Crimes division of the Chicago PD."
Brian regarded Raoul a moment, "French name, but you don't look French."
Raoul smiled, "Right on that, I was born in Zanzibar; I'm ethnically Parsi."
Brian clapped him on the back, "I won't hold it against you, mate."

Raoul set the sheaf of papers down onto Nick's desk, "Sign that contract and we hire you at your full daily rate for a minimum of two weeks, with an option to renew. We won't pay for expenses but it's steady work."
Nick closed his eye and then opened it, looking up, "Can't Jessica expense things to the city, though?"
Raoul nodded, "Sure but we won't pay YOUR expenses. I imagine she'll use up more gas and eat extra food these next two weeks, though."
"Alright then, when do we start?"
Raoul looked at the screen, "After I've kicked both of your asses at IK+ for a while."
Brian laughed, "Oh, challenge ACCEPTED mate!"

Towards the evening, Merrick stepped out of his Mercedes-Benz AMG. Nick stealing his clothing had been annoying, but it was nothing that put him out too terribly much. His thought right now was more business. There was money to be gathered. While Merrick did not agree with money's existence, he understood it was a requirement to have power in the white man's culture.

This was the last thought Merrick had for now, as a .308 Winchester round struck him directly in the left eye. The hefty engine block of his vehicle provided a good backstop to the round after it had passed through Merrick's head. It would be a good day, maybe two, before Merrick could gather his psyche together from the shock of sudden death and shape another Skinstealer to the form he customarily took.

"Good fucking shot, Brian!" Nick said, applauding.
"Cheers, mate," his old friend responded, "rather quiet like I said, wasn't it?"
"You're goddamned right it was," Nick responded, "How is that even possible?"
"Sub sonic ammo. Sure, means I need to get closer to my mark than otherwise but it sounded much like a cracker going off, didn't it?"
"I'll be damned, it really does."

Late the following evening, Jessica stabbed her half-smoked cigarette into the half-emptied soda can. "Okay, say Merrick is... okay really, Prettyboy, run that by us again?"
Nick pointed to Raoul, "Actually it was his idea, I'm just theorizing how it would be possible."
Raoul shook his head, "No it wasn't, Nick. MY theory is a lot like Jessica's, that he's gathering brains to research... whatever he's trying to do."
Nick held his hands palm out, "Okay, fine this IS my idea, but it was your idea that set up the spark for my idea. If you are correct, why is he gathering athletes to clone?"

"Kind of... Well because he is going to want shock troopers, and he'll need good, fit sorts."
Jessica nodded, "It makes sense to me. You can't take a city over by force without some people who HAVE force, you know?"

Nick shook his head, not directly against anything she said, but to show he was against the idea in general. "If that were the case, we'd have heard about soldiers going missing, not scientists, athletes, and a psychotic killer."
"Sociopathic," Raoul interjected.
"...the hell is the difference?" Nick asked, almost grabbing the can Jessica had just fouled for a drink.

Jessica gently moved the can well out of Nick's reach. "A psychopath tends to have the appearance of a normal life, albeit one full of shallow relationships. They kill in such a way as to minimize risk to themselves. Andreyko had no friends for long, never held down a job and didn't really plan anything he did, he just sorta... did things. He's a sociopath."

Nick gave her a thumbs up, "right okay, I have learned something new today, and just sorta proves my point... Merrick is clearly a psychopath so he wants a sociopath in his little group."
"Yeah," Jessica said, "I'll say. Just quit sidetracking us and lay out your theory."
"For the record, he started this sidetrack."
Raoul chuckled, "Tattletale!"
Jessica lightly slapped the table, "Mommy doesn't care who started it, she just wants quiet."
"Oooh, spank me, mommy!" Raoul said with a grin.

"Sorry, while you are a very pretty boy, I only spank one particular one."

"And we sidetracked again!" Nick said, laughing, "Okay, here's my theory: he's not gathering people to make troops in any direct manner, I think he is gathering those with genetic traits that would be useful to them, and using the eggheads to isolate those traits... somehow."
"The Skinstealers have never shown any inkling of that ability before," Raoul pointed out.
"They also couldn't mimic people on any more than a very general level before the bit with Jess here... or at least nobody noticed it."
"Okay, so I guess their powers do evolve."

"So I'm thinking Merrick wants to make one perfect super-soldier. One that will probably be a crude biomechanical weapon, able to control prostheses in ways better than us."
Jessica exhaled, "That's a scary thought, Prettyboy. I'm not saying I buy it... but I'm not ruling it out, either."
"Gives us something to think about, at any rate," Raoul said, "Let's call it a day, meet back tomorrow afternoon fresh and alert."

The following morning, Merrick had gathered himself and re-formed. He sank into his plush leather chair, and stared at his intercom a moment. At moments like this, the need for him to fit into the white man's culture annoyed him. What did he need an intercom for? His secretary was one of his creations. "She" did his bidding with a thought.. But there were powerful men Merrick had to truck with, and they would be confused if he did not play the dumbshow of pretending to call her in for her assorted duties.

But then there were the other things the white man's culture provided which he did enjoy. When Merrick took the silver top off of his snack bowl, he found snickerdoodles inside. He smiled wryly. Jessica had first brought those into his life.

At first Merrick had only known her as a white woman, but as time passed he came to understand how much more she was. Jessica was a nature spirit, and had she been born a short two hundred years earlier things may have gone differently. Had they met at an earlier time, she might have even been a friend to him, an ally in his endeavours. It was true that the white man brought Dryads with him from their home, but the Dryads were of nature.

Nature spirit as she may be, Jessica was born into the white man's culture; and through her he was forced to admit that it was not all bad. After time Jessica surprised him with these cookies one day; her mother's recipe handed down and carefully guarded. Since she had gone... Even before he had decided he would make her his queen, he had sought to have her recipe duplicated. Time and again it was a failure, but he could honestly say that he had never had an awful snickerdoodle.

Anticipating the pleasure, Merrick raised the first of this new batch to his mouth and bit off a piece. As the cookie first hit his tongue, Merrick smiled. This was as close as it could possibly be. Whoever made this batch had paid well and direct attention to his specifications, and had, for all intents and purposes, duplicated Jessica's masterwork. Merrick munched happily on the cookies as he checked his email, one right after the other. When that first order of business was done, and it had only taken 10 minutes, Merrick had eaten more than half the bowl.

Merrick pressed his secretary's mind to find out which bakery these had come from. Dinkel's Bakery over on Lincoln Avenue. Merrick had tried them twice before and found they could not match the recipe. He did allow his underlings a lot of free will, and one had clearly engaged their services again. He would find out which had shown such initiative and reward it greatly. This bakery would also receive a healthy chunk of business from Merrick's companies.

Looking at the bowl again, Merrick spotted movement and light under them. Sated and full of rare good nature, Merrick let pure curiosity drive him and removed the cookies to see what was underneath. It was one of those tablet computers everyone seemed to obsess over these days. Merrick preferred the tactile feedback of a keyboard to lifeless touchscreens, but he was not utterly ignorant to their operation. The tablet under the cookies had a flashing arrow that said "swipe a heart pattern to see our secret ingredient!" Merrick rolled his eyes a moment and did as instructed.

His light smile turned instantly to a frown when he saw the video that played after. There was his queen, wearing one of her ridiculous anime t-shirts, giving the camera two middle fingers. A few moments later, a man's member came into view and she pointed at it with one hand, and gave a thumbs up gesture with the other. The camera cut to a wider shot... it was Nick's cock, and he was masturbating in the presence of his queen. Another cut to his ejaculation, which Jessica caught in her cupped hands like she was receiving manna from heaven. She then dumped it into a bowl, shaking her hands to get most of it off. The last she cleaned with her own tongue... and then brought a plastic mixing spoon into view. She stirred. One more camera cut... to Jessica scooping balls of dough from that bowl onto a cookie sheet.

Merrick seized the tablet and threw it against the wall, shattering it before he had to see more. He vacated the body that he was in and willed it to find lighter fluid to cover itself in and set itself aflame. That now blank Skinstealer left to obey its final command, and Merrick went into one of the backups he always kept nearby.

Even as he began to take himself into the new body, Merrick could not control the physical revulsion he felt.

At the same time, Nick was munching on a cookie while Jessica was applying her makeup. It was nice how she was no longer even remotely shy about nudity around him... the shirt she was wearing did nothing to hide that muscled butt from him. The workouts Jessica had been doing combined with her far lower consumption of alcohol were doing wonderful things to her legs and ass. They were doing great things to other parts of her body as well, but Nick couldn't think of any of them in this particular moment. His thoughts were on the leg show and the snickerdoodle he was eating. "These are some pretty awesome snickerdoodles."

Jessica blotted her lips to ensure her lipstick covered only what she wanted it to, "Yep. They're my mom's recipe."
"See," Nick said, "I've never had a snickerdoodle before. I just thought snickerdoodle was a name disgusting people called each other. Instead I come to find out a 'snickerdoodle' is a good cookie. I've never had other snickerdoodles to compare this to, but I'm willing to bet as far as snickerdoodles go, these are good ones."
"You know what's kinda... I'm not entirely sure which batch we actually sent to Merrick."

Nick looked at the cookie, sniffed it a moment, and then shrugged, "Eh. Who gives a damn. These snickerdoodles are awesome. I didn't know that one of the things I was missing in my life is the simple joy of a snickerdoodle. Just think of all these years I wasted. A new era has begun. I shall refer to those dark years as 'BJS'... Before Jessica's Snickerdoodles."
"Say snickerdoodle one more time, Prettyboy. Watch what happens to you."
"Snickerdoodle!" Nick said and then ducked.

Jessica turn and poked him in the gut, "You know what? You are really asking for it, Prettyboy."
Nick grinned lopsidedly, "Bring it then."
"Oh, I'll bring it," she said, putting her hands on her hips, "I'll bring it so hard you'll end up in a new zip code."
Nick rolled his eye and held his left hand up and mimed a mouth opening and closing, "All talk, no action, that's my girlfriend."

Jessica went low and tackled Nick to the ground, making him lose his air when her shoulder first hit his gut. When Nick was able to breathe again, he began laughing as his hands came up to hold her thighs fondly. He stopped almost mid laugh and made eye contact with Jessica. She looked back at him wondering why he had suddenly gotten so serious.
"Snickerdoodle."

Jessica balled her hands into fists and pounded on his chest several times, making hollow thudding sounds each time. Nick's shirt was not yet buttoned, and thus had fallen open when she knocked him down. She stopped pounding on his chest and flattened her hands. She ran them up and down him, working the flesh under her hands. His muscles relaxed under her ministrations as she looked him over, feeling the heat of her desire rise. There was such a dichotomy to him.

Nick's face looked so soft, feminine, with the Japanese features that clearly dominated his genetics, but all one had to do was peel back his clothing to see how overpoweringly masculine her man really could be. She had seen him every day working on the weights and keeping his kata up, it had inspired her to work on her own body as well. He did it not of vanity, but out of a genuine desire to remain in prime fighting shape should the need to defend himself or others come up. Jessica liked knowing she didn't need to protect him during a fight, and she would never even think of complaining about the other benefits. Better to have the best of both worlds; this man was genuinely kind, funny, and also hot.

They remained like that for a few moments, Jessica massaging him and Nick touching her thighs. Belatedly, Jessica became aware that she had been rubbing herself against his Activision boxers, and his cock underneath the thin fabric responded in kind. She stopped moving entirely, closing her eyes to let the passion of this moment wash over her. When she moved again it was to fish her man's rigid member out the front hole of his boxers. In a moment she was on him, moaning as he filled her.
"I love you, Prettyboy."

He returned the sentiment in Japanese. She did not speak the language at all, but she could read the intent behind it easily enough. She began to ride him quickly, her pent up need driving her to take him into her over and over, as deep as she could. Within minutes she was gritting her teeth as she tightened up around him. Nick was clawing at the bath rug, trying to hold out as long as he could for her benefit. She smiled as she recognized that… it made her feel good to not only be exciting him this much, but to know he was thinking of her pleasure. She clamped her muscles down hard and gave him two more as she was reaching for her own climax. He gave out the little whining howl Jessica had come to love as he surged out into her. Jessica used her fingers to bring herself the rest of the way over even as Nick's seed leaked out over him onto his belly.

Jessica collapsed onto him, "I do, Prettyboy, I love you. Thanks for being so patient with me. It meant a lot. Though I do wish you had done more laundry so I didn't have to know you used my socks to help you BE so patient."

Nick touched the back of his head, "Err… sorry?"

Jessica looked down at him with mock pity, "You can't help your foot fetish. You're Japanese! Come on, Prettyboy, let's go clock in and see about scaring up some new leads.

Nick kissed Jessica's forehead gently, and then reached up to take his telephone off the dresser edge. He swiped it open, tapped it three times, and Lonely Island's "I Just Had Sex" began to play as Nick danced under her, lip syncing the song.

Jessica rolled her eyes and had to laugh, "I know you had that ready and so wanna be mad at you."

"Doesn't matter had sex!" Nick sang along, as Jessica shook her head and cuddled back in.

Chapter Sixteen:
- "Merry Something to You", Devo

Raoul very carefully placed his coffee down, "Okay. What are we gonna work on today?"
Jessica lit up a smoke, "I was thinking maybe Nick and I could go poking around at the scenes, canvass the witnesses again?"
"May I offer a suggestion?" Nick asked.
"That's why you're here, Nick," Raoul responded as he took his first sip. He winced slightly. The coffee was incredibly old. So be it, old coffee is still coffee.
Nick blew a kiss at Jessica before he spoke again, "I was thinking, since we are keeping Merrick off balance anyway, why don't we go after him? Take the head off and the rest of the body dies."
"We can't 'go after' Merrick, Prettyboy. That's why we're fucking with him." Jessica said as she slapped the invisible flying kiss down onto the table and squashed it, "Speaking of, I no shit went with the 'bucket of paint on top of the slightly open door' gag. You shoulda seen his reaction it was epic."

"Look, Jess, Raoul, I know you kill him he keeps coming back, what do you theorize he IS, exactly?"
"I'm guessing some sort of spirit," Raoul replied.
Nick pointed at Jessica, "Dryads are nature spirits capable of hiding in trees and reforming their bodies from other trees, yet if you shot Jessica in the head she'd die and I'd kill you before killing myself."

"That is probably a lot harder than you think," Raoul said, "But I get where you're coming from. It's entirely possible Merrick has a 'true' body."
"I know I'd have to drive flint through your heart to kill you for good," Nick said with a nod, "But, yes, that's where I am coming from.

Raoul look genuinely surprised, "How... how the hell did you know that?"
Nick thumbed his upper ears, "I go places and hear things."
Jessica decided to head them off before they went into a tangent, "This doesn't follow, Nick. Just because my race can do things like that doesn't say anything about Merrick's nature.

"What's your theory, Jessica? That he's a disembodied spirit? I refuse to accept that. That's fucking irrational," Nick said as he shook his head, "The fact that he can directly assume control of Skinstealers indicates he's either their hive queen or we're just straight out fucked and there's no way to stop him and it's just a matter of time before he kills us all."
"You know what?" Jessica asked, "my gut tells me you're right. Somewhere there has to be a 'Merrick' that we can track down and kill.

Raoul slugged down his horrible coffee in three more gulps, "You know him better than anyone else, Jessica. What motivates him?"
"Aside from me now, apparently, he REALLY hates white people."

"That's a little odd," Nick said, "Why does he hate white people so much, did he ever say?"
"He says white people stole the land from the Natives."

Nick's ears perked comically and Raoul leaned forward. Raoul responded first, "Well, that's a very odd way to feel about that. Isn't he an Amerind himself?"
"Well, the body he has looks like one, but that doesn't mean he himself is one."
Nick laid his hand on the table and tapped the pencil he was holding on it. "So he is clearly a supernatural creature that has a beef with white men taking Chicago from those he feels it belongs to by right."
"Then that's where we need to start," Raoul said, "We need to find out everything we can about the natives of this area."
"To the res!" Nick said.
"No," Jessica said, "first to the library to read up so we don't look like complete assholes when we go poking around."

Two hours later, they were in Nick's GTO, on their way over to the American Indian Center over on Wilson. Given the general flow of traffic, it was probably going to be another half hour or more before they got there. "I swear I can hear my car crying. She's not meant for this crap."
"What the hell am I here for, mate?" Brian asked.
"Well that's simple, Brian," Jessica answered, "It's almost impossible to get mad at a British person no matter how many stupid questions they ask."
"You're right there, these are some really stupid questions you've got me asking."

Nick reached back to clap his old friend on the shoulder "Yup, so do your thing and British it up!"
"Looks a bit of time before we get there, innit?"
"There you go! Like that!"

Nick's left ear flickered, "Well, there's only one way to pass the time in true British style. Uh, let's see... Baker Street? Yeah that's what I'm doing."
Brian laughed, "Gonna take me on with the Birghton-Milligham variant then? Okay... Edgware Road."
"The one on Hammersmith Circle or Bakerloo?" Raoul interjected, "If I'm going to jump in here, I have to know."
Nick looked up in the rear view mirror, "You play?"
Raoul shrugged, "I admit it's been a decade or more, but I think I can catch onto the new rules as we go along."

Jessica screwed her face up a bit, "How the hell can you? I have no idea what they are doing. It makes no sense to me."
Raoul smiled pleasantly, "It's quit simple, actually. We'll pop around to Barnes and Noble and pick up a copy of Rules and Origins for you."
"Out of print." Nick and Brian said at the same time.
Raoul could only shrug, "well, listen in. It's not too hard to pick up if you think it over."

"Right then," Brian said, rubbing his hands together, "Bakerloo."
"Well, that means I can cut to Goldhawk Road, since you didn't block off the Hammersmith back route."
"Hanger Lane for me," Nick said.
Brian scoffed, "What a pedestrian move. Heathrow 4th terminal."

Raoul shifted his wings a bit. Unable to find a comfortable way to sit in the cramped back seat, he simply vanished them, "Taking us both on at once? Knightsbridge."

"Wait, is that legal?" Nick asked.

"It's not a move I've seen in years, but I don't think it was ever specifically outlawed."

Nick set his jaw and nodded, "Fine then, Raoul, we'll work together on this. Marylebone."

"Kensal Greene," Brian said, "as the insufferable yanks say, 'come at me, bro'."

"I've never said that in my life, or even heard anyone say that," Jessica said as she shook her head.

"Come on now, Jessica, " Raoul said, shooting her a look, "You know better than to interrupt your partner while he's working. North Wembley."

Jessica rolled her eyes, "It's just a silly kid's game."

The three men in the car looked at her, aghast, and Nick spoke first, "Jess? Just... no. Chess is a game of 52 card pickup compared to the concentration and tenacity, never mind the raw intellect, and study of past masters to play Mornington Crescent. North Wembley."

Brian shook his head, "Not gonna corner me that way, boys."

"He talks big but we've got him on the run, Nick. Upminster."

Nick broke out into a grin, "Good flank! I'll flush him out. The other Edgware."

Brian gritted his teeth, "You rat bastards. Brent Cross."

Raoul buffed his nails on his immaculate shirt, "Vauxhall."

"You... dirty backstabber!" Nick said, exasperated, "Uhh... Roding Valley? Yeah, Roding Valley. Up to you now, Brian, I did all I could."

Brian was deep in thought for thirty seconds before he finally responded, "If you hadn't pushed me so hard I... I know! Park Royal!"

Nick's ears went flat and he spoke sarcastically "Great move there, Brian. Really truly a masterstroke. Stovington himself would be in awe of THAT piece of shit move."

Raoul cracked his knuckles, grinning, "Gonna go ahead and slide over to Hornchurch."

Nick gritted his teeth, "Cockfosters. Best I can do."

"Well, that's an easy one," Brian said with a smile, "Northwood. Wait!"

"No take backs, buddy," Raoul said with a smug expression, "Mornington Crescent."

Brian sighed, "I meant Northwood HILLS. You knew I meant that."

Raoul shook his head, "If you meant it you should have said it."

Nick turned and gave Raoul a high five, "Well played, man. You kicked our asses."

Jessica pointed forwards, "Traffic's moving now you goons. Eyes on the road."

Nick turned forward, "Right, right. When we get there we'll drop you off and go park. Then I'll come in and join you, play the clueless Japanese tourist. You find Angela Darius and we'll start asking her about the religion and whatnot, find out what we can about possible shapeshifters and whatnot."

"I may not be professional investigators like you lot, but I'm not completely barmy."

Nick pulled up in front of the American Indian Center and let Raoul out and then set about the nearly impossible task of finding parking in downtown Chicago.

Brian stepped in and headed right for the receptionist; who was rather cute in a mousey sort of way, what with those glasses. She was an orc woman in a smart suit, and her size did nothing to make her intimidating to him. "Pardon me... oh, you're a pretty bird, aren't you?"

The woman looked Brian over, prepared to be annoyed. Brian did cut quite a figure. Clearly getting up there in years but not yet an old man, Brian had a sturdy, powerful body and a mouth full of immaculate white teeth which contrasted sharply against the gentle brown tone of his skin. She found herself actually blushing as she responded clumsily, "Oh thank you! How... how can I help you?"

"Well firstly you can direct me to where I can find one Angela Darius, would you love?" Brian asked, "and perhaps on my way out you'd give me your phone number? Tell me what time you're off work miss..." He looked at the nameplate, "Ellen?"
The orc blushed deeper, and looked him over, "Mr..."
"Brian," he said, doing his best Timothy Dalton, "Brian Braddock."
Ellen glanced at his hand, "You... you're married, Mr. Braddock."

"Brian, please. And I know my wife will simply love you as well. She's a wonderful little Japanese girl, I think you two will get along smashingly."

Ellen felt if she blushed any harder she'd pass out. She thought this over for a few moments, looked again at the man in front of her, and took her cell phone out, "I never call myself. I have to look up my own number."

Brian took his own phone out. As she named off the digits, he entered her into his contact list, "Pretty bird Ellen. Now to make sure you've got my number..." Brian sent her a text message that said, "Tell me your favorite dish and if Noriko cannot prepare it, we'll have it ordered in."

Ellen bit her lip and smiled, "I... I like pizza, actually."

"Nothing wrong with the basics, Ellen," Brian said with a charming smile, "But once you've tasted the best of Noriko, you'll never go back to what you've eaten before." Brian's eyes widened a moment, "Oh my! That was a rather unintentional double entendre. But I feel as if we should leave it just like that, don't you, Ellen?" Ellen nodded, speechless as Brian continued, "Now if you could just direct me to Ms. Darius, I'll ask her some questions about culture and whatnot, and then I'll tell Noriko to prepare for a guest, sound right love?"

Ellen nodded again, "Mrs. Darius actually is over working on the new archery exhibit on the second floor. Shall I tell you she's coming? I mean! Shall I tell her YOU are coming?"

"You're planning on calling her later tonight to let her know when I come?"

Ellen had to laugh, and she pointed up the stairs.

Nick walked up and met Brian as he walked off, "That was pretty smooth, you perv."
Brian's grin showed up in a mime of Nick's lopsided fashion, "You're one to talk about being a pervert. Jessica dished a bit about you to my never-to-be-blushing bride."
Nick stuck his tongue out at Brian, "Hey, you have the things you do with your girl, I have things I do with mine."
Brian shook his head, "Just yankin' your chain, mate. Now, make with the 'no speaky Engrish'."

It was not difficult to spot the person they were looking for, she was a simply stunning elven woman of Native descent. Her raven black hair was as straight as Nick's, and she wore some beads in it. Nick was fairly certain that it was not a cultural thing so much as a fashion choice. He strode up and took a picture of the exhibit, half completed, with the flash on his phone on despite the ample lighting conditions. The woman blinked and looked over, "Can I help you, sir?"

Nick looked down at his phone and typed some Japanese into it, then looked up, "Yes purease, thank you. Are you Angera Dariusu?"
She nodded, "Yes, I am."
Brian stepped half in front of Nick, "Sorry, for my friend, his English is just a bit dodgy as you can tell. I'm afraid we've made a bit of a pig's ear of this already, wot?"
Nick nodded, "Purease and thank you! Niko Sakamoto nice to meeting with you!"

Angela laughed, "Okay boys, you can drop the show. I know exactly who you are Mr. Sakamoto. You helped the

228

woman who is now my assistant escape from a life of sexual slavery last year in that club."

Nick sighed as he grinned lopsidedly, "Curse me and my desire to protect the innocent while looking completely memorable."

Angela pointed at a woman across the hall, and as soon as Nick looked upon her, he felt an odd kinship, and was able to identify her even before she turned. The last time he had seen her, she had long blonde hair, not short purple, and her nine tails had not been not visible. Nick waved to her when they made eye contact, and she suddenly found her work super interesting. She stole a few sidelong glances at him, giving him a shy smile when she noticed he was still looking.

Brian elbowed him, "Lookit that, would you? Her tails all went right up just a bit. Clearly she fancies you for some how's your father. Go! Go, Nickyboy! Mount her! You mount her and have it off right now in front of the staff and that primary school field trip!"

Nick rolled his eye, "You'll have to pardon my friend here. He wasn't playing too much of a role. He's so cripplingly British that it prevents him from functioning in society properly."

"You wot now, mate?"

Angela shook her head and laughed, "You two should take this act on the road. So what brings you here today?"

Nick grinned lopsidedly, but Brian answered first, "Nicky is here doing a little research so we can see about saving the day."

"Oh?" Angela responded, "what can the Culture Center do for you then?"

"Well, I am tracing down the origins of a supernatural creature, and I thought there's a chance you might be able to help?"

Angela sat down on the edge of the display, "Well, sir, as you can surely tell given that you could see my soul with the lack of eye on the left side, the supernatural is very natural. If I had your gift I wouldn't cover that, I'd just learn how to use both at once. In addition to being an elf, I was also born with a... sense for these sorts of things."

"I'll say you do," Nick said, taken slightly aback, "How did you know all that?"

Angela shrugged, "I just do. I get these insights from time to time, and it's led to great success in my chosen field."

Nick pressed her a bit further, "I can't just let that drop. That's not in my nature. I need to know more"

Angela smiled indulgently, "The world is changing Mr. Sakamoto. Once the elves returned, you had to expect that magic would as well. Stroke of luck that my human father was a shaman, isn't it? But you're not here to learn about me, so let's move on."

Brian raised his hand, "I'm certainly here to get to know you if you've the inclination."

"I'm afraid I'm married, sir." Angela said.

"Well, so am I," Brian began, "but that's never stopped my wife or I from taking home folks we fancy for some drinks and a shag."

"Anyway," Nick said, disappointed that his line of inquiry had been shut down so soundly, "Our adversary takes the appearance of a Native American man, and has a dislike of white men, specifically how they 'took' Chicago and soil it. From what I'm told he talks like he was around since before this happened."

Angela nodded, "I can see why you'd look into our legends, then. If that's not an angry spirit it's certainly someone pretending to be one."

Nick's left ear flickered, "Oh, we are absolutely sure he's not ordinary crazy. He's shown VERY unique abilities."

"What can he do?" Angela asked.

"He's the leader of the Skinstealers, first and foremost."

Angela's eyes widened, "That's a big fish you're after there."

Nick nodded, "So, do you have any theories?"

Angela thought for a moment, "Coyote is a shapeshifter, a trickster, but doesn't have the patience for this sort of thing. Bear has the patience but not the abilities nor the inclination. Raven would change it's own from to fool man, but would not do so for more than root curiosity."

"You seem awful certain we're dealing with an animal spirit," Brian interjected.

"Good sir," Angela responded, "a white wolf who lives to avenge the sins of mankind stands right next to you, and you doubt that the entire world is about the Earth and her children? I wouldn't go so far as many of my brothers and say technology is an aberration, but it does distract man, make it difficult for him to understand how one should treat the world."

"White wolf?" Nick asked, "Why is it I understand dogs so well, then?"

Angela smiled, "Didn't take a zoology class ever, did you? All dogs come from Wolf. We're getting off topic here again. It's not a wolf, because... well, Nick, do you think someone like you could be capable of the atrocities committed by the Skinstealers?"

Nick lowered his gaze a moment, "I'm capable of some pretty terrible things."
"The business of avenging sins is rarely pretty." Angela said with a sad little smile.

Nick felt it necessary to stop the topic drift himself, this time, "What is most likely to be angry that it is no longer revered, and hold a long grudge."
Angela was thinking again, "Boar. Skunk. Bison. Salmon. Moose. Fox, maybe? Elk."
"Which of these associates with tricksters?"
"Everything has met with Coyote at one time or another. There is a story of Bison turning Coyote's own tricks back against him."

Nick's ears perked at that, "Really? That sure feels in my gut like that might be important."
"A wolf should always listen to his intuition. That's one of the things you're most known for."
Nick shrugged, "Not sure I accept that 'wolf' thing, all due respect. I... a dog is familiar and friendly, but can snarl with the best if things go south."
Angela shrugged back, "You don't have to accept it for it to be true."

Brian coughed and then spoke, "do we have any way to confirm this?"
Angela shrugged, "I'd start with finding a bison and taking a good long look at one."

Nick's lopsided grin turned into a childlike one "Awesome! I have an excuse to take Jessica to Brookfield Zoo!"

Chapter Seventeen:
- "White Man", Queen

Jessica took a big suck from her seasonally inappropriate grape ice... slush... thing... and could not stop herself from smiling. Since the moment they arrived at Brookfield Zoo, all decked out for Christmas, Nick was firmly in 'oversized 12-year-old' mode. She could not fathom why Nick doubted himself, feared himself a monster. True, he was capable of incredible brutality, but he never turned it towards her or anyone else that didn't deserve it. It wasn't just that, however, it was this. It was how he was wide-eyed here, his tail wagging constantly since he first saw the entrance with the Christmas trees flanking it. How could he think himself evil when this was inside him? If anything, THIS was closer to his true nature than anything else Nick thought he may be.

Nick spotted a young girl wearing a Daniel Tiger's Neighborhood jacket, and a Detroit Tigers hat trying to push her way through the crowd to see one majestic female tiger who had a tail that seemed to have been cut short. Nobody was moving for her, or paying attention to her mother whom was, in a small voice, asking for someone to please move. He tapped the mother on her shoulder, "I think I can help, Miss?"

She looked at Nick, wary at first of the male voice. When she saw Nick's perked ears, kind expression, and lightly wagging tail her apprehension melted away, "Would you, please?"

Nick nodded and crouched down to the girl's level, "What's your name, miss?"
The girl looked at her mother, who nodded, and replied, "I'm Gia."
"Well, Gia, it's a pleasure to meet you. I'm Nick. Nick Sakamoto, PI."
Gia giggled at him, "What's a PI?"
Nick flickered his left ear, "Why I'm a man who finds lost things for a living, like lost kitties."
Gia reached up and tweaked one of Nick's upper ears, then squealed, "They're real!"
Nick comically leaned into the touch and slapped the ground repeatedly with his right hand like a normal dog being scratched just right.

Gia giggled again, and Nick grinned at her lopsidedly, "You wanna see the tigers, Gia?"
She nodded enthusiastically, and Nick leaned down very low, "Climb on my shoulders… it's okay I won't let you fall. You're not afraid of heights, are you?"

Gia shook her head and did as Nick asked. Nick took hold of Gia's ankles to keep her balanced and safe, and then stood up. She laughed and held onto his hair as he stood. Nick grimaced but when he was standing she let go and tweaked his ears again. Over the next few minutes Nick and Gia talked about these tigers in specific and cats in general.

Jessica took several pictures of this and found herself smiling as she watched him.

On a whim, she sent a text message to her mother with one of the pictures attached, saying, "God damn, Mom, in some ways he really reminds me of Dad."
The response came back after four minutes, with an attached picture. Marion apparently had used her phone's camera to be able to send her a copy of a print photo. It was of a much younger Jessica at the same zoo, with her father pointing at the tigers as she giggled about something. Also was this message, "Good men are good men the world around, sweetie."

Jessica thought for a few moments, considering how she was going to phrase her next message. Now seemed as good a time as any to get this out of the way. "Did you know that we met him before, in Hawaii?"
The response was a little bit delayed, "Yes, sweetie. There honestly didn't seem any reason to bring it up, and I can't see any reason to ever bring it up again."
Jessica watched the goings on for a moment before a thought occurred to her, and she sent another message, "If my kiss didn't save him, yours was going to?"

"There's no reason to bring this up again, Jessica. Since you did I'll say this. The fact that yours did is plenty for me. I've had my one great love in your father. I'm not one to waste my thoughts on 'what could have been'. It was a weekend fling with a hot guy. I don't know if my kiss would have saved him, but I sure would have tried."
"It's all sort of awkward for me."

"Not for me. As soon as your kiss saved him, I commissioned your wedding dress."

"Are you insane?"

"Look at what you just sent me a picture of and tell me honestly you couldn't spend the rest of your life with that man? I remind you I had married your father the same week we met. You're a Dryad, and a Dryad knows right away, sweetie."

Jessica stuck the phone back in her pocket and walked up next to Nick and Gia. She put her hands on her hips and shook her head, "I always knew a redhead would steal my man away from me."

Gia laughed as she rubbed Nick's ears some more, "I don't have a big enough dog house or I would keep him!"

Jessica maneuvered herself around Gia's leg to give Nick a kiss, "He's not a shelter doggie, he already has a home."

Gia pouted as Nick put her down, "Well, looks like my owner is tugging the leash, Gia. It was a pleasure meeting you!"

Nick gave one last wave as they walked away. They were holding hands, and Jessica was the one who initiated that.

"This has been a shitload of fun, Prettyboy," she said, going up to get another light kiss. She knew that Nick wasn't always comfortable with displays of affection when in a large crowd; some leftover of his Japanese upbringing, so he didn't get the kiss she wanted to give him right now.

Nick smiled at her, "Yeah, but I think rather than paying ridiculous zoo prices for food we should go take care of some business and then go get some McDonald's?" Jessica reached up to rub his left ear, and he closed his eye a moment, exhaling. She let go, "We'll leave when your owner says we do. What business could we possibly have here?"

"I... already told you that right after I talked To Ms. Darius."
"Right!" Jessica said, "mumbo jumbo about you looking at a real bison to see if we're facing off against a nebulous animist concept that has no rational basis?"
"You're right. Dryads existing at all, and finding one that can order black widows around is TOTALLY rational."
"Touche. Alright, Prettyboy, let's go see the bearded cows!"

Despite Nick's verbal insistence on leaving early and not spending 27 dollars on 8 dollars worth of food, there they were an hour later with a fully loaded hot dog and a big sloppy Italian beef as they wandered into the Great Bear Wilderness attraction. They saw the polar bears swimming, the grizzlies snoring, and even a bald eagle. It was not the bison that gave them first pause; it was the gray wolves that made Jessica tug on Nick's sleeve.

"Hey, Prettyboy?" Jessica asked as she looked at the wolves.
"Yeah, Jess?"
Jessica took a bite of her hot dog. It was once a fearsome beast, but now her last attack had reduced it to a

ridiculous little relish-coated nub. "You can talk to canines, right?"

Nick nodded as he booped her nose, "Yeah, but they honestly don't have a whole hell of a lot to say."
Jessica poked his side, "Go on, say hello."

Nick sighed and barked at the wolves. The ones closest gathered nearby, and Jessica didn't need to be able to speak canine to tell they were confused. The wolves yapped to one another for thirty seconds before an old wolf came forward, scarred and with one lop ear.

"How can this possibly be, human?" the wolf asked.
Nick's left ear flickered, "Because I'm not entirely human."
The wolf regarded him, "You may be domestic with the humans but you are almost entirely not one of them."
"You giving me guff for being domestic?"
The wolf sat on his haunches, "Frankly I don't know what to make of you. Usually domestication turns us into idiots. I hear them around us when the nights are quiet. 'Can you hear me?' 'Is it dinnertime where you are?'. If they were born here I'd have them torn apart and their mothers would applaud me for doing so."
Nick crossed his arms, "And yet here you are, enclosed in human cages and looked upon by them every day of your lives."

The wolf huffed annoyance, his breath visible in the chill of the air, "Man may have us here, but there is meat and there is safety. What little cost to us except to try and show their young what a true warrior looks like? They're soft, weak. They need examples of how to behave."

Nick thought it over, and then nodded, "I suppose that is true enough. But can't you see that being mankind's partners can-"
The wolf cut him off with a sharp yip, "I've heard them talk about their dogs, and talked to their dogs sometimes when they are close enough. They're not all imbeciles. What they call a German Shepard is a fine warrior, a good protector that understands a pack mentality."

Nick looked over to Jessica, "Huh. The wolves have a word for German Shepherd."

The wolf snarled at him, "I'm not interrupting our conversation to talk with my mate right now, show me the same respect."
Nick raised up his hands, "My apologies. I'm just a bit taken aback at the wisdom and complexity of your thoughts."

There was silence for a bit, before the wolf spoke again, "Go on with your recreation with your mate, boy. Come back on another day once my irritation with you has subsided. I'll teach you some things about how to raise a pup with that mate of yours."

Nick shook his head and looked over at Jessica; knowing the wolves were done with him for now, "That was weird. That pack leader was very well spoken. I... hmm..."

Nick barked to the wolf again, "I want to know more."
The old wolf looked at him, tongue lolled out in annoyance, "I told you I'd teach you later."

Nick thought about it, then spoke with contrition in his 'voice', "I want to know about the bison."
The wolf now sat up, "The bison? Now that's an interesting topic. You are a man and a wolf, but you are also surrounded by now servants of a bison who look like men. Any man they can taste the body of. Sometimes a man comes to this part of the... enclave in which men keep us, and that man becomes replaced by one of the servants. I doubt their mates know."

Nick's left ear flickered again, "Old wolf, my mate and I are not here just for recreation. We are seeking to learn about an enemy of ours. One who wronged my mate repeatedly in the past, and seeks now to take her from me by force. Once we track him down we intend to lay his guts on the pavement. May I talk to her about what you've told me?"

The old wolf went on his haunches, "I once had a mate who was a warrior, not like the feeble broodmares I had before and since, fit only for suckling my sons and daughters. If your mate is such as this, it is no insult for you to pass on what you have learned from me."

Nick turned to Jessica and spoke in Japanese, "I don't suppose you're faking it and really speak Japanese?"
Jessica looked in thought and bit her lip, "I watch enough anime to know you asked me if I speak Japanese?"
Nick sighed and nodded. Switching back to English as he lowered his voice, "That wolf just told me... If I understood him correctly... That a bison over where the bison are keeps servants around that look like men, 'any man they can taste the body of'. He makes it sound like the staff over by the bison are Skinstealers."

Jessica looked at the wolf, who met her gaze steadily. "Let's get over there and look for green where red should be in tired eyes?"
Nick held his hand up, "In a moment."

Nick returned his gaze to the old wolf, "My mate wishes to take leave so we can learn more about our enemy. The more we know, the better prepared we are to meet him and his... servants. Which of the bison holds these thralls?"
The wolf tilted his head, "The oldest one, did you expect otherwise?"
"Honestly?" Nick answered, "I was hoping it might be. How old is he?"
The wolf yawned and sat down to rest, "Many, many seasons. More than you for certain, and maybe... yes, I am almost sure, more than I."
"How can I thank you, old wolf?"
The wolf sneezed, "By fighting alongside your mate and winning the day, so that you may bring your pups to me and learn how to raise them."

Nick wanted to respond, but the wolf laid his head down and slept. And why not? Everything that needed discussing was talked out already. He turned to speak to Jessica, and found she was already heading towards where, he assumed, one could view the bison. Jessica turned back to smile at him, and beckoned him to follow her, swaying her hips. Nick could only think to follow her until she stopped, outside the gate, halfway across the parking lot to Nick's Judge.

"This is a hit, Prettyboy. Almost every staff member attending to the Great Bear... thing we were in had the green in their eyes."

Nick ran his hand down through her hair, fingers spread. As always, her silken tresses told him playful lies of getting caught inside. Her hair yielded easily as he combed through it with his fingers. "Is that enough to go on?" Jessica shook her head, "No, but something else is." Nick sniffed the air as he was wont to whenever he was apprehensive, "What have you got, Jess?"

Jessica resumed her walk to Nick's car, "I know Merrick's eyes. I saw him. I wouldn't have known to look for it unless you brought it up. Merrick is in there, and he pretended not to notice me. I… I seriously fucking pray that he thinks I didn't notice him."

Chapter Eighteen:
- "Sympathy for the Devil", The Rolling Stones

Jessica Dombrowski had a lot to think about just now. How to handle the situation with Merrick, for example. How does one get away with killing a random bison at a zoo without creating insane amounts of negative press for the police department?

Why the hell did Satine Reigns suddenly decide to open a bar not ten minutes' walk from where Nick and Jessica now lived? Jessica had been going to the Succubus for years now so she had just assumed it was a bar that had been there for a very long time. While that was technically true, Satine had purchased it with cash shortly after Nick had moved to Chicago. What was she, some sort of obsessed stalker?

These thoughts and so many others like them could easily keep Jessica trying to work her life out all day. What's the deal with that fluffy large cat that keeps visiting? Was her mother wrong about how "a Dryad knows" right away? What the hell do you get a dork like Nick for Christmas when you don't know the first thing about 1980's video games? How the hell does it work that she is able to order black widows around… could she order around say... Australian Redbacks? It was certain that ordering around other spiders didn't seem to work.

She was not letting any of these things occupy her thoughts right now. What she was up to this lovely late December morning, with the sun out as bright as a summer day yet utterly incapable of melting any of the snow? Trying to puzzle her way through installing a Windows program under this Linux thing that Raoul "helpfully" put on her laptop a week back when she complained of having to run weekly malware and virus scans.

It was bad enough she'd spent nearly 200 on this program to learn Japanese and now was spending all this time trying to find a way to make it work on this "superior" OS.

After asking on message boards and receiving such helpful comments as "this question was already answered" and "write an abstraction layer yourself, that's the beauty of open source!" for several hours, she finally got the program to run. Jessica's smile returned once it was running. She always picked up languages fast, and was told this series was great for self-paced learners. Her smile turned quickly to a frown when it would not pick up input from her headset. And so it was back to searching and the forums…

Deep into her fifteenth attempt to change the sound driver system, she was brought out of her battle by a kiss to her cheek from her beautiful boyfriend, who now whispered into her ear., "Were you listening to anything I just said?"

Jessica turned to face him and deadpanned, "Well, that's an odd way to start a conversation."

Nick rolled his eye, "I was just telling you that I finished that damn bug sweeping job for Mr. Martin."
Jessica tilted her head, "You mean the paranoid dwarf who thinks Bill Clinton is eavesdropping on his conversations about lizard people hiding amongst us?"
Nick shook his head, smiling, "V was a great series but damn, it's not my job to judge my clients' sanity, it's my job to do what they ask for. So what are you up to, my alluring arthropod?"

"Well, I thought it might be nice to learn Japanese for you, but I can't get this stupid thing to WORK!" Jessica said with clear annoyance.
Nick looked at the screen, "Ah! I see the problem right away! You're someone with a sex life who is trying to use Linux. Just put the recovery disc in and go back to the way things were."
"Weren't you the guy who talked for an hour and a half about how much more secure and versatile Linux is?"
Nick grinned lopsidedly, "Oh, yeah and I'll never stop using it but I have a dual boot configuration."
Jessica took a deep breath and exhaled, "Oh god, dual booting. Has it gotten better since I was a kid?"
Nick nodded, "Yeah, so long as you install Windows first it's pretty idiot proof."

"Well, time to get it ON!" Jessica said as she started digging around in her messy computer stuff drawer, "I know I've got the cd key for it around here somewhere."
"Hey, Jess? How about we order some Chinese and watch a movie?"
Jessica waved him off, "I am determined to get this going, Prettyboy. I'll just eat whatever you order. Let me do this"

The next morning, Nick shook his head as he watched Jessica get up and walk over to the coffee pot for the third time in the last 45 minutes. He was about to say something snarky to her about it. Perhaps suggesting she just drink out of the pot itself, but he decided instead to just enjoy Jessica for a moment. She turned away, with a fresh cup, and her hair slipped just a bit past her shoulders as she leaned her head down to make sure she poured the right amount of hazelnut creamer and sugar in. When she looked up at Nick, her viridian eyes locked a moment on his.

There it was again, that little shock that rippled over his body when he occasionally noticed how beautiful she was. Even tired and hung over from where her late night battle with the computer started becoming fueled by energy drinks mixed with vodka. She won the battle, but at the cost of this miserable morning. The thing was Nick found her, if anything, even more beautiful in moments like this; moments when she just was not paying attention to anything superficial. She had not bothered to put on what little makeup she wore day to day, or even combed her hair. She was in a grey pair of leggings and his Defender T-shirt like it was a dress over the tights.

Jessica caught his extended gaze over her, and touched her hair, "Yeah, yeah, I look like crap right now."
Nick shook his head, "You look amazing."
Jessica poked him, "You like seeing me in pain or something, Prettyboy? You're just trying to piss me off, aren't you?"

Nick grinned lopsidedly, "Those flashing eyes, those flushed cheeks, those trembling lips. You know something, Princess? You are UGLY when you're angry."
Jessica punched his shoulder, "DORK!"
Raoul had to join in the fun, "That's it... you and your dog are-"

"Please, please. Total humans, droids, if I may," the grey-haired dwarven man said, "You are in a judge's chambers, so how about you show some tiny little speck of decorum?"

Nick leaned back a bit, unsure if he had just been chastised. Judge Steinbeck closed the folder and looked over those in front of him. "So, I've looked over all the evidence and speculation you've presented me with and I just want to make sure we are extremely clear on this."

All three stood quietly. Nick's left ear flickered. When the judge felt they had calmed enough to make no more snarky remarks, he spoke softly, "You are asking me for a warrant to go into Brookfield Zoo, detain the entire staff for Skinstealer identification, and arrest a BUFFALO?"

"A... bison, Your Honor. Buffalo is just a mistaken term and-" Nick was silenced by the judge's withering glare a moment, and changed his tack, "Yes, Your Honor."

The judge looked irritated, "This scenario you've laid out before me is so unbelievable and idiotic even Tarantino would call it contrived. You're telling me that a hunch led you to talk to a Native American mystic, which led you to talk to a wolf, and that incited you to look at the crew around a buffalo..." he looked at Nick, eyes daring him to speak up about that again, "upon which time Officer Dombrowski here was able to identify this buffalo because, direct quote here, 'I recognize Merrick's eyes'?"

Raoul spoke up this time, "Yes, Your Honor. That's exactly what is going on here."

The dwarf swiveled his chair to look out the window, "You people are idiots. This is the kind of thing where the first I was hearing of this should have been that this buffalo was killed during a shootout of some sort. Now that you asked me to do this officially and I say no, Internal Affairs is going to know RIGHT where to look. I need to think how to handle this, because if you're right..."

Jessica took a step forward, "If we're right, then a whole lot of people, myself included, get closure. Remember that I was the first one they took. I was the first one they replaced. They took blood from me every night to use me as the vector to take so many others. Eventually Merrick took delight in telling me everything my doppleganger was achieving for him. Then he took delight in raping me to get those needed samples while telling me that it was so much better than essentially hanging on a wall being a blood bank. I started to believe him after a while. When I was rescued, that fucked me up, bad. So I have a very personal reason to want him."

She finished her coffee with two gulps, and looked at the judge as he turned back, "But here's the thing: I got to come back. Hundreds didn't, because Merrick decided that once a member was outed, they were useless to him.

Those people lost their wives, their husbands, their fathers and their children. And you know what else? They lost their loved ones in a way most people will never understand, because some of them... some of the Skinstealers chose to stay with their new families until the two days passed and they lost the ability to BE that person anymore. Some of them developed enough free will to truly love their partners... I know because my replacement got married, had a DAUGHTER with him, and then begged me to try to take her place."

Jessica put her hands palm down onto the judge's desk with a thump, "These people were told there was never any chance they would get justice, due to Merrick's nature. If we're right, we can bring justice to these people. Yes, I personally also get my revenge. It's not just my revenge, though. It's also for that man who lost a wife that looked like me, and their daughter who will never know her mother, only some lady who looks a lot like her. You have to see your way into helping, Your Honor."

The judge turned back to face them. "But what if you're wrong? What if all we do is end up looking like a pack of goddamned idiots by bringing a dumb zoo animal into custody?"

Nick touched Jessica's shoulder, "Yeah, and when you lay out the scenario like you did above, it sounds totally preposterous. You know what would sound equally preposterous to a judge in 1940? That one day a dwarf wearing the same robes would be standing in front of a literal Hellspawn, a Dryad, and a whatever-the-hell I am being asked seriously about a bison that was the hive queen of a race known for just... the worst kinds of atrocities. Look at the world around you, Your Honor. The world itself is likely heading to even more preposterous places, and sometimes you just have to take a chance on things to keep pace with the very real fact that we live in a preposterous world."

Steinbeck pondered for a few moments more, tugging on his beard, before nodding, "Okay, I'll give you your warrant, but you're doing this my way. I want you in there when there's no visitors and very minimal crew. Furthermore, you're going to do this when nobody is likely to be paying attention."

The three nodded, and the judge continued, "You're doing this Christmas Eve after the Zoo closes. You're bringing the SWAT team, and a full complement of foot patrol with you. I want this as controlled as possible. You folks work out the specifics but I want no chance for fuckups. Furthermore, you're not risking innocent lives. Once you're ready to enter the zoo, you will call security and warn them what is going down."

Nick tilted his head, "Your honor, that... could be bad. They'll fight."

The dwarf was now smiling, "The Skinstealers will fight. The humans will not. It'll be a fast way to sort out the innocent, as well as prove out your theory about this particular buffalo."

Raoul spoke, "He's right, you know. This will force Merrick into revealing who his agents are."

"Okay," Nick countered, "But what about the good men and women we could lose in this fight? I wish you'd just let us go in and handle it."

"Do you want your warrant or not?" the dwarf thundered, standing up. "We do this my way, or we don't do this at all!" The judge sat back down and took a few breaths, calming himself. "Make it a volunteer duty, only people who feel like Officer Dombrowski. Keep it top secret and make sure everyone who learns about it is not actually a 'Stealer. The best of both worlds. I get enough people to keep it as safe as possible, and you get your man. Your buffalo. Bison, whatever."

He signed the warrant and slid it over, "Now get the hell out of my office!"

As soon as they got outside, Jessica spoke up, "Okay. So we have to keep Merrick off balance until Christmas Eve. I've got a few ideas…"

Chapter Nineteen:
- "Broken", Seether ft. Amy Lee

Jessica held in her right hand a wreath, and in her left a wrapped present. Inside it was a small thing, an Iron Man action figure. She understood that every time Nick visited Bronswood he brought his son a new toy and she felt it would be right to do the same thing. She had never met the boy, but knew she would have loved him. How could she not? She loved his father more than she imagined she ever could love a man. That was what Jessica was really here about, her love for that man. She wanted to see the final resting place of Nick's first wife.

She stopped walking and realized how she had formed that thought to herself. First wife. She had not even verbalized the thought to Nick, but she was already seeing herself in a place that Akiko would become known as his "first wife". Nodding to nobody in particular, she continued to go deeper into Bronswood cemetery. It really was that simple. If they survived the upcoming fight she wanted this man in her life forever; it was as simple as that. Her mother's words kept coming back to her, over the years Marion had always told Jessica that, as a Dryad, she would know right away. She chalked it up to the fact that most adults had an overly romanticized view of their past, now she knew it to be true.

She hoped Nick was ready. Their courtship had not been very long, so he might say no. If he wasn't ready she would understand, but at least her thoughts on the matter would be out there. They had both endured incredible amounts of pain in their lives, pain that had caused them to shut down and become parodies of their former selves. It was true that Nick had some support and life in the form of Brian, as Jessica had in Raoul, but missing from their lives was someone they could be totally unafraid to show every part of themselves to. Jessica moreso was in the depths until she met him.

She stopped this line of thought through force of will; Nick was not her salvation, that's not a healthy thought. Dr. Thorne told Jessica it wasn't right to think that way, and she was probably right. She could not deny that she felt safe around him. He was not just the man she loved, he was also her best friend. She laughed at his cheesy jokes, and he loved her clever snark. They had seen each other's darkest sides and shrugged it off, so this was just... Jessica felt that if Nick didn't marry her, he was only delaying the inevitable. She would state that openly to him when she proposed to him.

She was shaken out of these thoughts brutally. As soon as she turned the aisle to where Nick's wife and child were laid to rest she saw the mess of dirt all over the ground. The cold gnawing at her breastbone told Jessica before she got there to confirm it with her eyes. The graves had been dug up, the caskets opened. A cursory glimpse showed her that the bodies had been removed as well. She took out her cell phone and looked up the number for the Hinsdale police department, keeping an eye out for anyone else in the area.

A female voice answered, "Hinsdale Police. How may I direct your call?"
"This is Detective Jessica Dombrowski, Chicago PD. There's been two bodies exhumed and removed from Bronswood Cemetery."
"10-4, detective. I'll send units over immediately," the dispatcher responded.

"Thank you. I'll secure the area while you're on the way." Jessica unzipped her jacket with one hand, "Not trying to step on any toes but… these corpses are my boyfriend's wife and son, so I'm a little interested in working this case. That and I've already got a pretty damn solid theory. Thanks."

The dispatcher came back before she could hang up. "Detective Dombrowski? We'll need a physical description of you so the officers don't mistake you for a suspect." Jessica shook her head, "Right, right. I'm 5 foot 10 with shoulderblade-length wavy.,. curly… something black hair. I'm in a zip up denim jacket that's nowhere near warm enough for the weather, and I'll clip my badge to my outer pocket. Gotta go in case there are suspects around."

Jessica withdrew her revolver from the shoulder holster and took a closer look at the area; given the tracks in the area it was obviously Skinstealers. Furthermore, there were shoe prints as well, coming away from the groundskeeper's shack to this spot, and then returning to it. Not even a cursory effort had been made by the grave robbers to hide their trail. Jessica shook her head and followed the tracks back to the shack.

There were many sets of prints heading to the grave, but only one towards the shack from whatever vehicle they had gotten out of. That meant whoever got out of the vehicle had left the shack to check on the grave work, and then had returned to the shack, staying there. The heat wavering out of the ventilation pipe atop the shack told Jessica that the little building was presently occupied. She pulled the little orange earplugs out of her inner jacket pocket, rolled them a bit, and put them in.

Jessica came up as slowly as possible, staying out of sight of the window. Before she got up to the door she pulled the hammer back on the revolver. No sense in wasting that split second. The door was a cheap wooden number, on an even cheaper wood frame. She judged that one kick right underneath the knob would be more than enough to break the latch out of the frame and open the door.

And she was correct. The door banged open easily. Jessica lost a little time recovering from the follow through, but she still managed to line up into a shooter's stance… and fire three rounds into Merrick before he could utter a single sound. Merrick had been leaning back in a chair, his foot up against the shack's table. He was trying to look relaxed. Merrick glared at her and drew breath to speak.

Jessica took three steps forward and stepped on his throat, cutting off his ability to deliver whatever stupid dialogue he had in mind. With sheer contempt in her eyes, she leaned down and aimed the revolver at Merrick's right eye. "I'm not interested in anything you have to say, shitheel. We're coming for you, did you know that? We're going into the sewers connected to your house. We'll find you. You'll have left eggs or something somewhere. Go ahead and try to pull out, it won't matter. Nick and I will track you. We will find you, and you will die." Jessica adjusted the weapon just a bit to the left and then pulled the trigger.

Sickened as always by the smell of burnt gunpowder, she went outside to await the arrival of the Hinsdale PD; sparing Merrick not a single glance more.

An hour later, Nick had returned by train and then raced over in his Judge. Jessica could hear the engine a good fifteen seconds before his actual arrival, and went out to the parking lot to meet him. Nick parked the car and got out, "Jess, I got here as fast as I could, what's…" he looked around at all the police cars and news media, "..what's going on?"

Jessica came in and gave Nick the best kiss she could possibly muster; her arms up around his neck. Her tongue came out and gently prodded at Nick's lips, and he opened them obligingly. She held the kiss, tilting her head slightly to get as close to him as she could, her body similarly close. When the kiss was done, she held onto him while he held her, looking him directly in the eye. "I love you, Prettyboy. A lot. I'm here." She let go of the embrace and took his hand, leading him to the grave. Nick tilted his head; Jessica rarely wanted to hold hands. This was serious.

Upon seeing the scene from a distance, Nick instinctively surged forwards, but a gentle squeeze from Jessica's hand slowed him.

Nick walked up to the scene. One of the officers addressed him, "Mr. Sakamoto? We'll find the-" he stopped when Jessica waved her hand at him. Nick stood unmoving except for his eye sweeping the scene. His jaw set after a short bit and he turned to leave. He did not let Jessica's hand go, "Merrick?"
Jessica nodded, Yeah, Prettyboy. He was waiting in the shack over yonder to gloat, I assume. I didn't give him a chance. I shot him down, told him we were going to search the sewers for him and kill him."
Nick's expression remained flat, "Misdirection. Good."

Nick walked her right past her car, and towards the Judge. Jessica let out a breath, she was afraid he'd want to be alone right now. She would have quietly let him go, of course, but she was happy that he didn't want to retreat entirely into himself. Nick did not come around to open the door for her, but he did lean across to unlock the passenger side. Jessica got in and was not at all surprised how Nick was already pulling out before she even got the door shut. Nick reversed it and pulled the wheel hard, spinning the car to face out of the parking lot.

Nick sat a moment, staring at nothing and letting the engine idle. His body trembled a bit with the barely contained rage. The Judge seemed to growl in his stead as Nick seethed. "We're going to hurt him. Bad." Jessica said nothing. Nick already knew how she felt about this matter, and all the latest of Merrick's many atrocities would do is harden her resolve to end Merrick once and for all. Nick raised up his fist and half punched at the dashboard and snarled audibly. The clenched fist went instead to the gearshift. They were into first for only an instant as Nick went out onto the road with a light squeal of the tires. Every shift after caused another slip, Nick was craving all the speed he could get, the car itself seemed to bristle angrily at the tight spaces the suburban roads offered it. .

When they got out onto 294, Nick could eat up the pavement and spit out the miles with everything the Judge had to offer. Since this particular Judge was equipped with a Ram Air V and aggressively tuned by a damn fine mechanic, that was a lot. It wasn't long before they were racing along at 130 miles per hour. The heavy body and wide tires gave Nick the stability to stay on the road at a speed during which Jessica's own Celica (itself no old lady cruiser) would have had dangerously low traction. They slalomed through traffic on the interstate until they were out at Northbrook. Jessica knew this was a very serious situation, but could not help just a little surge of desire. It was cliche as hell, yet there really was something overwhelming, primal, about a man controlling all that power with such ease.

Nick slowed down and brought them off and around to going back the other way. Jessica could almost hear the Judge spitting defiantly at Nick bringing it back under sane control.

Nick finally spoke, "How many people do we have in on this?"

"13 SWAT, four detectives, 10 regular patrol boys, and two National Guardsmen. I'm hoping we can lure some more foot patrol in to at LEAST help us cover the rest of the Zoo," Jessica answered, watching the scenery go by. "Also Brian I assume."

Nick made a scoff, "Of course Brian is coming. He's been itching to bust some heads ever since I explained what Merrick did to you. Do we really have to give him the warning?"

"Yes," Jessica said, "we really do. Not everyone there is going to be with Merrick, Prettyboy. Some are bound to just be normal staff members."

"Fine," Nick said, "But we really need to move fast to get him. And I will hurt him. For you, for me, for everyone that he took the joy away from. What the hell was he thinking, anyway? That this would break me?"

Jessica had to laugh, "Merrick is a lot of things, but how to deal with other men is a skill he never learned."

Jessica glanced at the clock, "Hey, do you know how to get to the Chicagoland Speedway up in Joliet?"

Nick glanced over, "I've been there a few times, why?"

Jessica lit up a smoke and cracked the window, "The kickass driving you just did got me thinking... Merrick likes to run the obstacle trials every Saturday in his Continental GT 3."

Nick pursed his lips, "What do you want me to do about that? He'd kick my ass. This car isn't built for tight corners at speed, never mind the fact that his engine is more powerful by like two hundred horsepower."

"Firstly," Jessica said, "it's more like 80 horsepower. Secondly, that's not what I had in mind at all. Though it would be fun to see. You showed me you can write and make blood appear on surfaces, right?"

Nick flickered his left ear, "Yeah, and to anticipate your next question; it's entirely possible for me to give him a message while he drives. I doubt he'll spook that easy though."

Jessica took one of the Dog and Spider Private Investigations cards Nick had given her. She took her pen to it furiously for several seconds. Satisfied with her work, she showed the card to Nick. "Can you give him this message?"
Nick saw the card and barked out a very genuine laugh, "Holy shit, that's genius! Yes, I can do that."

Jessica had covered the entire card back with ink to form a solid block.

Chapter Twenty:
- "Can't Fight This Feeling", REO Speedwagon

Jessica had been dreaming. It was an unusual dream, but not a bad one. They were students at a high school in Japan, and she was some sort of assassin for a revolutionary movement. Her mother was one of the leads of it, and her entire life had been controlled by that organization. Jessica had been sent to that school to kill Nick, and had failed in a ridiculous manner. Her mother later found out that her current boyfriend had literally been assigned to her by the organization and despised her.

Over the course of the dream, her mother had formed a splinter group and her life began to change. For basically her entire childhood her mother had been giving her orders, do this job, kill that person. Almost every day now her mother gave her a different order, "Go be a kid." As time went on, she first befriended and then eventually fell in love with Nick.

That was when she smelled it. Hazelnut coffee. No dream could possibly stand up against the reality of Nick's various takes on hazelnut coffee. She sprang up, not even bothering to put any more clothing on than her "ASK ME ABOUT MY FEMINIST AGENDA" T-shirt and headed down the stairs. The persistent beat of "Do They Know It's Christmas?" caused her to strut the last few steps down the stairs and towards the kitchen. Nick was singing along with the song as he worked on three different pans at once; Nick was preparing french toast on two pans and bacon on one. As Jessica came in, Nick had just flipped some bacon up in the air twice, and then over to their cat, who pounced on it and batted it a few times to cool it faster before gobbling the bacon up.

Nick turned and grinned lopsidedly, "See, Atton came in and his expression was all 'You have swine! I smell it!' so I had to feed him."

Jessica ignored her man utterly. On the table, glowing with a holy light all it's own, was what she had been smelling. Nick had made her a 24 ounce beer mug of hazelnut latte, topped with whipped cream and Christmas sprinkles. "See now THAT'S how you tell a Dryad you truly love her."

Nick snorted, "By ruining coffee? Mommy's insane, isn't she, Atton?" Jessica showed him her middle finger, which was starkly pale in contrast to the black nail polish she wore. It was Sinful Colors Black on Black. One thing Jessica learned ever since she started this girly shit was that given her active lifestyle, pretty much every brand craps out at the same time, so why spend a fortune? Nick rolled his eye. Atton's tail swished and he mewed gently. "See? Atton agrees with me"
Jessica tapped her fingers on the table, "Please, he knows the truth. He's just trying to grift you for more bacon."

Nick plated the food for them and sat down at the table, "So, here's my tentative plan for the day. I was thinking we'd go back upstairs, eat our breakfast in bed while we watch Rudolph. Then I'll give you a footrub, and we'll watch the Futurama X-mas specials. After that, we maybe play some Atari, have a pizza I'll make, watch some of the South Park Christmas episodes cuddling on the couch, and then a fast snack before we go fuck Merrick right up?"

Jessica munched happily on some bacon, and then her expression flattened a bit. She felt a gnawing, almost empty sensation under her ribs. Was this the right time? Would he go for it? She wasn't sure she could handle rejection right now. It made sense for her to be all casual about it, so if he reacted negatively she could play it off as a joke. "Sounds fun, but when are we going to fit a visit to the Office of the City Clerk in?"
Nick blinked and thought a bit. His left ear flickered, "I'm... I don't... why would we go there?"

Jessica took a big swig from her coffee and then spread butter on her french toast, "Where the hell else do you get a wedding license from, jackass?" Her voice was light and casual, but inside she was yearning to know his reaction as fast as possible. Too long and she'd lose her cool, do something silly like get down on one knee.

"Doo Wop Christmas" by Kenny Vance and the Planotones began on the sound system just then. Nick dropped his fork, "I... Jess?"
Jessica gave him that smile she had only for him, "Yeah, Prettyboy?"

Nick's face carried an expression Jessica just could not read. Was he about to laugh at her? He spoke, "Marriage... you... you want to marry me?" Jessica lifted her coffee again and took a big drink. She'd have cream on her upper lip from the angle but she did not want Nick to see her eyes right now. She nodded and took another swallow. He was quiet too long for her to fake this anymore, so she lowered her mug. His eyepatch looked a bit moist, and his good eye had the tracks of tears going down his cheekbone. His expression was one of wonder and joy. "Please say you're not joking. I... can't imagine anything that could possibly be better than to marry you on Christmas Eve! How do you do it in this country? Can we book a priest?"

Jessica gave him that smile again, trying to calm her heart and keep the red from rising up in her cheeks, "Well, we go show our IDs, get the license, and then get it turned in. If we go now, we can probably have an impromptu ceremony, then get it and my name change form back in before they close. We need two witnesses to sign the form also."

Nick exhaled. He was trying to look cool, but his tail was wagging madly. "Okay, uhm. I'm thinking Brian and... Raoul?"
Jessica shook her head, "Gotta be US citizens. I mean Brian can be the best man, but we need US citizens. My mom and Raoul?"
Nick, still trying to look detached and disinterested, swiped his smartphone alive, "I'll call Brian."

Jessica coughed, and her breath came out in a visible puff. The heat had not been on in the restrooms of the court, but where else could she get dressed and ensure her man did not see her? Her man was not just enough anymore... he was about to be her husband.

Feeling foolish in so many petticoats she turned and looked into the mirror. The hem of the dress hovered just above the floor, her black-painted toenails with the red hourglass on each big toe just barely visible.

The dress was made of a very light brown satin, with an overlay of cream colored organza that appeared to be floating over the satin. The skirt was flared and softly pleated to create waves of fabric. The bottom of the dress was adorned with fake leaves and almost flower-like black spider webs which crept up the dress like vines, as though she were rising out of the very earth itself. Something magical, some nature spirit of those dumbass legends. She laughed a moment audibly. As Brian might say, what the hell was she on about? Not "like" some nature spirit. She was a literal nature spirit. Jessica Dombrowski... soon to be Sakamoto... was a Dryad.

As she slowly turned she saw the skirt billowing out behind her, the pleats gradually smoothing out into a train, more leaves and flower-webs clung to the fabric. The back of the dress was low cut and cinched by a black ribbon crisscrossing down her back. The leaves trailed up and across the shoulders, clinging to the satin and organza which draped just barely off the shoulders. Slowly she turned again, the front of the bodice coming into view. It had a sweetheart neckline and the organza was held tightly to the satin.

The boning in the bodice was sturdy, and for the time being, comfortable. Her mother told her that she was lucky she wouldn't be wearing it long, a full length wedding would have caused her to have sweat clinging to her and the boning would have left marks on her skin by the end. It would have been worth it, though. Would that she could have this figure for all time, and without the use of shaping tools, but even a Dryad could get fat.

She felt sexy and beautiful, confident and amazed. Until she realized other people would be seeing her in this dress. She longed to tear it off and hide under her regular clothes. They were safe, they drew no attention unless she intentionally sought it. When she sought it, she could make a potato sack look sexy.

Tears started to form in her eyes as she gazed at herself. She seemed so out of place and yet she wanted to be beautiful, but she was so awkward, who could think she belonged in a dress like that? She was too plain, too ordinary. Too... dirty. Good enough for a one night stand, but not until death do us part, as they say.

What would Nick think? Would he find it funny she dressed up so much? Would he like it? Would he feel underdressed? What was he even wearing? Would she be able to walk in this?

As Jessica gazed upon herself again, she realized it was perfect. It was everything she could have ever wanted for a wedding dress; the dress was not wrong. Marring the picture was the fact that she was the one wearing it. That ruined the effect it gave. Gingerly she fingered the adornments, slowly warming to the idea of wearing this.

She wanted to wear it. She wanted to never take it off. She shook her head, trying to negate her own thoughts. There's no way in hell she could take Merrick on wearing this. Could she put it back on afterwards? No, that was incredibly stupid.

Belatedly, she realized her mother was standing close, a simple felt box in her hand. Jessica watched as the box was opened and a jeweled hair piece was removed from it. "This was mine, sweetie. I just had it fixed up for you. Didn't have time to find anything blue for you."

Jessica's chest heaved twice, she was about to sob. It took a Herculean effort to stop herself from bawling like a baby. "Have you SEEN the toys and life you gave me as I grew up, Mom? I may not have realized it at the time, but you offered me a princess' life. My very BLOOD is blue."

The headpiece sat on her head like a veil, though there was no fabric on it. The front was a simple band, the back a spider web. Just like that the tears pricking her eyes became ones of happiness. "This is a thing, isn't it?"

Marion Dombrowski could not help but throw her arms about her beloved child from behind, "It really, really is, kiddo. And very nice of Judge Steinbeck to volunteer his courtroom for this, considering how much he hates me." "Well," Jessica said with a light head shake, "He has an ulterior motive. He can make sure that Nick and I go after Merrick the way he wants us to now… he's already collected everyone that volunteered."

Marion smiled wanly, and Jessica could see that in the mirror, "I'm coming along for this ride also, sweetie. I brought my own weapon so you don't have to worry about me."

Jessica shook her head, "No way, Mom. Too many cops hate you."
Marion smiled, "I'll be providing sniper support and taking care of another project, sweetie. Your father taught me how, and made sure I always practiced. They won't even know who is doing the work."
Jessica shook her head, "This is my life. Get married, go kill a scumbag while my mother gives overwatch."

Marion tapped her head, a thing she had done when Jessica was a child. She would do that when she wanted the young Jessica to stand up straight and look presentable. Jessica found herself responding to that by instinct pushing her shoulders back and raising her chin lightly. Jessica then rolled her eyes. "Alright, let's go."

Marion held her daughter's arm a moment, "You look beautiful, sweetie. I'm going out with the Best Man, though."
Jessica grinned lightly, "Wait, if he's the Best Man, then why am I marrying Nick?"
Jessica's mother lowered her head and shook it, "I don't suppose you honored the fast, did you?"
"Fast?" Jessica asked.
"Oy, sweetie," Marion said. Her voice was playing up the Jewish Mother stereotype. "Judge Steinbeck is also a rabbi. He will be very disappointed in you, I bet you didn't observe kabbalat panim?"

"The what now?"
"You call this a kiddushin? I bet you didn't even set up a chuppah, did you? Oy, some kallah you are."

Jessica exhaled, "This is the part where I smile, nod, and say something about Hanukkah, right, Mom?"
Marion adjusted Jessica's collar line, "Do you even know what the meaning of Hanukkah is?"
Jessica looked deep in thought, and then held up her finger in recognition, "I know! They show these symbols on TV every year. That candle thing, a dreidel, a big fuckin' nose and a yarmulke, right?"
Marion shook her head, laughing now.

Jessica continued, "That's how we know that it's time for the Jewish winter holiday! You know the one, where instead of putting lights on a tree and sticking good presents under said tree we light candles and get a shitty one every night for like a week?"
Marion punched her daughter on the shoulder, "Smart ass!"
Jessica blinked, realizing that was a mannerism she used on Nick also. She gave her mom a genuine smile, "the apple doesn't fall far from the tree."
Just then came a knock on the door, "Come on Mrs. Dombrowski, it's time to get this show on the road."

Marion gave Jessica a kiss on the forehead, "Stop fidgeting, Sweetie. You look amazing. You'll blow his mind." She then stuck her head out, meeting Brian's eyes, "Okay, let's do this."

The courtroom was not decorated in any specific way, although there was gentle music playing over the PA. All in all this was not a terrible place to hold a wedding; since it had an aisle to walk up and they could stand in front of the judge's desk in front of everyone.

The string quartet Marion had hired was in the jury box. Nick only had Noriko and Satine on his "side" of the ceremony, so the police, firemen and paramedics who chose to attend were spread out on both sides. It was a bit unusual in that they were all in uniform… with their equipment ready to go, but what about this courtship had been normal at all?

Marion and Brian walked arm in arm, and Brian leaned over to whisper… Marion shook her head, "Jessica warned me about you. No, I'm not interested in sleeping with you and your wife."
"Aww," Brian said, comically looking sad as they parted to stand on their respective sides of the courtroom.

Nick stepped into the courtroom now from the men's room, and drew a little murmuring and turned heads. He was wearing his old black wedding kimono from when he was first joined with Akiko. His sword was sheathed at his waist, and the insignia of the Saotome clan was embroidered on the back. He began to second-guess his choice of wedding attire, wishing he had not listened to Brian's suggestion. He took his position, nodding at Brian and Judge Steinbeck and tried his best to look stoic, though his tail was twitching nervously.

The courtroom door came open and Raoul, wearing a full and proper wedding tuxedo that matched Brian's, held the door open. The quartet began playing the finale from Handel's Water Suite, and Jessica came around the corner into view. Nick's attempt at stoicism fell apart upon the sight of Jessica. She looked like something supernatural as she was led by Raoul down the aisle. Raoul took measured steps as tradition would demand, but Jessica? She seemed to glide down the aisle like leaves carried along the surface of a flowing river. Her hair was held in place by the headpiece, tamed back and tight except for two wavy strands that hung down in front of her ears. That was a Japanese wedding hairstyle, and it pushed a lot of Nick's uncertainties about his own mode of dress away.

"Close your mouth, mate," Brian whispered.
Belatedly, Nick did so. When she reached the altar, Officer Traficant cheered a bit. Steinbeck's glare silenced the other dwarf, and then the judge spoke.

"Ladies and gentlemen, thanks for coming today. Today we are gathered here for two purposes, one important to the city, the other important to the world in general. Love is something that's in short supply in this world. The world is a changing place. I'm evidence of that. Before World War 2, the existence of the other races existing was ridiculous nonsense. Magic is being reborn. The problem is that these changes in the world threaten to drive us apart. I'm not going to waste your time quoting a Beatles song, but they are correct. All you need is love. And so we are here to celebrate the joining of these two in the sacred bonds of marriage. Step forward and speak your piece, kids."

Nick stepped forward, leading Jessica by her hand. When she was with him, Nick took her other hand, "Jessica, I'm not gonna call this a storybook romance. We are not great people. I mean… the first time I saw you, you were just popping up after blowing a guy under the table at the bar, and I was dealing with a hangover that I'd gotten from drinking until 7 am by… going to the bar for more drinks. For me it got to be something of a pleasure to see you there, eventually I wanted to get the courage to speak to you. And I know you noticed me looking. You ran a background check and even had other cops look into my life, see if I was gonna be a creepy stalker. And who knows? With enough booze I might have convinced myself that was the way to go… but you were already making me a better person by accident. I found myself drinking in your beauty more, and drinking well… the booze less."

Jessica blushed a bit, and whispered, "You didn't have to tell them I was blowing a guy, you jerk."

Nick smirked and continued, "And I know when you took me home, you were mostly doing it to fuck me and help me get it out of my system."

"Well," Jessica said, squeezing his hands, "to be perfectly fair, it also helped that Lori used to brag about how good you were in the sack and how none of us could land a guy like you."

Nick squeezed her hands back, "And that night turned out way different than either of us thought. Ever since then, it seems like color came back into the world. I'd been going through the motions, loving for just the shortest instants. Fucking whoever I could to give myself flashes of light before moving onto the next dull task in an increasingly gray world. Then you came into my life, no more flashes of light; it's just... a much brighter place. To... probably mangle a quote from one of my favorite shows.. Everything I do is more fun when you're doing it with me. Even time spent without you is more relaxing. It's not just that I need you in my life, Jessica, I mean. No, let me walk that back a little bit. I spent years of my life looking for someone to come along and save me. Someone to give me a reason to live again. And then I met you, and I realized something important: I never needed anyone to save me, some magical princess to hold in esteem above me. All I needed was someone to walk the path of life with. To be strong where I am weak, that I may let myself admit those weaknesses. That I can do the same for her. We both have a lot of pain in our pasts, and a lot to work through, but we're taking that walk together now. They say that everyone is looking for their 'happily ever after'. I know I was too. But when I look into your eyes..."

Nick leaned in just a bit, gazing at those viridian pools, "I see forever. I see lazy Sundays, I see exciting adventures. I see terrible fights, I see amazing holidays... I see years with nothing to even mark the passage of time except for a calendar. I see there's pain yet to come and joys I can't even yet conceive of. I see children, I see the lives we will build, helping each other along the path.

Jessica? I'm not calling this 'happily ever after'. This is more that our real lives begin together today."

Jessica was crying at the end of that, eyes wide, left almost entirely without words. She had come into this intending to tell a few jokes, leading into a discussion of what he meant to her, but found that when she opened her mouth what came out was this:
"You're so pretty. It's not just here, either," Jessica said as she touched his cheek, "It's in here." Jessica ran her hand down his chest, flattening her palm over his heart. "You are the most beautiful soul I've ever known. It's true I don't think a lot of myself. I heard all the stuff you said above and was all 'who the hell is he talking about? Can't be me!' But you are. It's your last chance to run, Prettyboy. If you do... it won't break me. You showed me that life doesn't have to suck. You made me a better person. I may have been the town bike but..." she blushed again, "You see so much more in me than I thought I ever would. But I see it now. My world won't be destroyed. I'll mourn the loss of all those things you talked about, but I will go on. I want all those things you talked about, Prettyboy. And now that I found you, I think I get to have them. What's it gonna be?"

Nick turned to Judge Steinbeck, "It's gonna be man and wife is what it's gonna be."
Steinbeck's expression was one of joy, "Do you have the rings?"
Nick nodded, as did Jessica.
"Then place the rings on each other's fingers and say 'With this ring, I thee wed'."

Jessica held her hand up, and Nick slid the cobalt gold ring onto her hand, "With this ring, I thee wed."
Jessica closed her eyes a moment, took a deep breath, and did the same for Nick; his ring a matching black cobalt. "With this ring, Prettyboy, I thee wed."

Judge Steinbeck smiled, "With the authority vested in me by the State of Illinois, I now declare you man and wife. You may now break the glass, and kiss your bride."

Marion set down the glass, bagged up in a purple velvet sack, "This can symbolize a lot of things but... I prefer to think of it like this. When God made the two of you, he made you a single soul. He then split that soul in half, so you two could become ready for the day that you were brought back together. Now, Jessica, I know you don't believe in God; and Nick... I know you're something else; but I believe this with every fiber of my being: the two of you were meant to be together. Let this symbolize the barriers between the two of you finally being broken down."

Nick grinned at Jessica, and as he raised his foot; so did she. They stomped on the glass together. Nick raised her hand high, and with his other hand placed at her hip, spun Jessica a full turn and a half before he dipped his bride for a kiss. She punched his shoulder and attempted to say "Dork!" before he muffled her with his kiss.

"Okay, people," Officer Traficant said, "I hate to cut this short, but the zoo closes in 45 minutes, so we need to get a move on." Her mother and her partner stepped forward to sign the marriage license as witnesses, even as Jessica was signing her name change form.

Marion Dombrowski.

Farrokh Bulsara.

Chapter Twenty-One:
- "Awake and Alive", Skillet

At 5:15 the speakers positioned all across Brookfield Zoo blared to life. "Attention Zoo staff. This is the Chicago Police Department. We have every entrance, including sewage linkups, under heavy guard. You are all instructed to lay on the ground and wait with your hands behind your head for an officer to arrive and escort you off the premises. We know a lot of you are Skinstealers. We will be checking everyone we take in. Anyone who is even STANDING will be taken down with appropriate force, and if anything that even resembles a weapon is in your hands… you will be taken down with appropriate force. You've been warned. Officers are on the move in thirty seconds."

The speakers clicked off a moment, and then came back on "We know where you are, Merrick, you son of a bitch, and we are coming for you. If it didn't rightly belong to Detective Dombrowski I'd mount your fucking head right over my mantle."

Nick Sakamoto pulled the band on his hat a bit tighter to ensure he didn't lose it. His upper set of ears would be a bit raw after this fight; sure. Nick adjusted his holster a bit as well, to make quick draw and reholstering easy. It was entirely likely he'd have to make use of his sword, so he wanted to be able to switch weapons as fast as possible. The sword itself rested on a specialized magnetic pad across his back Cynthia had made him almost six months ago. Such James Bond gadgets have little use in day to day life, but the quick release and return abilities would be useful today. He looked to his right.

What an incredible beauty this woman was. Tonight she wore it in a different way than he had seen it for quite some time. Here it was like it had been that night in her shitty old room at the motel. Her eyes were filled with righteous indignation once again. This time Jessica Dombrowski... Sakamoto, she was Sakamoto now. She had chosen him, taken him as her man forever. He tried to get his train of thought back and failed utterly. What did it matter? He took a deep breath and then let it out, prepared at last to face whatever may come.

Jessica Sakamoto pulled the carbine up to shoulder a few times from its sling position, limbering up and trying to get a bit of last minute practice lining the red dot sight up as fast as humanly possible. Satisfied at last, she let the Hi-Point 4595TS RD carbine fall back into its rest position. She and Nick already had a .45 auto theme going here, so the weapon seemed a perfect fit. Her shoulder holster fit as perfectly as always, the weighty revolver promising her potent backup if needed. Like Nick, she was carrying spare ammunition in every pocket she could find, in addition to the pre loaded magazines and moon clips mounted in easy-to-reach places.

She looked to her left and smiled, a chill going over her that had nothing to do with the weather; it had everything to do with her man. Jessica liked the way his jaw was set, his hat tilted just so; his trenchcoat flapping lightly in the evening winds. She knew how much time her husband spent perfecting this act at work for effect. She supposed that he was probably very aware what an imposing figure he cut right now. Not just that, she knew that the little ego boost it gave him would help in the coming battle. Inside of every man is a little boy who wants the world to know his name, to see him as a hero.

"Let's go!" Traficant yelled. The strike team, comprised mostly of SWAT officers, headed straight for the Great Bear Wilderness, while other officers fanned out from each entrance to secure the rest of the zoo. Raoul fired first, hitting the first Skinstealer who stepped out from behind a rock right between the eyes. The group continued in. "Fan out!" Traficant yelled, "I want groups of three, go around and secure the sides. Lovebirds, go for the bison pen! Delacroix, you're with them! Braddock, if you'd do me the honor? Let's go clear the service tunnels." Brian looked over at Nick, then shrugged, "Probably be a bit more action that way. Let's go, mate. Who dares, wins!"

Raoul nodded, "I suggest we take it slow and steady, we are going to meet the most-" a Skinstealer dressed as a janitor opened a staff only door, carrying a shotgun. Jessica took him down with three shots to the midsection. "Slow and steady my ass!" Jessica said, "We need to move!"
"Jessica's right," Nick said, "Live fire zone. This isn't an arrest and you know it."
Raoul holstered his pistol. His hands and eyes lit with an eerie green fire, "You know what? You're right. It's time to cry havoc and let loose the dogs of war."
Jessica pointed at Nick, "We've only got one"

Nick raised his pistol, aiming down the path leading to the bison. A male and female Skinstealer, proving exactly how intelligent they were not. They were armed with shotguns, and making no attempt to go for cover Nick was fast, but could tell he wouldn't be fast enough to fire first. He threw himself to the ground as the buckshot whipped just barely over his head. He propped his elbows from prone and fired three times, praying the others had gotten out of the way as well. His first round took the female in the kneecap, one went wide, and the third hit her in the heart, a lucky shot. Nick adjusted to fire again, but found it was not needed. A green fireball sailed towards the Skinstealers, igniting the male. It burned to bones in seconds.

Nick looked back, "Holy shit, Raoul, that was awesome!" Jessica dropped to one knee and fired down the path again. A cry and gurgling told Nick he didn't need to check, just get up and keep running. Which he did. "Not too far from the bison pen."
"A thought occurs to me-" Jessica said, snapping off a shot to her left, "Did any of us bring anything big enough to actually kill a bison?"

Nick holstered his empty pistol, and drew his sword, "This thing can cut through-" he stopped talking a moment to stab the blade through the nearby wall of the Bear Crossing gift store. A female voice cried out and trailed off. "-just about anything. Plus you know... gay demon guy with hellfire... launching... hands."
Raoul crossed his arms, "Bisexual. Daemon. The rest of that is pretty accurate."

Jessica looked over as they were running, "Okay, firstly... Nick, I can't believe you heard that Skinstealer, and second... bisexual? I've never even seen you LOOK at a woman."
Raoul grinned a bit, "It has been a few... decades."

A flying leap took Nick down into the bison pen. Jessica was a step behind him, and landed right next to him, carbine out and covering the area. Nick was instinctively covering opposite the way Jessica was. The bison... what ones were awake... looked at the pair, bored. "I'm going to make sure the inevitable ambush doesn't take you off guard," Raoul said.

Jessica scanned the bison for only a moment, then pointed, "There he is." The bison she pointed at snapped his head up and glared directly at Jessica. Jessica dimly heard Raoul fighting, but figured he could take care of himself. "Come on Prettyboy, let's go hunting." Nick was tugging on her sleeve, "Jess?"

Jessica turned to see what Nick was on about. Skinstealers. Lots of them. Dozens of quill throwers. Hundreds of the lesser stealers. Elves. Dwarves. Jessica whirled and shouldered her weapon, peppering Merrick's body with the entire magazine. She did very little damage, and Merrick retreated into the nearby caves. The rest of the bison formed up in front of the cave, an impenetrable wall of fur and muscle. "Son of a BITCH!" Jessica screamed out, "If we coulda dropped Merrick, the rest of this shit wouldn't happen!"

Nick touched her cheek, "He probably won't kill you."

"Oh, yeah, YOU get to die. I have to be his 'queen'."
Nick's left ear flickered, "Good point. Do you want me to kill you?"
Jessica huffed her breath out, "I... I actually think I'd really prefer that, Prettyboy."
"Unless someone or something comes along to save us? Cavalry?" Nick said, hopefully. He looked around as the Skinstealers began their approach.
"Not gonna happen, Prettyboy. Want a last kiss before you do me?"

Nick reloaded his pistol and re-holstered it, working fast to reload his spare magazines, "Honestly, Jess? I think I'd rather go down fighting."
"Fuck it," Jessica said, doing the same thing with her carbine, "Try to take me out before you go. I love you."
"I love you, Jess. Are there a lot of black widows around?"
"What? Why?" Jessica asked.
"Because I thought it might be kinda fitting if we die to black widow venom after we go down fighting?"
"Great idea Prettyboy!" Jessica said, adjusting the red dot sight, "all we need is 40 bites each and about 12 hours to figure out if it will kill us or not."
Nick's left ear flickered "Have I mentioned I love you when you're snarky? Hit it!"

The newlyweds approached the crowd at a fast walk, firing liberally first at the quill throwers. The Skinstealers were absorbing the casualties happily with no response other than jeers. "Looks like they're going to do this the old fashioned way, my arachnid Aphrodite."
Jessica rammed a new mag in and racked the slide, "Wanna try to run?" she asked.

Nick's response never came. The loudspeakers blared to life with some electronic music, and Virus surged into the crowd of Skinstealers. In seconds, they had infected several. The Skinstealer formation split apart as they moved to engage the new threat, but the Virus were not to be denied. Their army was growing quickly.

"Is that... the Canadian national anthem?" Nick asked Jessica shook her head in disbelief, "Yes. A techno O Canada." Cynthia, in a new version of her armor, waved at the pair from the edge of the bison pen, "That's right! The mounties are here!"
"Cynthia!" Nick yelled, "How the hell did you do this?"
"Science!" Cynthia yelled. At a whispered command, what appeared to be a quad-barreled rocket launcher came... most of the way up over her shoulder. Cynthia muttered a few curses and smacked the rocket launcher a few times. It finally snapped to place.

"Get down!" Cynthia yelled. Nick covered Jessica with his body as he pulled the both of them down. Nick heard sizzling as the rockets cut through the air at half the speed of sound. Three large explosions followed by one more, and then the scent of cooked bison meat. Nick looked up and back at the cave. Sure enough, Cynthia had wrought unspeakable horror on several dozen members of a threatened species. The polite atrocity had, however, opened a path to Merrick. Nick sprang up, "Move, Jessica, move! He probably has some sort of getaway plan!" Jessica did not need to be told twice.

After they had been running down the cave for thirty seconds, Jessica spoke up her concern, "Prettyboy? We still don't have anything bigger than your sword to handle this."
"He's a bison, Jess. Once we take his legs out we could drown him with urine if we felt like it."
"Sure," Jessica responded, breath huffing out, "But I'd prefer we do it... holy shit!"

They had come into the deep part of the caves, which were well lit. This was the area the caretakers of the Great Bear Wilderness gathered to plan their day and give out assignments. Merrick was butting the double doors at the back, desperately seeking escape. That wasn't what caused Jessica to swear, though. It was the monstrosity that was waiting for them in this area.

Nick immediately thought of Strogg Troopers from Quake Wars. The good news was that the gun arm was replaced by a spinning buzz saw arm. The bad news? A spinning buzzsaw arm would still be pretty damned effective in these tight quarters. Nick held his sword out to Jessica, whispering, "Try to get Merrick before this thing kills me." Jessica was about to fire off a smartass comment, when she got a better look at Merrick's guardian. She nodded slowly as she took the blade, "Good... good luck, Prettyboy."

Nick took off his trench coat and shirt. He turned to face his enemy. The tattoo on his back was that of a white wolf in front of Mount Fuji, baying at the moon. The wolf's eye seemed, to Jessica, to be leaking blackness.

Nick jerked his neck to the left, and his right ear flickered as a light clicking sound was heard. Nick reached into his pockets, drawing forth a pair of fingerless gloves. He dropped his gun belt after pulling them on. His missing eye was showing his own life as being very short right now. His lip curled up in a snarl, revealing his teeth. So be it. If this was to be, at least Jessica would survive to win the day. Her soul's aura was bright, she had years to go. Nick dashed in towards the much larger cybernetic creature.

The beast roared and seemed to look smug. "Yup. You're probably going to smear me into paste. No need to be an asshole about it."
"Prettyboy?" Jessica said, sounding unsure.

"PAPA!" came a small voice, followed by a gentle, melodic female one, "Niko-chan." The black fire in Nick's eye went out as he turned to face the voices. The monstrosity advanced on Jessica, intent on holding her away while Merrick made his escape. Nick's arms fell slack a moment.

His son was running at him, tail wagging madly. It all happened in slow motion for Nick. He crouched down, extending his arms to catch his son. This was his chance to get it all back, wasn't it? Merrick had built these from their corpses, so they would have memories from just before they died. They were almost as good as having his family again. He could make love to his wife once again. Watch his son grow into a man. What was the difference after all? If Jessica's double could bear a child and the stretch marks that came with that, surely his son could grow up?

He looked up and over at the Dryad. Of course he could make love to his wife. She was right over there holding his sword. Nick changed his position to that of a three point stance. Once the false-Kazuo got almost the rest of the way to him, Nick sprang forward. Though he knew these images would haunt him in the nights to come, this had to be done. His gloved hand caught the child Skinstealer by the neck.

He hurled the doppelganger at the monstrosity, and continued his run, regaining the lost momentum. The beast wearing his wife's skin? He could see it's aura fading now. He brought his fist up, ready to strike, when the ersatz Akiko's eyes opened wide. A 45 caliber slug entered one side of her head and came out. It hit the wall and bounced away, dragging a fountain of blood, brain and skull fragments behind it. Nick turned to Jessica and nodded, then dashed towards the beast, which had just stomped on the doppelganger of his son. Another sight that would torture him for years, but it didn't matter right now. They had a job to finish.

Nick knew there was very little chance of defeating the beast in front of him, but he was going to try anyway. He had to, Jessica needed time to catch and deal with Merrick. When Nick got within striking distance, the beast lifted its leg to catch Nick with a forward kick. Nick was taken by surprised, he had thought it would be slower. Nick got his arms up in time to cushion some of the blow with a block. Nick was pushed back several inches; but did not let the creature recover from the attack. Nick stepped forward and danced around the retracting leg, leaping up to reach its neck with a punch. The blow landed solid and a crunch was heard. Nick grinned lopsidedly, he had just crushed it's trachea. This not being his first rodeo, Nick sprang back just in case. His caution paid off, because the creature made one coughing sound, and it's neck swelled back out to normal proportions. Nick had to leap back again, as the buzzsaw would have cut his chest open otherwise.

Nick decided now was not the time to think, it was time to try a bunch of shit until something worked. The abomination was a little top heavy on the buzzsaw arm side; so it would lose some balance on the follow through. Nick stepped lightly in again and then juked to the right, delivering a straight kick to the creature's kneecap from the side. As expected, he couldn't break the knee, but it did trigger the counter attack. Nick stepped inside of the attack, caught the arm over his shoulder, and then grunted. Using it's own momentum, Nick managed to roll the creature over his body flat onto its back.

The agile man mounted the creature's chest in the blink of an eye, and began to throw heavy punches into the fleshy parts of it's face. This? This was doing some damage. It was beginning to bruise up. Nick overplayed his advantage however, and the creature's other arm struck at his face. Nick raised his arm, again, to block, but it helped little. He was still thrown off, and the blow landed on his head anyway. Nick pulled himself up to hands and knees, shaking his head rapidly. The creature was also getting up; and Nick was faster. It was only to it's knee when Nick arrived. Instead of running directly into the beast, he took a step back, raised his elbow, and used his other hand to help piston that into the back of the creature's neck. He then dropped prone. As anticipated, the buzzsaw sizzled through the area where he had just been. Nick scrambled forward as the beast continued its turn. It stood, and Nick wiped the sweat from his forehead. Gosh, the abomination in front of him was awfully big.

Nick gathered his strength, and danced in, narrowly avoiding another attempted kick from the creature. He pulled a classic Taekwondo combo, setting up a turn back kick with a same leg push kick. The push kick he aimed at the creature's hip opposite the heavy arm, and his theory paid off. The creature was taken off balance. The turn back kick landed as well, right in the gut. Nick stepped away fast, he knew he had not done much damage.

The creature roared and charged him. It had lowered its head. Nick had to time this right... he balled his fist and gathered his energy. Right before impact the creature fell to the ground, twitched, and then just... stopped moving. Nick kicked it's head doubtfully. The eyes were devoid of what little intelligence they had possessed before. Nick stood, desperate fighting spirit giving way to confusion. "What?" Jessica asked, "Why the hell are you so surprised? He's just a goddamned bearded cow. You expected him to put up any fight?" Jessica raised the head of her tormentor, "And a damn fine job your sword did, also."

Nick went down to one knee on the ground, the strain of it all suddenly getting to him. "I… thank you for killing Akiko for me, Jess."

"I wouldn't have done it had you not rejected the Kazuo clone already."

Nick tried to form a response, and instead pulled Jessica down into his arms.

Chapter Twenty-Two:
- "Hall of Fame", The Script, feat. will.i.am

Cynthia was making small talk with the gathered officers. Once the Skinstealers were dealt with Cynthia had simply issued an idle command to her small army. And so they did exactly that, running only basic life support processes.

Raoul crossed his arms and shook his head. His partner always had such a flair for the dramatic, Nick really was a perfect match for her. Nick was wearing nothing to cover his upper body, but did not seem to even feel the cold. Jessica hefted Merrick's head, and the gathered officers exploded in applause. Against all odds, the casualties on the side of the blue fury were very few. Merrick and his men simply were not ready for this. That beast was only a prototype, and Jessica made sure that Nick barely had to actually fight it.

The cheering was infectious, it drove Nick to clench his fists and look up at the moon. He pointed at her, and uttered a prayer of thanks to her. And then raised both of his arms and ripped forth with a howl of victory. Jessica punched the bison head up towards the moon as well, seeking only solidarity with her man.

Raoul stretched his wings wide. "Let's go get some dinner, Cynthia. Bound to be something open tonight." Cynthia looked over at him, then shrugged, "Sure, what the hell, why not?"

Nick was handed his trench coat, which he quickly buttoned up. The adrenaline was finally wearing off, and he was getting cold. A microphone was suddenly thrust into Nick's face, "Judge Steinbeck tells us that you and Detective Dombrowski ended the Skinstealer threat for good tonight. Do you have any comment?"

Nick put on a look of confusion, "Who the hell is Detective Dombrowski? The woman standing next to me is the spider that crept into my life, who found all the holes in my heart and spun her web to close them with her love. This is Detective Jessica Sakamoto, the Spider to my Dog."

The reporter drew her mic back a moment, "Spider to your dog? That's... an unusual statement." She pushed it back towards Nick.

"Why would you think so? We are, after all, Dog and Spider Private Investigations." Nick let go of Jessica a moment to stand his full height and push his chest out. Impossibly, through all of this, his hat had stayed on, and he pulled it down to shade his eye as he looked at the camera. "Do you suspect your husband is getting a little on the side? Did a former friend run off after accruing some debt? Do you think someone is embezzling? Do you miss your kitty and want to find out where she is? Then call Dog and Spider Private Investigations! If we can save the city, we can save your peace of mind!"

Fifteen minutes of official police statements later, Nick had his GTO Judge warmed up and ready to go. Merrick's head was in the trunk, Jessica in the passenger seat, and Brian behind them. "Righteous as can possibly BE, mate!"

Brian said, clapping him on the back, "But there's only one thing to do now to cap this off on the ride home."

Nick looked up into the rearview at his best friend's face, "Fine, fine, I saved the world, I can kick your ass as well. Baron's Court."
Brian rolled his eyes, "Predictable. Knightsbridge."
Nick opened his mouth to answer when Jessica cut in, "O'Hare Transfer..."
Nick looked over at Jessica, "Pardon?"
Jessica smirked at him, "Well, since I married you, that basically makes me Japanese, so the Satoshi clause applies. I'm getting to England."

Brian leaned forward, "What's all this, then? Who taught you the Satoshi clause?"
Jessica gave Brian a sad smile, "I'm sorry. I haven't a clue."
Brian exhaled, "Well, I can fend a newbie off easily. You take your turn, Nicky."
"North Acton."
Brian stroked his chin, and nodded, "Well with Jessica on her way I suppose you'd have to. Let's see... Holland Park."

Jessica sighed, "Only move I can make now is Docklands to Canning Town."
"Well, fuck," Nick said, "I thought for sure you'd head for Stratford."
Jessica looked offended, "I'm a new player, not an utter imbecile."
Brian smirked, "Nick would make that move."

293

Jessica held her hands palm up, "Well, like I said, I am not an imbecile. I simply married one."

"Oh, that's low," Nick said, "Just for that, Upminster Bridge."

"You can't possibly think I'm going to ally with you, Nicky? Noriko simply wouldn't stand for it. South Woodford."

Jessica wrinkled her nose a moment, "I'm gonna say… North Wembley."

Nick snorted, "That would normally be a great move, my love, but if you're invoking the Satoshi clause, we have to stick to the Mitsubishi variant."

"Fine, fine," Jessica said, "In that case… Elm Park."

"I guess you weren't kidding when you told me you liked me spanking you. I'll crossover to Chigwell."

Brian laughed, "Suckers! Ickenham!"

Jessica rolled her eyes, "Epping, how new do you think I am?"

Nick slapped the dashboard, "Oakwood!"

Brian coughed, "Well bravo on blocking me… I have to retreat to Pimlico."

Jessica cracked her knuckles, "That's right, run! Canada Water!"

Nick shut the car off, they had arrived at their house. "Really, Jessica? Mornington Crescent."

"I KNEW you were going to stab me in the back!" Brian said.

Jessica threw her hands up, "Honest mistake, Brian. I'm not as experienced as you guys."

"Sallright, love," Brian said, "You can make it up to me by inviting me for a drink."

"Absolutely not," Nick said, "It's my honeymoon night, and I'd really REALLY like to fuck my wife."
"Bah," Brian said, "Birds come and go, but a right proper Crimbo drink is a rare occasion."
Jessica leaned back to give Brian a light whack on the head, "Get outta here, you ponce. He's my man now."
Brian sighed dejectedly, "I'll miss you."
"One last kiss, love?" Nick said as he leaned back.
Brian scoffed, and then got out of the car.

As Brian stepped off to his own car, Nick came around to the passenger side and held the door open. Jessica extended her hand, "Be a proper gentleman." Nick took her hand and helped her out, then dipped down to pick her up. Jessica stepped off, "Easy there, Philip Marlowe. We gotta get the bloody bison head out of the trunk."

Nick shook his head, "Not sure why we took that with us in the first place."
Jessica shrugged as she popped the trunk, "I dunno. Throw it in the garbage, I guess?" She reached in to grab for the sack, which was open, and paused for a moment, "Hey, Prettyboy. Check this out."
Nick peered over, "That's kinda weird. Looks like it's mummified."
"Great," Jessica said, "That mean he's gonna come back?"

Nick pondered a moment, and then shook his head, "No. The natural order of things is simply returning. This buffalo should have been dead maybe centuries ago."
"Bison," Jessica corrected.
"Gah. Now I'm doing it." Nick left to go open the door.

Jessica picked up the sack and slammed the trunk. She yelped out surprise as Nick picked her up in the traditional marital carry, "What the hell, Prettyboy? We've already crossed this threshold like a bajillion times."
Nick nuzzled his nose against hers, "Not as man and wife."

Jessica wrapped her arms around his neck and leaned her head against his chest. As soon as Nick opened the door, Bonecrusher slid out and headed for his home. Nick chuckled, "That's right, Boney, get back to Jen before she decides she needs to hire me again."

The bison head bounced against Nick's back as he walked in, then paused. "Holy shit!"
"What?" Jessica asked, turning her head, "I… oh my God."

The back wall of their tiny kitchen was missing… as the back of their house had an addition. The walls extended another good thirty feet out, into a lushly furnished and decorated den. Candles, dim lighting, and a fully stocked bar ran along the left side of the den. Along the right were a pool table and several couches with coffee tables. Along the back wall was the cherry on top of this sundae: a classic brick fireplace with two comfortable looking leather chairs in front of it. Their Christmas tree had been set up to the right of the fireplace.

Jessica gasped, "It's… it's beautiful. Thank you, Prettyboy, how did you manage this?"

Nick shook his head, "I was about to ask you the exact same question." Nick scanned the area for danger or clues as to what, exactly the hell had happened.

Jessica pointed, "There's an envelope on the bar. That might answer some questions." Nick set Jessica down, and she strode over to pick it up. "It's addressed to Mr. and Mrs. Sakamoto. The paper feels expensive... is that... a... gold seal?"
"What are you, the narrator?" Nick asked, "Open it up and read it already!"

Jessica cleared her throat, "'Hey, kids, it's Mom. As soon as I saw your house I knew it just wouldn't be big enough. I hope you don't mind but I moved your bedroom from one of those tiny things to upstairs in the addition. Admittedly, this is all made from prefabricated parts, but what are you gonna do? I only had 10 hours or so to get it all finished. I hope my boys did good work for you. Don't forget, the first night of Hanukkah is tomorrow, my beautiful daughter!'"

Nick looked around, clearly amazed, "In one day? All this? And I thought us Japanese were fast."
Jessica stepped forwards and set the dried bison head on the logs in the fireplace, "To be fair, Prettyboy, she IS a Mafia overlord. If she says this is done on Christmas Eve in ten hours, well? Look around you. Hey, Prettyboy? Go ahead and start a fire, I am going to slip into something a little more erotic."

Nick's tail began to wag, "The fire will be bright and warm when you return, my luscious Latrodectus." Over the next five minutes, Nick built the fire. It was something he was already familiar with; a fireplace was one of the luxuries Akiko's father had ensured they had. He was taken back a bit when the flames reached Merrick's head... they consumed all but the bones almost as if there was nothing but flash paper involved.

There was nothing to do now except wait for his bride's return.

Nick sat back in the chair, and turned on the news. A pitcher full of what Nick instantly recognized as eggnog and blackberry brandy was placed down on the table between the chairs; Jessica had managed to sneak up on him entirely. He turned back to speak, and his throat suddenly dried up. He poured himself a glass and slugged it down.

Jessica was standing by the bar, one foot up on a lower rung of one of the bar stools. She was dressed in an almost see-through black negligee with a spiderweb pattern all over it. It was ankle-length, with a wide collar and puffed sleeves that went halfway down her arms. Underneath it she wore black cotton panties along with thigh high black nylons which displayed a different web pattern. The finishing touches? Jessica had refreshed her black lipstick, as well as the polish on her nails. Her toes were on display with three and a half inch heeled open toe sandals with black ribbon tied up her calves.

Nick poured another, shakily. Nick's lopsided grin appeared. "As I recall, this isn't all, is it, Jess?" Giving Nick that smile which was just for him, Jessica put her foot down on the ground, and turned away from him. She placed her hands onto the bar stool in front of her, and bent slightly for him to see. The back of her panties had a hole in them, with silken ruffles sewed expertly around the rim of the hole.

Nick had to take a deep breath before he could finally speak, "I remember these panties, my domesticated widow. My latter-days June Cleaver."

Jessica spread her legs in the pose a bit, and then brought them together and stood up on the balls of her feet, "I should hope so. I was wearing these when you first met Merrick." The movements made a heart-shape of Jessica's ass, and allowed him just a peek at her.
Nick took a deep breath and let it out, "I thought you wanted me to get tired of doing that, anyway?"

Jessica nodded lightly, "Prettyboy? I was going to give my man something, and Merrick stopped me from doing it. And now that he'll never bother us again, we can finish what we started. Right in front of that fire where he can watch us do it. Indulge my crazy. You agreed to do that until death do us part."

Nick set his drink down, and his left ear flickered, "Don't take this the wrong way, Jess, but… are you sure this is what you want for your wedding night?"
Jessica wiggled her hips slowly, "There's Astroglide on the pool table, Prettyboy. Though if you'd prefer, I can put some jeans on and we can go attend Midnight Mass somewhere?"

"No!" Nick said, raising his hand, "not necessary. I just wanted to point out to you this is our first carnal act as man and wife. Twenty years from now-"
"I'm about to head upstairs for jeans!"

Nick shut the hell up and swiped the bottle, opening it quickly.

Nick and Jessica Sakamoto finished what they had started, in front of the now fire-bleached skull of Jessica's tormentor. When it was all done, they sat on the chairs and idly sipped the eggnog. There were no words needed; they silently basked in the joy of being with one another; stirring only to refill their drinks or add logs to the fire. The hours were spent watching Christmas specials, themselves on the news, and a late night monologue before finally retiring to their new bedroom. There they made love again. Afterwards, Atton curled up between them, and the family slept, awaiting Christmas Morning.

"Our hearts grow tender with childhood memories and love of kindred, and we are better throughout the year for having, in spirit, become a child again at Christmas-Time"
- Laura Ingalls Wilder

Satine Reigns answered her phone, "Yes. Yes. He's in a consecrated union now, and genuinely happy. I have... I don't think he's going to become a true Terror. The Brit almost made me for a prior person, I think."

She listened a moment, "Yes. Yes. Thank you. And if I may? I would very much like to be taken off this duty."

More listening, "Yes, of COURSE that's the reason why. I want to go back to Japan and be left alone now. I've done enough jobs for you to earn my freedom."

More talking on the other end, "The fox? No, the old gods... no. She won't awaken." The voice spoke with a bit more precision and less patience. Satine responded, "I don't think the vampiress is going to be a problem either."

Satine was quiet a few moments longer, "The Vatican? Allright. I'll be there as soon as I can." Satine pressed her head against the wall and exhaled. Would they ever let her just live her own life? She hung up and got ready to book a flight.

Made in the USA
Lexington, KY
07 April 2017